LOVE ON THE LINE

DIANE HOLIDAY

CITY OWL
PRESS

LOVE ON THE LINE
Love Beyond Danger, Book 3

CITY OWL PRESS
www.cityowlpress.com

Cover Design by MiblArt. All stock photos licensed appropriately.

Edited by Mary Cain.

For information on subsidiary rights, please contact the publisher at info@cityowlpress.com.

Print Edition ISBN: 978-1-949090-56-7

Digital Edition ISBN: 978-1-949090-55-0

Printed in the United States of America

This book is dedicated to all military members past and present. The sacrifices they and their families make to keep this beautiful country free allow me to pursue my dream of writing. I'm forever grateful.

PRAISE FOR DIANE HOLIDAY

"*Love on the Line* is an excellent story in the vein of time-honored romance--suspense, love, and characters who keep you turning the pages." — *Contemporary Romance Author and Golden Heart® Award Finalist, Christina Hovland*

"Two people looking for the opposite things in life find out they might be a perfect match. But danger lurks when they fall under the spotlight of a madman. *Love on the Line* is a suspenseful read." — *USA Today Bestselling Author of Historical Romance, Renee Ann Miller*

"*Love on the Line* delivers a romantic suspense with strong characters you'll remember long after you read the last page." — *New Adult Author and Golden Heart® Award Winner, C.R. Grissom*

"Well-plotted, beautifully written and completely engrossing, *Love on the Line* is absolutely the best romantic suspense I've read this year." — *Jessie Gussman, author of Sweet Water Ranch*

"Both intense and hot, *Love on the Line* keeps readers flipping the pages! Sexy romance and thrilling suspense--there's nothing else one could ask for!" — *Young Adult Romance Author, Miguella Twosias*

"*Love Uncovered* blends the tension of a high-stakes corruption case with the charm of a well-realized small-town setting to create a fun, fast-paced story." — *Publisher's Weekly*

"Diane Holiday's debut, *Love in Hiding*, kept me hooked from the first page to the last." — *USA Today Bestselling Author of Historical Romance, Renee Ann Miller*

"Holiday delivers another fast-paced read with heart and humor in *Rock Bottom Romance*." — *USA Today Bestselling Author of Historical Romance, Renee Ann Miller*

"*Love in Hiding* combines the laid-back atmosphere of country life with the suspense angle of a crazed stalker beautifully. Great characterization, perfect pacing and witty dialogue top off this exceptional read." — *Jessie Gussman, author of Sweet Water Ranch*

"Full of moments that will make you smile. *Rock Bottom Romance* is a feel-good novel that will have you rooting for the hero and heroine right from the moment they meet." — *Young Adult Romance Author, Miguella Twosias*

"This was an amusing read with relatable characters I couldn't stop rooting for." — *Historical Fiction Author, KA Nelson*

"A fast-moving, exciting novel. The main characters are the perfect combination of charming and complex. This contemporary romance delivers electrifying heat between characters with a sprinkle of humor." — *InD'tale, Tina Donovan*

"A strong heroine, sexy hero and downright scream-worthy villains—a page-turner with spunky dialogue and suspense that kept me up way past my bedtime because I just couldn't put it down." — *Contemporary Romance Author and Golden Heart® Award Finalist, Christina Hovland*

"Solid storytelling featuring a classic hero and a daring heroine." — *New Adult Author and Golden Heart® Award Winner, C.R. Grissom*

"A man scarred by guilt, a feisty woman, and a villain who is totally evil make Diane Holiday's *Love Uncovered* a fast-paced read that sizzles with both romance and suspense." — *USA Today Bestselling Author of Historical Romance, Renee Ann Miller*

"Diane Holiday's well-crafted romantic suspense stories keep readers turning the pages, ready for the next twist! I always look forward to her books." — *Contemporary Romance Author and Golden Heart® Award Finalist, Christina Hovland*

"Holiday writes romantic suspense with just the right balance of heart and heart-pounding action." — *USA Today Bestselling Author, Dylann Crush*

"What begins as a cruel bet...soon becomes a terrifying, life-threatening game of cat and mouse. The chemistry between Holiday's protagonists is intense and believable." — *Publisher's Weekly*

LOVE BEYOND DANGER SERIES

BY DIANE HOLIDAY

CHAPTER 1

ANNE COOPER EYED the tray of tequila and kamikaze shots on the high table. Her friends grabbed one of each. Much as she'd like to join them, as the designated driver, she'd stick with water, and her stomach would thank her in the morning. Mixing shots was the kiss of death.

Mostly, she wanted to be there for Emily, who worked nonstop and deserved a night out to celebrate her birthday. With a spreadsheet and a calendar, Anne had compared everyone's schedules. Finally, she'd managed to find a date that worked for all of them. Thanks to her careful planning, she had all of her friends together. Her heart swelled with satisfaction.

Emily ran a hand through her curly red hair and pouted. "Have a drink. I want you to have fun. We can get a ride."

"Relax, I'm enjoying myself," Anne shouted over the band blasting alternative rock music from across the sports bar. Besides, she was more of a wine-sipping kind of girl. Hard liquor went straight to her head, and she didn't like to feel out of control.

She glanced at the guitar player jamming on the small stage. Maybe she could ask the band to play Emily's favorite song. Approaching a singer and drawing attention to herself made her pulse skitter, but what the hell. She'd do it for her best friend, who always had Anne's back. Besides, at thirty-two it's not like she was some shy teenager.

Trish, their server, was nowhere in sight. Anne pointed to her empty glass, using it as an excuse to slip away. "I'll be right back."

She weaved through the crowd, dodging servers carrying trays with pitchers of beer and fried wings. Baltimore Orioles pennants and Ravens pictures covered every inch of the walls. Even though she didn't follow sports, she at least knew the team colors, since her fifth-graders proudly wore their purple football jerseys to school.

The band announced they were taking a break, and the noise level returned to normal. Perfect. She'd grab a water and muster up the courage to make a request.

She spied an empty seat at the bar and hurried to the only open spot. As she slid the chair out, a man in the midst of an animated conversation waved a hand, bumping her shoulder. Cold soda spilled on her arm, and she jumped.

He whirled around, his mouth agape. "I'm sorry. I didn't see you behind me."

Her breath caught as eyes the color of emeralds stared down at her. Way down, because the guy stood an easy foot taller. Blond hair highlighted his tanned face, which would be flawless if not for a few faint scars and a less-than-perfectly-straight nose that somehow added character.

Her heart thumped in her chest, and she blinked.

He snagged a handful of cocktail napkins as she held her arm away from her body so the drink wouldn't drip onto her jeans or shoes. At least some part of her brain hadn't seized. He placed a warm hand under her elbow for support and dabbed the napkins over her wet arm.

"Um…it's okay." She fumbled to take them from him, paying no attention to his bulging biceps. Not at all.

"Nice move, slick," came a voice from behind him.

Anne glanced at the beefy, dark-haired man with a shit-eating grin on his face.

"That's John. Ignore him. He has no manners," Mister Biceps said. He released her elbow, wiped his palm on his jeans and extended his hand. "I'm Wyatt."

She shook his hand, and an electric current tingled up her arm. Something in his eyes flashed. Maybe he'd felt it, too? Her gaze traveled from his massive chest to his broad shoulders. Either the place had shrunk, or this giant of a man had filled it. "I'm Anne."

"Hey, you gonna buy the lady a drink or what, superjock?" John asked.

Wyatt must have given a quick kick to John because he jerked on the bar stool and laughed. He leaned across the counter and said something to the bartender, who nodded, not breaking his rhythm pouring shots.

"My friend has a good point. Can I buy you a drink to make up for this?" Wyatt waved at her arm, which had bits of paper stuck to it from the napkin dabbing.

She brushed back a few strands of hair. Her stomach clenched. The guy was smoking hot, and the scent of his cologne was making her heady. Even so, she couldn't go there. The next guy she dated wouldn't be someone she met in a bar and knew nothing about. She'd closed that door and sealed the windows. But there he stood, jiggling the locks.

"Well ..." She glanced across the room to her table. "I'm with friends."

The bartender placed a drink with a pink umbrella in front of Wyatt, and faced Anne.

"What can I get for you?" he asked.

"A water, please."

He filled a glass and slid it over to her.

Wyatt shook his head, plucked the umbrella from his drink, and twirled it in front of John's face. "Seriously? You ordered a Shirley Temple for me?"

John smirked and took a pull of his beer.

Anne bit her cheek to keep from laughing. This big, manly guy holding a pink paper umbrella was too much.

He dropped it on the counter and sighed. "I can't take him anywhere. My team lost tonight, so I'm the DD, but I *don't* drink Shirley Temples."

His eyes twinkled with humor, and her heart slammed against her ribcage. She needed to leave. Walk away right now before he made her laugh again. "Well, I gotta go."

Yet she didn't make a move.

Her gaze fell to the writing on his T-shirt. "No softballs here. We play hard."

This time she did laugh. Wyatt glanced down and winced. With a grin, he shrugged. "I'd regret the shirt choice, except it made you smile."

He made her smile.

"There he is. Hey, superstar." A tall blonde wearing stilettos, sprayed on jeans, and a clingy halter top strutted over, followed by an entourage of look-alikes. She gave Wyatt a peck on the cheek. "Sorry we're late. I see the party has already started."

Giggles came from the peanut gallery as they surrounded Wyatt, pushing Anne to the end of the bar. She shuffled in her Skechers. Sure, she liked to dress up and wear heels once in a while, but if she tried to pull off sky-high stilettos, she'd be limping for a week. Jeans and the T-shirt she'd bought off the clearance rack at Target were no match for these women's sexy, hip vibe. Heat crept up her neck like back in school when the popular girls called her a nerd.

Time to go to her table. She didn't fit in with this crowd. Picking up her water, she turned to leave, but Wyatt tapped her arm. He'd moved away from the women to stand next to her.

He rubbed his jaw. "Hey, I don't want to keep you, but..."

Her gaze flew to his, and he must have seen something in her eyes, because he didn't finish his sentence. He rocked back on his heels and shoved his hands in his pockets.

Great. She'd scared him away. Just as well. Didn't need a hot guy with groupies and an ego that probably needed constant stroking. She'd steer far away from that type.

When she dated again, it would be with a stable, responsible man. Someone who had a work ethic and wouldn't impulsively quit his job and expect to mooch off her. Someone she could count on, who wouldn't perpetually stand her up or not be able to commit to any plans for fear of missing something else more "fun."

Nope. She was so done with those guys. Looks didn't matter. Only, she couldn't deny that Wyatt's looks...well...the looks he gave her made her insides quiver oh-so-pleasantly.

"We usually come here after the games. Maybe see you around some-time?" He hitched an eyebrow.

John shook his head and coughed over what sounded like, "Coward."

The minions encroached on Wyatt, their laughter pealing. Still, he held Anne's gaze.

Something in her chest fluttered faster than the wings of a bird taking flight. Doubtful she'd run into him again, since she didn't get out much. "Maybe. Nice meeting you."

She hurried away before she changed her mind. Whatever expression he'd seen on her face had stopped him cold from asking her out. All for the best. Teaching, interviewing for vice principal jobs, and volunteer work kept her super busy. That's the way she liked it. Besides, she needed some space to get over the last breakup and time to do her homework on anyone new. He'd have to tick off the right boxes on her growing list of important attributes.

The band tuned their instruments, getting ready for the next set. She took a deep breath and pushed through the crowd to get closer.

The lanky lead singer, with sleeve tattoos and multiple piercings, paused to pick up his drink. She stood on her tiptoes and waved to him. "It's my friend Emily's birthday. Do you take requests?"

He leaned down. "Depends. What song?"

She told him, and he nodded in an I'm-so-cool way. "You got it."

His fingers fiddled with the guitar strings as his gaze wandered down her body. "Why don't you stop back when we take our next break?"

"Thanks, but I'm with the girls tonight."

"Bring them with you." He jerked his head in the direction of the drummer and bass player. "We love a party."

"Maybe next time." She smiled and walked away. Her face was on fire, but she'd done it.

His voice came over the mic. "Got a request from a pretty lady. Can't turn that down. This one's for Emily. Happy birthday."

Anne's friends let out a whoop from their table as she returned.

"Oh my God. My favorite song. Did you do that?" Emily high-fived Anne as the girls moved to the music. Worth the nerves to make Emily so happy.

Anne glanced across the bar at Wyatt. The group around him had grown. A guy clapped him on the back and another passing by gave him a fist bump. She ignored the tiny sinking of her spirits.

Wyatt was out of her league, and she'd promised herself she'd stick to her plan.

No room for players in her life.

CHAPTER 2

DEVON BLACKWOOD DROVE into the Corner Bar parking lot and hit the brakes. Neon beer signs blinked like beacons in the windows of the cedar building. He double checked the GPS to make sure he'd gone to the right place. Whenever he and Paul met for drinks to discuss their next bet, they picked a different bar. They'd started the whole thing back in college to make life more interesting. Paul must have misplaced his glasses or something when he'd chose this dive.

After zigzagging through a pot-holed maze, Devon parked his BMW in a spot far away from the jacked pickup trucks. A cold January wind blasted his face, and annoyance grew with every step he took. His shoes would need polishing after the trek through the dirty gravel, and his car would need washing.

He opened the heavy, paint-chipped wooden door and stepped inside. His nose wrinkled in disgust at the stench of stale beer and fried food. The scent took him right back to his father, passed out drunk on the couch, reeking of alcohol.

No need to relive those days. Now Devon was in control, always in control. He slid out of his coat. First thing tomorrow, he'd call the dry-cleaning service to pick up his suit and jacket.

His gaze swept the room. Mostly a blue-collar crowd wearing T-shirts, flannel, and jeans. Servers grabbed plastic pitchers of beer from the bar, while a band blasted music as if volume could make up for their lack of talent. A peanut shell crunched under his designer shoe, and a vein pulsated in his forehead.

Everything about the place made his skin crawl, including the women who elbowed each other as he passed, like he'd give any of them a second look. Tall, with dark hair and a martial-arts-trained body, he commanded attention. Females were putty in his hands.

He spotted Paul at a table away from the band. Even the finest clothes couldn't make up for his small stature and the receding hairline that highlighted his pastiness. Both of them were thirty-five, but Paul could pass for mid-forties.

"Haven't seen you in person for a while." Paul took off his glasses, wiped them with a lens cloth, and put them back on.

Devon sat across from him. "No need any more with a virtual world."

"Probably for the best, considering the *sensitive* nature of our business."

"You have a problem?" Devon arched an eyebrow. "Because I can easily find someone else to keep the books for what I'm paying you."

"Nope." Paul shook his head. "I'm good. Don't need to know the details. See no evil, hear no evil—"

"Exactly, Paulie. Remember that." Devon wasn't worried. Paul liked the finer things in life and wouldn't do anything to risk losing his lucrative income.

Paul's lips drew into a thin line. "You know I hate it when you call me Paulie. I wish you would drop that old college nickname."

A brunette server, who he'd guess was in her late twenties, stopped by the table. "I'm Trish. What can I get you to drink?"

Devon frowned and eyed the bar. "Scotch on the rocks, the highest quality of whatever you carry in this place."

Trish stiffened, and the smile fell from her face. She took Paul's order for a merlot and walked away.

Devon's head ached from the noisy band. "Why on earth did you pick this slum to meet?"

"The online pictures made it look much nicer." Paul shrugged. "We're just here for a drink and to set up the next bet."

"I hope it's something good. My boredom has reached an absolute high." And so had Devon's tolerance for the bar.

"A man of your means and money really shouldn't be bored," Paul said.

"That's why we started this game, isn't it?" Devon sat back in his chair. "What's the challenge when I have the money and influence to get whatever I want?"

Paul nodded. "True. It's made life more exciting."

"What I wonder is why you even bother anymore. You never win." Devon snorted.

"Oh, I won once. Remember back in college when Lynn picked *me* over you?" Paul smoothed down the edges of his cocktail napkin and blew out a breath.

Devon's ears burned. That bitch. He'd been shocked when she'd turned him down, choosing instead to go out with Paulie. The first woman to ever reject Devon. He fisted his hands under the table.

Trish returned with their drinks. She plopped Devon's down, smiled at Paul, and placed a bowl of nuts next to his merlot. "Would you like a menu?"

"No, thank you." Paul said. As she returned to the bar, he waved a hand at her back. "You really charmed her, didn't you?"

Devon glared at Trish, his face heating. She had ignored him, fawning over Paul, who had a lot of nerve bringing up that ancient-history bet that he'd won. Like Devon could ever lose another bet over a woman. "I wouldn't spend a second trying to impress some low-class waitress. I can have any woman in this bar that I want."

"Really?" Paul took a sip of his wine and rolled his eyes.

"What's that look for? You think I'm kidding?" Devon glanced around the room. "Fine. That will be our next bet. You pick someone here, and I'll get her to go out with me."

Paul sat up in his chair. "Hmm. This could be fun. Only..." He tapped a finger on his lip. "Let's make it a little more challenging."

"How?" Devon swirled his scotch.

"I imagine you could buy or charm a woman into your bed if you put your mind to it, but as far as I know, you've never had a lasting, meaningful relationship. Whoever I choose, you have to date exclusively for three months." Paul smiled a Cheshire-cat grin.

A thrill of anticipation climbed up Devon's spine. This would be the easiest wager he'd ever won. He'd come a long way since college when he'd lost that one over Lynn. Sure, he'd been popular back then, but nothing compared to his status now. Wealthy, handsome, respected in the community, he had his choice of women. Any of which would marry him if he ever proposed.

Paul had no idea how much power and lure Devon had over the opposite sex. They always wanted more, but he tossed them to the curb once they bored him. He wasn't sharing his fortune with any gold diggers. Date some cheap bar chick for three months? Hell, he could do that in his sleep.

"Tell you what, Paul-ie." He dragged out the name. "I'll up the ante and get the woman to agree to *marry* me in three months. Put a ring on her finger."

"Really?" Paul's eyes widened. "You actually think you can?"

"I don't think it. I *know* it."

"I can't wait to win this one. I'm pretty sure I've already found the woman, but first I need to set up a little test."

Devon rubbed his chin. "What kind of test?"

"You'll see in a second." Paul jerked his head. "Take a look over there."

Devon followed Paul's gaze to a table of five women who appeared to be in their late- twenties or early-thirties. Trish brought them a tray of drinks. They all knocked back shots except for a short-haired blonde, who drank from a soda glass. She stood and slung her purse over her shoulder, saying something to a tall redhead before leaving the table.

She headed toward the restroom and passed by without a glance in Devon's direction. That was a first. Women always noticed him. His gaze raked down the back of her body. Nice ass and curvy in all the right places.

"You thinking of her?"

"Maybe. Her table has been pretty rowdy all night, so I've noticed them. I'll need Trish's help, though, to see if that blonde is the right person for the bet."

Devon snapped his fingers as Trish passed. She flinched, but continued on, carrying a tray with pitchers of beer and mugs. Slowly pouring them, she chatted with the men at another table.

Total ignorant bitch. She'd just lost her tip. He would leave her a one-cent tip so she'd know he didn't forget it.

She finally came to their table and spoke directly to Paul, with no smile this time. "Ready for another?"

"We'd like to order a round for the ladies over there." Paul gestured to the group of women.

Trish nodded. "Okay."

* * *

When Anne returned from the restroom, Trish showed up with another tray of drinks.

"Some guys bought you a round," she said.

"Who?" Anne asked.

Trish pointed across the room. As Anne turned to look, three men at the next table stood, blocking her view.

Anne frowned. Free drinks were nice, but who'd sent them? "I can't see who ordered these. Is it a group of guys or what?"

"Nah. Just two. One of them seems kinda nice, but the other is a jerk. Can you believe he snapped his fingers at me to get my attention?"

"That sucks. I waited tables when I was in college. I hated when people did that."

Trish cocked her head. "And he looks like he stepped out of a magazine, wearing designer clothes and acting snobby-like. I mean, what's he doing here anyway?"

"Hmm. That is kind of strange." Then again, there was no law against dressing nice.

"For what it's worth, I think the guy's a jerk. It's a gut thing, but I've learned to trust it." Trish gave a curt nod.

Emily snagged one of the shots and raised it in the air. "Bottoms up."

The girls picked up the others and drank them.

The back of Anne's neck tingled. Something didn't feel right. She lowered her voice and spoke to Trish on the side. "I don't like it. One time a group of men followed us after they bought us a round of drinks. I don't want to make a big deal out of it, though. Can I pay you separately for these, and you tell the guys we said, 'Thanks but no thanks'?"

"I'll be happy to deliver the message." Trish clamped the drink tray under her arm and left with a bounce in her step.

* * *

Devon glanced up when Trish returned to the table.

She faced him, meeting his eyes with a smug smile. "The ladies paid for the round you sent over and said, 'Thanks, but no thanks.'"

Heat flushed through Devon's skin. He didn't give a flying fuck about whether the girls accepted the drinks. It was Paul's deal, not his. No one smirked at him and got away with it like this bitch of a waitress with a stick up her ass.

She must have realized her mistake because the smug look disappeared, and she swallowed, taking a step back.

Paul clasped his hands together. "Great. We'll take our check."

Trish blinked, and her brows furrowed like she was trying to figure out a puzzle. "All right then…I'll get it."

She hurried toward the bar. Good, she should be nervous. Devon would have a word with her manager before he left. He dragged his attention back to Paul. "Why are you so happy those girls paid for the round?"

"It confirms I've chosen the right person for our wager. The blonde is the only one who spoke to Trish."

"So, what of it?"

"I've been watching her. She's obviously the designated driver, been taking care of her very tipsy friends, and now refuses free drinks." Paul leaned across the table. "She's a person of character, which I think will make it harder for you to win her over with your usual tactics."

"Just wait and see." Devon scoffed and held out his hand. "We have a deal?"

"Absolutely."

They shook on it as Trish came by with the check.

Devon snagged the bill and said to Paul, "I got this. You'll be paying up later."

Paul stood and grinned. "Good luck. I believe this will be harder than you think. I look forward to winning."

"We'll see about that."

After Paul left, Devon slid his credit card onto the tab and waited for Trish to return with it. On the tip line he wrote, ".01".

Standing, he shot a look at the blonde again. Not hard on the eyes, but clearly beneath him. He'd have her eating out of his hand. This was going to be fun.

Let the games begin.

CHAPTER 3

WYATT GLANCED AT JOHN, sitting in the passenger seat. "What's the cat-that-ate-the-canary grin for?"

"Nothing. I'm enjoying my DD ride. Losing sucks, not that I'd know." John slid a hand to the top of his forehead and formed an "L" with his fingers. He let out a long sigh.

Wyatt snorted. "Wait 'til next week."

"Yeah, yeah."

"You're a real dick, you know?"

"Yup, and I try *hard*." John closed his eyes and faked a snore.

"I'm not even going there." Wyatt held in a laugh. Smart ass. "Why don't you make that snore real and zone out?"

"I should. Monday morning I'm back to work."

A pit formed in Wyatt's stomach. His best friend put his life on the line every day as a Baltimore detective.

John waved a hand. "What was up with that chick you dumped your soda all over?"

"What do you mean?"

"You know what I mean." John slid a heavy-lidded glance in Wyatt's direction. "I haven't seen you wimp out like that since middle school.

Why did you? Women ask *you* out. Professional football player and all the hero-worship shit."

Wyatt stopped for a red light. "That's former player, and she didn't exactly seem like a fan."

"No. She didn't faint at the mere sight of you."

The light turned green, and Wyatt checked for jaywalkers before accelerating. On Saturday nights, the city streets crawled with people.

"Doesn't matter." John shifted in his seat. "You have plenty of other fans."

"Maybe I'm tired of that."

"What?" John did a double take and straightened.

"Just saying, it's getting old. Something about Anne was…different." Refreshing. The second he'd seen her, he'd fired to life. With gorgeous blue eyes and dimples that popped when she smiled, she'd caught his attention. Never mind the curvy body her understated T-shirt and jeans couldn't hide. And when he'd held her elbow, she'd blushed. All his fault for spilling a drink on her, yet she'd taken it in stride.

John dragged him back to the present. "You saying your playboy days are over?"

Wyatt shrugged. "I don't know. I mean, with sports and travel I've kept my dates casual. Then my mother needed me." A heaviness settled over his heart. He cleared his throat. "With her gone now, it's just me. I'm not sure what I even want anymore."

"I'm sorry, dude. That was some heavy shit to deal with."

"Yeah. Not that I don't like spending holidays with your family, but—"

"Stop right there. If you tell me your biological clock is ticking, I swear I'll revoke your man card." John held up a hand. "I get it. I get it."

Wyatt waved at him. "Nah, it's not that."

"Good, because I think at thirty-three your swimmers still have plenty of stamina."

"Christ, does everything go there with you? Your mind's always in the gutter."

"And I drag you right down with me, bro." John settled back in the seat.

"I can't even think about having kids. And besides, if I get that offensive coordinator job at USC, I'll be moving to California." Wyatt switched lanes and kept his eyes open for pedestrians. "What about you? You ever consider having a family?"

John gazed out the passenger window, street lights flickering over his face. "Not many women are lining up to be a cop's wife. Especially if they want kids."

Silence hung between them. Wyatt had no words. The truth was the truth. Most women couldn't handle the stress of their husband on a job from which he might never come home. His shoulders pinched, and tension ran a track through his body. His friend bled blue, as did generations of his family. They all deserved a medal and a chance to have children.

John brushed a hand down his pants. "So, what are you going to do about this Anne?"

Wyatt let out a slow breath. Maybe she'd come back to the bar, maybe not. What was he even thinking? They'd had one short encounter, but somehow, she'd gotten to him. "Beats the hell out of me. All I got is her first name. Not much to go on."

The way her eyes had grown wide had stopped him from asking her out. He didn't pressure women. He never put them on the spot. Probably best to forget about her.

Only, the cute way she'd tried to stifle her laugh at the pink umbrella, and the electric current that came from touching her refused to fade.

"Yo, Romeo." John nudged Wyatt's arm. "About to miss my turn."

"Oh, right." He hit the brakes.

"Are you sure you aren't the one who's been drinking? Never seen you like this."

"Yeah." Just hung up on a girl he barely knew. And kicking himself for not getting her number.

"All right. We still on for poker night?"

"Yup. Bring an extra shirt, cuz you're gonna lose one." Wyatt pulled up to the curb.

John opened the door. "In your dreams."

"Hey." Wyatt leaned over as John got out. "Be safe out there."

"Don't worry." John winked. "I never leave home without protection."

Wyatt groaned and pulled back into traffic. He'd let this whole encounter with Anne get way too much into his head. He had a dream life. Enough money, fame, and plenty of women interested in him. He didn't need anything more. Tomorrow he'd wake up and shake the whole thing off.

Yeah, he'd forget all about those honest blue eyes, adorable dimples, and the way his heart had launched like never before.

Right.

CHAPTER 4

DEVON SLIPPED BEHIND the wheel of his car and waited for the blonde and her crew to leave the bar. His black BMW blended into the darkness in the farthest spot on the lot. Once the women pulled out, he followed from a safe distance.

Paul had been right. The blonde seemed to be the designated driver, dropping off her passengers. Three of them lived in small row homes in downtown Baltimore. He noted the addresses of each. Might come in handy later.

The next drop off was a half hour west of the city. He stayed back as they traveled the hilly country roads. Out of nowhere, a town popped up, and they were in the middle of civilization again. He raised an eyebrow when the Honda pulled into an upscale apartment complex. This was a far cry from the row homes.

The redhead got out and used a key to open the outer door. She wobbled before turning to blow a kiss to her friend, then disappeared inside. His blood warmed. Too bad Paul hadn't picked her. She looked easily fuckable and lived well.

The small-town lights dimmed in the rearview mirror as he continued to follow. Ten minutes later, the Honda slowed and turned into the entrance of a small apartment complex. This made more sense.

The ugly car fit right in with the others in the lot. The blonde parked. Open concrete staircases led to the apartment units above. She climbed to the third floor and entered a unit on the left.

Devon's pulse quickened. Easy access. No cards to swipe or buttons to push for admittance.

He cruised the parking lot. Not a single BMW, Lexus, or Mercedes to be found. He'd need to rent or buy a vehicle that would blend in with the others while he watched the place. The muscles in his neck bunched. He unclenched his jaw and blew out a breath. His days of driving crappy cars should be behind him.

As much as it sucked, he needed to observe her routine and the others in the complex, so he would deal with a shitty car when surveilling the place. He could always take his Porsche or Lamborghini out for a fast, hard drive afterwards to expunge the putrid feeling of being encased by cheap vinyl and standard speakers.

He made another sweep of the lot, pausing to take down the license plate of her car. By morning, he would know her name and phone number. As he drove away, his lips curved in anticipation.

CHAPTER 5

ANNE FLUNG off the covers and leaped out of bed. Pain shot up her leg and she cried out.

She'd rolled her ankle. Damn. She didn't have time for this. In less than an hour she needed to be at a teacher's conference in Baltimore.

The sun filtered in through the white, lacy curtains, happily punctuating her tardiness. After indulging in a moment of self-pity, she shook her head. No one to blame but herself. She'd left her phone on vibrate and hadn't heard the alarm. Maybe because she'd been dreaming about Wyatt.

Ever since their encounter two weeks ago, she'd tried and tried to get him out of her head. One short exchange with the guy should not have affected her so much, but it had. His touch, his scent, the way his eyes had sparked when their gazes collided. She'd never had such a reaction to a man. Pointless because she'd probably never run into him again. She needed to get back to reality.

Gripping the sideboard, she pushed up to a standing position. She took a tentative step, then cringed. Painful, but she could put some weight on her foot. Forget about heels, though. She'd have to wear pants instead of the skirt and blouse she'd laid out.

She showered standing on one foot and sat on the toilet lid while she dried her hair. Of course she dropped a contact in the sink, losing more precious time. Her fingers froze as she filled a plastic bag with ice to put on her ankle while she drove. At least it was her left foot. Guess it was going to be water and a granola bar for breakfast. No time to boil water for tea.

She descended the stairs, gripping the handrail for dear life and cursed living on the third floor. Thank goodness her car was parked close.

Keeping an eye on the clock, she drove as fast as she dared. When she finally got to the assigned banquet hall, she eased the door open. She had to walk a distance to reach a seat in the cavernous room. A few people looked back as she slinked to an end chair in the last row.

A minute later, another latecomer entered the room. She was digging a pen out of her purse when a pair of crutches came into her peripheral vision. Since the seat beside her was empty, she slid over to make space for the person to sit on the end. She moved her bag and purse out of the way as a man sat and placed his crutches in the aisle.

People in front of her turned around, some whispering and pointing in his direction. Anne glanced over to see what the fuss was about and did a double take. Wyatt sat beside her.

His green eyes grew wide, and a big smile lit up his face.

Her cheeks flamed, and her heart jumped, like when she'd found out she'd passed her teacher's certification test. She'd never expected to see Wyatt again. What was he doing there?

Anne didn't talk to Wyatt, instead focusing on the speaker giving the presentation, but the fragrance of his cologne distracted her to the point of zero concentration.

Every time she dared to glance his way, he caught her. Or maybe she caught him, because he sure as hell didn't seem to be paying attention to anyone else besides her.

She forced herself to breathe and relax. He didn't know he was starring in her dreams. They weren't on a date. He just happened to be at the same conference.

When they got a break, he turned to her. "So, you're a teacher too?"

"Yeah. Fifth grade, how about you?"

"High school health."

No surprise there. The guy could be a poster child for "fit." She'd convinced herself that the crowded, cramped bar area had made him appear so much larger than life. Nope. He loomed just as big in the huge conference room.

She forced herself to break eye contact as every nerve in her body jumped to attention. Gesturing to his injured leg, she asked, "What happened?"

"Touch football gone awry." He grimaced. "And I owe John another DD night now."

A woman approached Wyatt and hovered by his crutches. He glanced at her. She licked her lips and held up a pen. "Any chance I could get your autograph...for my uh...nephew?"

Wyatt smiled, nodded, and took the composition book she held out to him. "What's his name?"

"Christy."

Wyatt gazed up at her. "Christy?"

The woman touched her neck and cleared her throat, a blush creeping up to her cheeks. "Yes. He's um...Christopher...but he goes by Christy."

Anne's throat tickled with a giggle, but she held it in check, feeling bad for the poor woman. Her face had turned bright crimson, and sweat gleamed on her forehead.

Wyatt jotted a message on the paper, then handed it back to her. She read the note and smiled. "Thank you so much. This means the world to...him. I mean, it will mean the world to him."

She clutched the notebook and walked away, glancing back at Wyatt twice before taking her seat.

"Hey, you wanna cup of coffee?" He gestured to the banquet table with shiny, silver urns across the room.

Nice try. He wasn't going to pretend *that* hadn't just happened. Who was he? "Hold on. Everyone seems to know you. Why? Are you famous?"

He clicked his pen a couple of times, staring down at it before tucking it into his binder. "Eh, I played football for a while."

"In college?"

"Yeah, but also for the Ravens. I retired a year and a half ago. Soon enough, I'll be old news, and no one will want my autograph."

"I have no idea about that, but yes, I know of the Ravens. My students come in wearing their jerseys sometimes."

Wyatt blinked, and a slow grin formed on his face. "You don't follow football, I take it?"

"Sorry." She shrugged. "I don't watch sports. I like to read."

"To read?"

"Yes, you know, fiction. I prefer that to television." Oh no, now she'd offended him. "I mean, there's nothing wrong with sports. People like sports. And I like people who like sports." Dear God, she needed to *shut up.*

Wyatt's shoulders shook. "Let me make sure I got this straight. You like people who like sports, but *you* don't like sports."

Now he was laughing at her. But she couldn't blame him. She sounded like an idiot. Somehow, she had to fix this. "Yes. I mean, no. I mean, for example, my father likes sports. He'd watch with our dog."

Wyatt squeezed his eyes shut and he didn't even try to control his laughter now. "Is it fair to say you also like dogs that like sports? That is unless you didn't like your"—his chest rumbled, and he had to stop to take a breath—"dog?"

Heat flamed a path from her neck to the roots of her hair. God, what the hell was she rambling about? He had to think her a complete moron. She didn't babble or speak before thinking. The crazy chemistry or whatever it was between them had rendered her stupid. "Never mind. Can we get that cup of coffee now?"

"Sure." He held her gaze for a moment.

Laughter still in his eyes, they sparkled with mischief. The space between them seemed to shrink. She swallowed and broke eye contact, reaching for her purse. "I'll bring you a cup. How do you like it?"

"Thanks, but I'll get it."

"Really, I don't mind. I'm getting some for myself anyway." Even though she usually didn't drink coffee, she wouldn't mind a cup, and he might need some help.

Wyatt was up in a flash, despite his leg, and pointed a crutch toward the banquet table. "After you."

So, he was stubborn, too. She smiled and walked ahead. He might be able to get the coffee, but walking back to the chair with it would be a challenge on crutches.

She hummed as she added cream to hers. No point in rushing. He leaned on the crutches and poured his own cup. Stirring her coffee, she waited to see what he would do. He took a sip, then paused as his gaze went from his chair back to where he stood. It wasn't nice to take pleasure in his predicament, but she couldn't help herself.

He swung one crutch forward and leaned on it while he switched the coffee to that hand.

"Are you always this stubborn?" she asked.

He grinned and nodded. "So I've been told."

She reached for his cup.

With a sigh, he handed it over and followed her back to their seats. He tilted his head and squinted. "You did that on purpose, didn't you?"

"Did what?"

"You know what. You took your sweet time fixing your coffee so you'd be standing right there when I made a fool of myself."

"I'd say I availed myself of an opportunity to help someone."

Wyatt hitched an eyebrow. "I think you're in the wrong career. You sound more like a lawyer than a teacher." He sipped the coffee. "Did I imagine it or are you hurting too?"

"Huh?"

"Looked like you were limping?"

Her face heated again. "Oh, it's nothing. At least not compared to your injury."

"Didn't look like nothing. Trust me, I know. I'm the king of lame." He opened his mouth, then shut it. "That didn't come out right."

"Believe me. I understand." He had nothing on her 'I like people who like sports' gibberish. She glanced at him.

He squared his shoulders, like he was bracing himself for something. "Hey, I've been kicking myself for weeks. At the bar I wanted—"

"If everyone could please listen up, it's time for us to break into groups," the moderator announced over the microphone.

Anne's stomach dropped to the floor. He was going to ask her out. A part, a really big part, of her wanted him to. And that was the problem. He seemed like a decent guy, but he was a former football player with a bunch of groupies. Not what she was looking for at this stage of her life. He had women drooling over him left and right, and she had no desire to compete. Never mind that he smelled like heaven and made her insides quiver. Attractive, popular guys were not on her wish list anymore. She needed to find a man of substance.

"We're running a bit behind, so elementary teachers please head to the back doors and high school teachers to the side," the moderator said.

Wyatt frowned. "I wanted—"

"I'll see you later. They seem to be in a rush." Anne picked up her purse and hurried away before he could say anything else, her heart beating double time.

* * *

Wyatt tapped his thigh, his gaze on the instructor, but his mind elsewhere. The conference was a waste on him. Good thing he already knew the material. He couldn't focus on anything all afternoon. Well, that wasn't true. More like he'd focused on only one thing. He'd failed again to get Anne's number.

What the hell was wrong with him? He didn't get tongue tied or nervous about asking a woman out. If someone turned him down, which didn't happen much, he moved on. For some reason, he couldn't shake off Anne. He'd nearly split a rib laughing at her attempt to explain her lack of interest in sports. She'd stepped right in it, and the more she said, the worse it got. Didn't help when her cheeks turned pink, sending a wake-up call to his parts down south.

Yeah, she lit up his scoreboard, which left him scratching his head. What was it about her? Her pants suit covered most of her body, but not enough to hide the sweet shape of her ass when she'd walked to the banquet table. She kept her nails short and neat, wore minimal makeup, and didn't even like football. Not his usual type. But those big blue eyes of hers got to him. So many emotions flickered in them.

Maybe that's what drew him to her. She talked to him like a regular person, not a star-struck sports groupie. Hell, she'd even made fun of him about the crutches and the coffee. The woman had spirit *and* intelligence. Beautiful, but seemed unaware of it. And like an idiot, he'd managed to let her slip away before even getting her number. Although, she hadn't slipped away as much as run away.

The back of his throat tightened. She had issues. But that made her all the more human. No pretense, no flirting, no trying to win him over. Just…honest and real.

His ears perked up as the instructor turned off the smart-board and thanked them for coming. Shit. They weren't going back to the big conference room. That meant he wouldn't see Anne again. Oh hell no. He'd find her. Maybe her session hadn't ended, wherever that might be. He grabbed his crutches and stood.

"Do you need any help?" asked the woman with the "nephew" named Christy.

"Uh, no thanks." He wedged the crutches under his arms, but couldn't move forward because she stood in the way.

"I wanted to ask because, you know, you were so nice to sign that autograph for me." Her mouth curved, and her face flushed. "I was wondering if…"

Ugh. He didn't have time for this, but he hated to hurt anyone's feelings. "I don't mean to be rude, but I'm late meeting someone."

"N-no problem," she stuttered and backed away, once again, her face beet red.

Well, hell. He crutched a step and leaned in toward her. "Hey, tell Christy I really appreciate my fans and thanks."

A huge grin split her face. "I will. I will."

Phew. Nothing worse than making someone feel bad. He hurried to the door, his mind racing. Everyone had to leave through the lobby. His best bet would be to look for Anne there, unless she'd already left.

Loser mentality. No room for that. He jammed the down button on the elevator and adjusted his crutches. The muscles in his leg contracted. He could have run down the stairs in half the time if not for his stupid knee injury.

At last he reached the lobby. He exited the elevator and scanned the people milling around. No sign of Anne. A weight dropped in his stomach.

Refusing to give up, he crutched over to a spot where he could survey the entire lobby and leaned against the wall. He wiped sweat off his brow and stared down at his damp hand. What the hell had come over him? Running around a hotel like a maniac in search of a woman who clearly didn't want anything to do with him? He'd lost it. Disgusted with himself, he pushed off the wall, and his gaze locked on Anne, coming out of the restroom.

His heart smashed against his ribs.

Purse hitched on her shoulder, nibbling her lip, she glanced around the lobby as if looking for someone. She strode to one of the lounge chairs and settled her purse on the cushion. Taking a seat, she pulled out her phone. She swiped and typed, but kept looking up from time to time.

Could she be searching for him? Damn the insecurity he'd never felt in his life. And damn the feeling this one mattered. Like he might not get another chance if he screwed it up. And why that bothered him compounded the whole thing.

He made his way across the lobby and caught the exact second she saw him. Yeah, he caught the way her eyes got wide and the quick flush of her cheeks as she stuffed her phone back into her purse. And yeah, he liked the way that made him feel because she *had* been searching for him. But she also had that skittish look to her. Like a curious cat that got too close to the fire and had to make a dash for it.

Anne stood and ran a hand down her pants. "Hi, again."

"Hey. How was the session?"

"Good. I always learn something." She glanced at the rotating door of the lobby.

Not a good sign.

Wyatt took a breath. Enough of this. He wasn't some cowering high school kid. "Can I buy you a cup of coffee?"

She blinked and cocked her head. "Thanks, but no. I have papers to grade."

"No. I didn't mean now." Strike one, but he wasn't giving up yet. "I meant maybe this weekend. Would you like to get coffee? In a place where they bring it to you so you don't have to carry mine? Come on, I owe you."

Retreat blazed in her deep-blue eyes. She forced a smile. "Thanks so much, but I'm not really a coffee drinker."

"But you had some today."

She shrugged, and the cute way her mouth twisted to the side made his belly flip. Oh man, she probably had gotten a cup just so she could help him with his. Another reason to like her.

He dragged a hand down his face. "So, you don't like coffee?

"Not so much."

"But you know people who like coffee, and you like them?"

Her eyes narrowed, and her lips twitched. "I like people who like coffee."

He might still split a rib. "Does your dog like coffee?"

Anne laughed. A pure, sweet, sound that reverberated through his body. And holy crap, her entire face lit up brighter than stadium lights when she smiled. It made him want to do whatever it took to keep her laughing.

Refreshing.

She shifted and pressed her lips together. "I really should get going."

Uh-oh. She'd retreated again. Maybe he could buy some time. "Did you park in the garage?"

She nodded.

"Me, too. I'll walk you out."

"Can you drive?" She gestured to his leg.

"Yeah. Right leg's fine."

"Oh, of course." She glanced at the elevators. "You don't have to walk me to my car, especially with the crutches."

"I'm pretty sure I have to."

"Why?"

"My mother. She would have killed me if I let a woman walk alone to her car in a dark parking garage."

"I managed to get here okay." Anne shrugged.

Wyatt shook his head. "That wouldn't have mattered to my mother."

"You're persistent, I'll give you that. Okay." She made her way to the elevators and pushed the button.

As she stared at the lit-up floor numbers above the door, he couldn't help but stare at *her*. Freaking adorable. She had a cute, perky nose and straight blond hair tucked behind her tiny ears. At least for now. The wisps tended to slip out, and for some crazy reason he wanted to be the one to brush them back the next time.

When they got in the elevator, Anne stood in front of the control panel and pressed the parking floor button. Wyatt balanced on his crutches. The doors shut, and a flowery, soft scent filled the space. Amazing. The woman smelled as sweet as she looked.

She gave him a quick, polite smile, and then looked up at the descending numbers.

Awkward silence. Shit. He needed to say something. Anything. Sweat tickled under his ears. He could talk to a wall, for God's sake, but apparently not to Anne.

Ding.

The doors opened, and he held a crutch out, gesturing for her to exit.

"You first," she said. "I'll hold the door button."

"Nope. After you." He shook his head.

"I'm already holding the button, go ahead."

"Nope. Remember what I said about my mama? Same thing with the elevator." And he meant it. Chivalry wasn't dead.

"Oh my God. It's not the dark ages. I—"

"You're holding the elevator hostage. What about all the people upstairs waiting for it?"

She pursed her lips and huffed. "Fine. I'll go."

The look she shot him on the way out meant he hadn't scored any points, but she still held an arm out to block the door from closing.

"You know you're stubborn, right?" she asked, a hand on her hip.

"And you don't like to let people do things for you, right?"

"Why would you say that?" She thrust her chin up.

His gaze dropped to the base of her throat, where her pulse beat a rapid rhythm. He'd love to press his lips against the spot. And her sweet scent floating in the air didn't help. Focus, he had to focus. "It's a hunch. There are givers and takers, and you're a giver. At least from what I've seen. And for the record, I appreciated the help today."

She blinked and swallowed, dropping the hand from her hip.

There. That did it. Now *she* was speechless. And not looking so ready to go to battle. But he'd only spoken the truth.

"I really need to get going." She adjusted her purse on her shoulder.

"Which way is your car?"

"It's over there." She pointed across the parking garage to the far end. "But I'm fine, thank you."

"Eh, that's not far from where I parked. Lead the way." He gestured with the crutch again.

Her hand went back on her hip. Shit. Now what? Everything he did seemed to get under her skin. And he didn't have the slightest clue what to do about it. No woman had ever challenged him.

"You're used to getting your way, aren't you?"

He kind of was. Not that he thought about it much. "Well, I'm not right now."

"How's that?"

Not sure what to say, he took a step closer. She glanced up, and her eyes did that flicker thing, heating his blood. Licking her lips, her gaze dropped to his mouth. He might not know what was going on in that head of hers, but he knew desire when he saw it. At least it went both ways.

All or nothing. His gut said he had one more shot. The muscles in his neck bunched. This mattered. Why, he had no idea.

When he blew out a breath, her gaze flew back to his.

He softened his voice because he didn't want to scare her off, which seemed like a real possibility. "I'm not getting my way because I've been kicking myself ever since I didn't ask for your number at the bar. And now that we've spent some time together, I'm kicking myself even more."

She gave the slightest shake of her head. "Wyatt, you seem like a nice guy, but—"

"I am. Give me a chance. All I'm asking is for one cup of coffee. Or tea. Or juice. Or whatever you want. No pressure, and if it doesn't work out, I promise I'll never bother you again."

He held his breath.

She closed her eyes for a second, and then opened them. "Okay. I guess a guy who doesn't want to disappoint his mother can't be all bad."

Yes. Virtual fist pump. "How about the diner on Main Street, Friday after school?"

She slowly nodded. "Sure."

He dug his phone out and handed it to her. "Can I have your number in case anything changes?"

She hesitated, but took the phone and punched in a number. After handing it back, she dug her own out. "What's your last name so I enter you alphabetically?"

Alphabetically? Most of his contacts were one-word nicknames—Bones, Jones, Jewels.

"Pearson." He forced a straight face and waited for her reaction.

None.

Tension tightened his belly. She really didn't know anything about him. He'd be starting fresh with her. Just a regular Joe. This woman didn't care about his fame or fortune. Going back as far as he could remember, women came to him. He'd never had to pursue anyone. Hell, he'd sweated bullets trying to get Anne to agree to cup of coffee. Scratch that—tea. And if she didn't even like sports, how would she ever understand him? Maybe he should stick to what he knew.

She slipped her phone back in her purse and held out her hand. "Anne Cooper."

Her dimples popped when she smiled and gave him a firm shake.

His heart slid sideways as her face lit up once again. He couldn't help but grin. "Now, can I walk you to your car?"

She squared her shoulders. "Thank you, but I'm fine."

This woman really didn't want help from anyone. But she'd agreed to tea. That was a start.

"Okay, I'll call you." He wasn't going to pressure her.

As Anne backed out, Wyatt's phone vibrated with a text message.

Angela. Flight attendant and a hot Redskins cheerleader he hooked up with from time to time. "Angel" had no business being part of her name.

I'm back in town. Come to my place tonight?

Wyatt glanced up at the tail lights of Anne's car leaving the parking garage. Since when did he not want to see Angela? Another first. He typed a quick note back. *Sorry, can't do. Maybe catch up another time?*

She replied with two face emojis. A frown and a blowing-a-kiss.

What the hell had he gotten himself into? He *never* turned down Angela. He brought up his contacts and searched for Anne's number.

Cooper, Anne.

Dynamite in a petite package. He shook his head, tapped edit, and changed her name to "mini-cooper."

He had a feeling he might be in for a wild ride.

CHAPTER 6

THE PAPER SHOOK in Paul's hand as he read the invitation for his college reunion. Would Lynn be there? His pulse skipped a beat. Lynn...the one and only girl he had ever loved. Sure, it had started out as a bet with Devon over who could win her affections, but it quickly became more than that to Paul.

He hadn't seen her since college when she'd disappeared and he'd lost touch with her. Now, he and his wife shared a comfortable life, but she had never stirred his blood like Lynn.

The image of her sitting up on the rocks when they went hiking back in college would burn in his mind forever. Her long, dark hair blowing in the breeze as she smiled shyly at him. Under the shade of a tree, Paul kissed her, and she kissed him back. That was the day Lynn told Devon she wasn't interested in him, and Paul won the bet.

The next month was a blur. Paul lived and breathed to spend time with her, and for some crazy reason, she acted the same way. When he finally got the nerve, they had sex. She was giving, loving, and he tried to please her to the best of his inexperienced ability.

That was the last time he saw her. His heart broke when she left town without a word. They'd both graduated, but she hadn't even shown up for the ceremony. None of her friends would talk to him or shed any light on the situation.

With no other choice, he'd licked his wounds and gone on with life. What would he even say to her if he saw her at the reunion? Regret gnawed at his stomach lining.

He picked up the phone and dialed Devon's number. "Hey Devon, how are things going? Haven't heard from you lately."

"I've been busy."

"Trying to win our bet?"

"I'll win. You just be ready to pay up. Is this all you called about?" Devon asked.

"No. I was wondering if you were going to the reunion." Tension pinched Paul's shoulder blades.

Devon scoffed, "Hell no. I haven't kept in touch with any of those people."

"I figured as much." Good. He wouldn't be there to make fun of Paul if he did see Lynn.

"Why? Are you actually thinking of going?"

"Probably not." Paul tried to sound casual. "On other subjects, I wanted to let you know the wire came through and everything is settled with that last purchase."

"Perfect. Thanks. Anything else?"

"Nope. I'll catch you later." Paul hung up and smoothed the invitation out with this hand.

College had been a struggle for him socially until he'd met Devon. He'd helped Devon pass some classes and climbed the social ladder by association. He'd been popular, and suddenly Paul was invited to parties and events. Devon liked to gamble and make wagers, which is how their game began. Paul didn't care that he lost most of them, because he had won the only one that mattered to him. Lynn.

He blocked off the date in his phone calendar and shredded the invitation.

No need to tell his wife about the reunion. She'd just think he had another late night at work.

CHAPTER 7

ANNE PACKED HER LUNCH, turned off the apartment lights, and headed to her car, taking her time on the steps, as her ankle still ached. Rituals were good. Rituals kept her from thinking about Wyatt and why she'd agreed to meet up with him. Rituals reminded her that he ticked off every block in her "men-I-should-never-date" column.

Handsome check.

Charming check.

Famous *double* check.

No. Her next date was supposed to be with an average, down-to-earth, reliable man. Someone who didn't need constant ego stroking. Someone who didn't draw a crowd wherever he went. She was a conservative, private person on a track to become a principal one day. Her reputation would weigh heavily in the decision of a school to accept her.

Only, when Wyatt had said that stuff about givers and takers, he'd gotten to her. And they'd just met. She was a giver. And it was as hard as hell for her to take anything. Her whole life she'd been the responsible one. Watching out for her sisters, teaching her students. Nothing satisfied her more than helping others.

Add to that the chemistry, or whatever the hell it was that caused her insides to melt around him, and...yeah, she'd said yes to coffee. Big mistake. She still had time to call and cancel. But the way he'd talked about his mother had touched her. Obviously, he cared about and respected his mom. That had to count for something.

A couple miles into the drive to work she groaned at the vibration followed by the *flap-flap-flap* sound of her tire as rubber smacked against pavement. Crap.

She got out of the car, zipped her coat up, and slightly limped over to the source of her frustration. Stupid flat tire. She itched to kick it with her good foot.

With a sigh, she headed back to the driver's seat. Once inside, she pulled her phone out and dialed the emergency roadside assistance number she had programmed.

Of course, she got a robo-voice asking for her account number and location. No real person ever manned a phone anymore. The robot informed her someone would be dispatched to her location in one to two hours. Shit. She needed to be at school in twenty minutes. Tension bit into her neck. The rearview mirror reflected nothing but a winding country road for miles.

She had a spare in the trunk, and she could look up how to change one. Couldn't be that hard. She had a wrench, tire iron, and first aid kit as well. Never hurt to be prepared. Hopefully the first aid kit wouldn't be necessary. But considering her lack of tire changing skills, she couldn't rule it out. She called the school office to let them know she'd be late.

As she hauled out the spare tire from the trunk, the smooth thrumming of a car engine caught her ear. The vehicle pulled up behind her and parked. Her heart raced. There wasn't time to put the tire down and get back into her car. What if it was some pervert or thug? Gripping the tire wrench in her hand, she stood as tall as her five-foot-four frame could muster and assessed the man getting out of a BMW.

He was tall, dark, and dressed in what looked like an expensive suit. The hazard lights on his car flashed as he approached with a friendly smile.

"Need a hand?"

She wasn't sure what to say. The guy was decked out like he'd stepped off a movie set. Certainly not dressed for changing tires.

"Are you okay?" he asked.

"Yeah. But I have a flat." Her gaze dashed over his suit. "I called roadside assistance."

The man shrugged. "Sure, but I bet you'll be waiting here for a long time. It'll only take me a couple of minutes to change it."

"Oh, I couldn't ask you to—"

"Not a problem." He slipped off his jacket and rolled up his shirt-sleeves. Glancing at the tire wrench in her hand, he said, "I have something better. Be right back."

He jogged to his car and returned with a bigger wrench and a cloth to kneel on.

After jacking up the car, he removed the lug nuts with quick, efficient twists. The guy wasn't big in a body builder kind of way, but he moved with strength and control. No doubt he got his share of female attention with his good looks, but he didn't ignite sparks in her belly like Wyatt did.

He yanked off the flat tire and his long, lean hands deftly replaced it with the spare. With a final twist, he tightened the nuts, then stood and tossed the flat tire into the trunk, thumping it shut.

"You should be good to go. Don't drive too long or fast on that little donut spare."

"Thanks so much. I really appreciate it." She wanted to offer to pay him, but he didn't look like he needed money and might get insulted. She held out her hand to shake. "I'm Anne, by the way."

Her gaze went to his hands, which were dirty from handling the tire. He picked up the rag he'd brought and wiped them. "Devon. Nice to meet you, even under such unfortunate circumstances."

They shook hands and he squeezed hers, holding it for a second, then let go and walked back to his car. With a quick wave, he pulled away and left her staring into the taillights of his BMW.

She shook her head. What was such a city slicker doing way out in the country?

CHAPTER 8

Anne parked in the lot next to the coffee shop. Red hearts adorned the lampposts lining the sidewalk. Several of the quaint shops had Valentine's window decorations. She'd forgotten all about V-day. Since she'd never had a boyfriend in February, it kind of fell off the radar. Soon enough, social media would blow up with pictures posted of flowers and candy. Sometimes it sucked to be single, but with standardized testing coming up, she didn't have time to wallow.

She couldn't bring herself to get out of the car yet, wishing she hadn't succumbed to some crazy attraction she'd felt with Wyatt that made her agree to meet, so she flipped down the vanity mirror to touch up her lipstick. One cup of tea, and she'd be outta there. Too late to cancel.

The scent of cinnamon buns and coffee swirled in the air as she entered the diner. Red streamers looped from ceiling lamps to booths, and cardboard Valentine's cut outs covered every conceivable inch of wall space. Nothing awkward at all about being surrounded by naked cupids with arrows pointed at her.

Laughter erupted from the far corner of the diner, where a group of people gathered. A pair of crutches leaned against a booth by them. Her chest tightened.

She stood on her tiptoes to get a better look at the table. Wyatt didn't have a monopoly on crutches. They could belong to anyone.

Tamping down the urge to leave, she approached the booth. As she got closer, a couple of people moved out of the way, and she spotted Wyatt. He craned his neck around the group and caught her gaze.

The full force of those jade eyes focused on her took her breath away.

As he slid out of the booth, people moved to make room for him. Someone handed him his crutches, which he waved away.

Almost as one, the crowd turned and stared at her. Heat crawled up from the core of her body. Everyone had gone quiet. Jeans, a soft pink T-shirt, and sneakers had seemed the right thing to wear for a cup of tea. But now? Not so sure.

She forced a breath. Why did she care? Just because Wyatt was some superstar didn't mean she should have to dress up. This was a diner, and it shouldn't matter what anyone thought of her. Yet all eyes were on her and hell yes, they did seem assessing.

"Hey, guys, my friend's here. I'll catch you later." Wyatt slapped a hand on the shoulder of the man beside him.

"Yeah, sure. See ya." The group broke up, but not before giving Anne the once-over.

She cleared her throat and faced Wyatt. Maybe this was her out. She didn't need the pressure of approval from his fans. "It looks like you're pretty busy. I don't want to—"

"No, I was waiting for you." And something in the low register of his voice sent a thrill through her. Which she didn't like at all. Or maybe too much. His teal polo shirt brought out the color of his eyes. As if they needed any help.

He gestured to the booth. "Please, have a seat."

She slipped out of her coat, and Wyatt hung it on the hook attached to the booth.

"I hope you weren't waiting long. I try to be punctual."

His lips curved, and he ran a hand over his mouth. "Punctual. You're punctual?"

She cocked her head. Was he making fun of her? Maybe he thought she was being flip. Or worse, an organized, planning, punctual bore, which was what her last boyfriend called her. Even though she'd been the one to break it off, those parting words had stung. "Yes. I like to be on time and not make people wait. Is something wrong with that?"

"Nope. What I wouldn't give to get my football and lacrosse teams to understand that concept." He waved to the booth again. "Please, have a seat."

Too late to back out now, so she eased into the booth. She had this. Get through the coffee thing and be done. She assumed her polite attitude. She knew how to do polite.

Wyatt sat across from her. "What's that look?"

"What look?"

"I don't know. That expression on your face." He scratched his chin, brows furrowed.

They stared at each other for a long, uncomfortable moment, and then a waitress came over. "Hey Wyatt. What can I get for ya?"

"Hi, Sally." He gestured to Anne. "Ladies first."

Guess he came there enough to know the waitresses. Since it was late afternoon, she'd best avoid caffeine. "Could I get a decaf tea, please?"

"Yup." Sally scribbled on her pad.

"I'll have a coffee." Wyatt leaned to the left and checked out the glass cake stands on the counter filled with pastries. He turned back to face Anne. "You ever had one of their cinnamon buns?"

"No." But the scent of them made her mouth water.

"You gotta get one. They're to die for." Excitement laced his voice.

Sally nodded. "He's right."

Eating pastries didn't fit in with her plan of a quick escape, but Wyatt obviously wanted her to try one. "Okay."

After Sally left, Anne pointed to his crutches. "How's the leg?"

"Better. Amazing what some therapy and a week will do."

"Why do I have the feeling you push yourself?"

He raised an eyebrow. "What makes you say that?"

"Because you wouldn't take the crutches when your friend handed them to you. I think I got your number." She placed a napkin on her lap. "Let me guess, you hobble out of PT after going to the max?"

"I'm kind of an all or nothing guy. If I'm there, I'm going to make the most of it. Besides, this crutching around sucks, and I want to get off these things."

"Ah, stubborn *and* impatient. Your therapist must love you," she said with a smile so he'd know she was kidding.

"My head's swelling from all this flattery. Any more and I won't fit out the door."

His eyes flickered, and a zap of awareness pinged her. She'd never had these reactions before. Sure, she'd been attracted to men in the past, but never this almost electric energy between them.

He settled his broad shoulders against the back of the booth. "So, you said you teach fifth grade?"

"Yes. I love that age. Trying to get them ready for middle school."

Wyatt shook his head. "Hormones starting up. That's a tough job. Hats off to you."

Sally returned with their drinks and then called over her shoulder as she left, "I'll grab your buns."

Wyatt chuckled. "She has no idea how that sounded."

Anne choked on her tea and willed the image of Wyatt's mighty-fine-ass out of her head.

His eyes danced with amusement, as if he knew exactly what she was thinking.

The hairs on the back of her neck prickled. She glanced around. Sure enough, four people sitting at the booth across from them stared at her. Two couples, who quickly looked away and whispered to each other.

"What's wrong?" Wyatt followed her gaze.

"Those people were staring at me, or us. Do you know them?"

He shrugged. "I don't think so. They look familiar, but I do come here a lot."

"Oh." Probably more fans. "I take it you were pretty good at football."

He paused, coffee mug halfway to his mouth, and grinned. "Segue?"

"It's just that everyone seems to know you. I mean, if you weren't any good, then…" Damn. This wasn't coming out right. Her ears burned.

"I didn't suck canal water, I guess." He smiled around a sip of coffee.

"Of course not. I didn't mean that. I meant…" She fidgeted and blew out a breath. "Darn it. I can't talk to you."

He put his mug down. "Why?"

"I don't know." Liar. She knew damn well why. Every time she looked at him her body revved and sentences failed to form right. It's like he gave her a brain freeze. Maybe if they discussed something less personal, she wouldn't fumble over words. She'd come prepared. "I looked up some football trivia."

"You did?"

"Yes." She straightened. "Did you know the huddle was first used in the eighteen-nineties by a deaf quarterback?"

Wyatt jerked his head back. "Really?"

"Uh huh. He was worried the other team could interpret his hand signals, so he brought his teammates into a huddle to call plays."

"No kidding?"

"I didn't research the trivia, but that came up on a football facts site." She ticked off the next one, since heck, he seemed impressed and interested. Not bored at all. "And kickers used to get way more respect. Touchdowns were worth four points and field goals, five."

He grinned and shook his head. "I didn't know that either."

Sally returned with the cinnamon buns and set them on the table. "Can I get you anything else?"

Wyatt pointed to Anne's cup. "You want more tea?"

"I'm good, thanks."

Sally nodded and left.

Anne gaped at the huge roll covered in rich, creamy icing. The heavenly scent of cinnamon and spice floated up, and she pulled a piece off. When she popped it in her mouth, her taste buds did a jitterbug. It's possible that she moaned. She licked the icing off of her finger and glanced at Wyatt, who gazed at her mouth.

At least she wasn't the only one fantasizing, if she read him right.

"This is sinful." She pulled off another piece.

He jerked as if someone had shaken him awake, and then nodded. "Told ya."

After a few bites, she asked, "Where did you play in college?"

"Syracuse."

"Oh wow. They get a lot of snow there. You must have been freezing at the games."

"No. They have a dome. But I used to shovel snow for money, and my first year there we got a hundred and sixty inches." He took another sip of his coffee. "I made a bunch of bucks that winter."

"That's crazy." She shuddered. "I would hate it. I like warm weather."

"The snow wasn't as bad as the cold. Below zero with windchills in the minus teens. A great city, but winters are brutal. You have to find creative ways to stay warm."

She blinked. Sheesh, was he talking about…

He grimaced. "Shit, that sounded bad. And I made fun of Sally for what she said. I meant we used to build bonfires next to the frozen lake."

"Gotcha." She nudged the plate with her half-eaten cinnamon roll a few inches away. Still might not be far enough, but she'd make herself sick if she ate the whole thing. "What position did you play?"

Wyatt wiped his mouth with a napkin, and then rubbed his chin. "I'm curious about something."

"What?"

"You googled football facts, but not my name?"

She squirmed. The temptation had been real, but she'd refrained. "I didn't think that would be fair."

"How so?" He rested an elbow on the table.

"Well, I mean, it's not like you could look me up and find out about my life. And besides, you never know what's true. I wanted to get to know you on my own." Even though she'd been *that* close to doing it.

He held her gaze, and said in a quiet tone, "You're really something."

She swallowed, and a warm wave washed over her. Somewhere along the way, she'd lost track of her mission to get out of the diner, and it had nothing to do with the dessert. Contrary to what she'd expected, Wyatt wasn't running for the hills, and neither was she. In fact, the complete opposite.

He sat back. "I played tight end."

A tight end? Oh God. Right back to the bun images.

He leaned forward. "Are you okay? You're flushed."

"Yeah, it's the tea I think." She tugged at the neckline of her T-shirt.

Sally came back to the table. "Need some refills?"

"No, but I'd like an ice water please," Anne said.

* * *

Wyatt bit his tongue to keep from laughing. Anne's face couldn't turn any redder. He'd bet the house she had no idea what a tight end was, and it didn't take a rocket scientist to know why she'd blushed right after he'd mentioned that position. Adorable.

"Go on, how long did you play for the Ravens?" She took another sip of tea.

"Eight years. Same position. *Tight end*." He couldn't help himself.

She choked and held a hand to her chest.

Shit, he wasn't trying to kill her. "You okay?"

"Mm-hmm." She took a breath.

Sally brought Anne's water, and she gulped the drink as Sally refilled Wyatt's mug. "Need anything else?"

"Just the check. Thanks." Wyatt said.

Anne set the water down. She seemed to be breathing normally again. "So, did you break any records? Like get the most sacks?"

God, she was so damn cute. "That would have been a nice trick."

"Why? You're famous and all, so I figured you must have broken some records."

"I did." He grinned. "But no sacks. A tight end plays offense. I was never on the field with the other quarterback."

"Oh." She frowned.

Crap, he didn't want her to feel bad. She was trying so hard. "It's okay. You told me up front you don't like sports. I'm not offended."

Her shoulders softened. "Good. I'm sorry."

"No need to apologize."

She nibbled her lower lip, and fire blazed a path to his groin.

"Hey." He leaned across the table. "You went out of your way to look up facts about my sport. A sport you admittedly don't even watch. And *you* told *me* things I didn't know. That means a lot."

Her tentative smile made his heart thump. She seemed to accept that he wasn't making fun of her. He sat back. "Enough about me. What about you? Do you have family here?"

She nodded. "I have two younger sisters. Sarah is only an hour away, but Maddie lives in New York, and my parents retired to Florida. How about you?"

"Just me." He held up his hands.

"You mentioned your mother when we met?"

A weight settled on his shoulders. "She was diagnosed with an aggressive brain tumor. They couldn't save her."

"Oh no. I'm so sorry." Anne reached across the table and rested a hand on his wrist. Her gentle touch radiated up his arm.

"Yeah, it was bad. That's why I retired. I don't have siblings, and my father died in a car accident the year before. She didn't have anyone to take care of her."

Anne pulled her hand back and stared at him. Her blue eyes teared up. "Wow. You lost both parents that close together and gave up your career?"

Hell, the last thing he wanted was pity. "I think of it more as being lucky enough to have the money and chance to spend that tough year with her. I'm doing fine. I have the dog."

"A dog?"

"Yup. I thought it might help my mom, you know, give her some-thing to love and focus on. I rescued a mutt from the kill shelter. And then I had to buy something to drive him around in, so he cost me a pickup truck, but he's worth it."

"That's really sweet. Is he a big dog?"

"Nah. Goober's medium sized with light brown fur. I think he's some sort of lab mix."

"Goober?" Anne's eyebrow raised.

"Yeah, he's not the sharpest knife in the drawer. A total goof, hence the name. But he loved my mother." And he wasn't the only one that missed her.

"I'm sorry you lost so much in such a short time. Do you ever think about going back to football?"

"I miss playing, but I've been out for eighteen months, and my replace-ment is tearing it up." He took a sip of coffee. "I interviewed for an offen-sive coordinator job out at USC. I'll start in the summer if I get the job."

"California, huh?" She sat back and crossed her arms.

Didn't have to be a brain surgeon to read that body language. But hey, he wasn't there to bullshit her. She needed to know he might only be around until summer, which was all the more reason to keep things casual. "There's nothing here for me anymore. I have no ties to the area."

Anne's mouth turned down at the corners and her eyes softened. "No relatives at all?"

"I have an aunt and uncle, but they live out west, so growing up I never really saw them."

"Yeah, even though New York isn't that far, it's still tough to get together with Maddie. And now both of my sisters are pregnant, which makes it even harder."

"Really? Both of them?"

"Yup. It's Sarah's second." Anne dropped her gaze and shrugged. "I always thought since I was the oldest, I'd be the first to have a baby."

She wanted kids? A punch to his gut went wide left. She had to be in her thirties, which meant her biological clock was ticking. Hell, he was nowhere near ready to go down that road, maybe never.

She glanced up and her eyes widened. "I'm sorry, I have no idea why I said that. I didn't mean…I mean…"

An awkward silence stretched between them. Time for a subject change. "No worries. So, you want to be a vice principal?"

Her hitched up shoulders lowered. "That's my goal."

"Well you seem like a planner. You're organized and punctual. My money is on you to land the job."

Her face fell, and her back stiffened.

Shit. He'd meant to compliment her. "What did I say to upset you?"

She glanced at him with sad eyes. "Don't worry about it. Just reminded me of something."

Like hell he wouldn't worry about it. He'd somehow hurt her.

Sally slid their check on the table and boxed the leftover bun. Wyatt dropped some bills on the slip, leaving a generous tip. "Thanks, every-thing was great."

Anne fumbled with her purse, pulling out her wallet. "Please, let me pay half."

"Call me old-fashioned, but I invited you, so my treat."

"Well, thank you." Anne quickly slid out of the booth and reached for her coat. He had to hurry to grab a sleeve and help her into it.

She picked up the box and thanked him again but avoided eye contact. Damn. His stomach fell to the floor. What had happened? They'd been getting along great, and then he'd told her he might move to the opposite coast, she'd brought up a baby, and he'd somehow insulted her.

Cold air blasted them when they left the diner. Anne crossed her arms and hugged her coat tight. Something he'd like to do, but that wasn't in the cards. She'd closed herself off.

Nerves fired in his chest. He didn't do nerves. Not on the field, not with women, not ever. Except big time now. Because despite the abrupt ending in the coffee shop, the thought of not seeing Anne again did unnerve him.

Once again out of words, he crutched his way to her car. Every step making him more determined to lose the damn things.

She hit the unlock button and gave him a polite smile, only it contrasted with the depth of emotion in her crystal-blue eyes. The same ones that had teared up minutes ago over the loss of his mother.

"Thanks for everything." She cinched her coat tighter.

"Sure." He fumbled for the right words to say because his gut said he was about to blow it big time. Maybe he needed a grand gesture. Offer to take her some place special. The other women he'd dated liked to dress up and hit the town.

"I better get going." She reached for the door handle.

He leaned back on his crutches. "Hey, there's a hot new restaurant in Baltimore that opened up a couple of months ago. It's booked solid and nearly impossible to get a reservation, but I'm sure I could swing it. What do you think? Would you like to go?"

"Mm." She shook her head. "I heard about that place. It's out of my price range, though, and I'd feel bad if you picked up that tab. But thanks."

Crap. That backfired. He had more money than he knew what to do with, but something told him that wouldn't matter to her. Should have figured as much when she'd wanted to split the diner bill.

As she opened the door, his pulse raced. He'd never met anyone like her. No pretense, no games, and the way she'd prepared for the date? Priceless. He had to find a way to see her again. Maybe casual would work. "Listen, I'm not looking for anything serious. Can we just catch a bite some place local then?"

She looked away for a long moment, took a deep breath, then faced him. "The truth is, I had a breakup not long ago, and I'm not sure I'm ready to date. I really shouldn't have gone out with you. I'm so sorry."

So that's why she had those sad eyes. He backed up a step to give her some space. "We can go as slow as you want. Slow as molasses, uphill, in the Syracuse snowbelt. Please, just give me a chance?"

She hesitated, and every second tightened the muscles holding his heart.

Uncertainty flickered in her eyes, and she worried her lower lip with her teeth. "I'm not sure about this, but I guess we can—"

"Yesss." Excitement and relief knocked the breath he'd been holding out of him. His crutch slipped from under his arm and he fell forward, right into the car door, which slammed against her shin.

"Ouch," she cried out as the back of her head hit the roof.

Holy shit, what a fucking klutz. He tossed the crutch to the side and grabbed the door handle, yanking it open farther. "I'm so sorry. Are you okay?"

She rubbed her head with one hand and her shin with the other, hunched over in obvious pain. "I'll...be fine."

"Here, let me help you."

He took a step around the door, but she whipped a hand up and said, "No, just stay where you are. Don't move."

Christ she must think him a total, uncoordinated dork. He winced. "Do you want me to get some ice from the diner?"

"No, that's okay." She eased into the driver's seat and dragged her legs in, glancing up at him. "Thanks for the tea."

Ugh. This must be what his students felt like when they got a bad grade on a health test. A total failure. "And the headache and the bruised shin? I'm really sorry."

She shrugged. "Remember, I was limping at the conference. I can do more damage to myself than you can, believe me."

"You're just trying to make me feel better."

"Is it working?" She angled her head and gave him a sweet smile that slid his heart sideways.

"It depends. Is it still okay if I call you?"

"Sure. I should be safe on the phone." She grinned, shut the door, and rolled down the window.

Wyatt laughed. "That was just mean."

"I was kidding. But seriously, be careful on those crutches."

He stood in the lot until she drove out of sight, half hoping she'd turn around and come back. How could he have lightning reflexes and perfect balance on the field, but not be able to put one foot in front of the other around her?

The crutches didn't help, but that wasn't the problem, and he knew it. She threw him off balance. This was all new territory for him. He'd never had to work so hard to get a date. When she'd agreed to go out again, he'd acted like an eager child tumbling down a flight of stairs on Christmas morning. He shook his head.

Yeah, they'd do casual. He could do casual. It's all he'd ever done. Only, for the first time, he might want something more than casual, and he had no clue how to go about it.

CHAPTER 9

PARKED in Anne's apartment lot, Devon drummed his fingers on the steering wheel of the dented, weathered pickup truck he'd bought. The piece of junk fit in with the other vehicles and wouldn't stand out at any hick bar she might go to again.

He'd done his homework and checked out Wyatt Pearson, the former pro-football player who had met Anne at a diner. Just like Devon's brother, another star athlete. Devon's gut roiled. Made him want to take Pearson down.

He jerked to attention when Pearson's Lexus pulled into Anne's apartment complex. The asshole must have managed a second date with her. Needles pricked Devon's backbone.

Anne opened the door and Pearson entered. A few minutes later, he and Anne came down the stairs and got into his car. Devon followed them to a chain restaurant with a full parking lot. Cheap bastard couldn't afford fine dining with all his franchise money? If this was Pearson's game plan, he'd be easy to one up.

With the crowd, dinner would take a while. Devon waited a minute to make sure they didn't bail, then doubled back to Anne's apartment.

Since it was dark, the old lady across from Anne's wouldn't be going out. He'd spent days and nights surveilling the place to get a handle on people's schedules. The hag never went anywhere after sunset, and she was the only one he needed to worry about being close enough to see him.

Devon picked Anne's lock, entered her apartment, and shut the door. The place was small and modestly furnished. It fit a teacher's salary. A few seashore pictures adorned the walls, and a gold-framed mirror hung in the entranceway. Wait until she got a load of his mansion, which she would, soon.

Too bad he didn't have time to snoop around and gather more information about her. Not worth the risk or the bother. He had her number. And he'd have her.

After he bugged the rooms and landline, careful to leave everything as he found it, he locked the door on the way out.

He scowled as he drove. Pearson might have some short-lived celebrity status, but Anne had no idea what Devon had to offer. He'd blow that soon-to-be-has-been out of the water.

His phone dinged. He stopped for a red light and glanced at the screen. A text from Jake telling him to call when he had a chance. He'd make the time. They went way back.

Devon had grown up in foster care after his family died in a fire. For five years he'd been passed from home to home and used by people to get government handouts. Hard to say which was worse, the fondlings or the beatings.

At age fifteen, he ran away and took up with the carnies. It wasn't a complete waste of his life. They taught him how to play poker, and he escaped the foster nightmare, but he was destined for better things. He waited for the right opportunity, which came when he decided to take his poker skills to the next level.

Vegas. That's where he met Jake and his life changed for the better. He'd worked his way into the high-stakes poker games when one day two bouncers escorted him to the casino owner's office.

"Been watching you, boy," said Jake.

"Yeah, why?" Devon asked.

The two guys who'd muscled him there stood in front of the door, blocking the exit.

"I'm trying to figure you out. I've never seen a kid play poker like you. Not a single tell, no matter what cards you're dealt." Jake leaned back in his chair and folded his hands across his ample belly. "No sunglasses, no hat. You're beating players twice and three times your age. I don't get it."

"Well I'm not cheating, so what's your beef?"

Jake's gaze bored into his. "How old are you?"

"Twenty-one."

"Bullshit." Jake stared him down for a long, silent moment. "Time to turn you in."

Devon said nothing. He sat perfectly still; his eyes locked with Jake's.

A slow smile formed on Jake's face. "Damn. This must be how you do it. You gotta be scared or pissed or fucking something, but I have no clue what you're thinking."

"Why am I still here?" Devon tapped his fingers on the arm of the upholstered chair.

"You're a cocky son of a bitch, aren't you?"

Devon merely shrugged.

Jake unfolded his hands and leaned forward. "Here's the thing. I could use someone like you around here. You help me, I help you."

Devon arched a brow, and after a pause, he nodded. "I'm listening."

Just like that, they were in business together. He raked in the money over the next few years and picked up a couple of perks along the way. One of the casino dealers was a martial arts teacher, and Devon trained until he earned his fifth-degree black belt. Damned if he'd let anyone ever push him around again.

Another one of Jake's employees was a computer genius. Devon paid him well to create documentation of home schooling, so he could apply to colleges. No one ever questioned it. Why would they when his SAT scores were near perfect? Devon didn't give a crap about college, he got in, but only wanted the diploma. His superstar brother had died in the fire at age sixteen, not living long enough to get one. Finally, Devon had beat him at something. He'd carefully rolled up the diploma and stored it next to the other trophies in his special place.

As far as brothers went, blood didn't matter. Jake was the big brother Devon never had, and always would be. Nothing he wouldn't do for Jake. When Jake had a heart attack and almost died, Devon ran the casino and kept it operating in the black until Jake could get back to work.

The light turned green, snapping Devon back to attention. When he got home, he picked up the phone and called Jake. "What's the news, Jake?"

"He's ready to sell. We got him by the short hairs. He lost a shitload of money last night at my tables, and the sharks are already after him."

About time. "He agreed to the Rembrandt?"

"Hell, yeah. He woulda agreed to his own mother. Can't get his hands on the money fast enough. He's scared shitless."

"Okay. I got a buyer lined up and ready. Get the painting to my shop, and I'll take it from there."

"You got it."

Devon's stomach churned. "Hold on. The selling price just went down on that item. Tell him he waited too long. Tell him a third less. We'll charge the buyer the original price and split the profit."

Jake whistled. "You're talking a lot of money, you sure?"

"He's desperate. He'll take it. What else is he going to do? Besides, it puts the message out there. People come to us to sell something, they better be ready to deal. We own this market."

"All right. Your call." Jake clicked off.

Devon rubbed his hands together. No one messed with him and didn't pay for it. After pouring scotch over ice, he sat at the kitchen counter and called Paul.

"Hey, Devon."

"Paulie. Got another shipment going out. There'll be a wire coming to my account soon. I'll call you later with the exact amount." He took another sip of his drink. "This one's big, so expect a nice cut."

"Perfect timing. I was thinking of taking the wife on a cruise. Any idea what my take will be?"

"Not yet, but I wouldn't skimp on the room." Like Paulie ever would.

"Excellent. Hey, on another subject, how are things going with our bet?"

"Making progress. You better be ready to pay up when the time comes." Devon sat back and swirled the ice in his glass.

"We'll see, Devon. We'll see."

"Just take care of business, Paulie, and let me worry about our bet."

"Okay, I'll be in touch."

Devon sighed. Another huge payoff. Who knew there were so many rich people out there with serious gambling problems and virtually no available cash?

Some guy racks up gambling debts, gets in trouble with the sharks, and needs cash fast. He's got a ton of valuable, insured stuff in his house. If he claims a piece is lost or stolen it takes time, which he doesn't have, and kicks off a massive investigation. So he goes to Jake, who tells Devon to find a black-market buyer. He and Jake split the money. Paul gets a cut for handling the wires and accounts without asking any questions. And the stooge goes back to gambling, setting Devon and Jake up for another score. A win-win for everyone.

Devon frowned and took another drink. The liquid burned a path down his throat. His legitimate front, meet-by-appointment antique shop, needed some attention. The paintings and sculptures were piling up. Such a time-suck finding buyers when the business brought in a mere fraction of the money he made on the black market. It ate the living hell out of him, but was a necessary evil.

The Rembrandt wouldn't be in the shop for sale, though. No one knew about the room beneath his antique store where he kept the black-market items until they shipped. He didn't trust anyone with that part of the business.

Or the other secrets hidden there.

CHAPTER 10

WYATT FROWNED AT THE SAD, wilted flowers. Sitting in the sun too long on the passenger seat had taken a toll. He rummaged through the glove box for a pen to black out the neon-pink price sticker on the cellophane wrapper.

No luck. Maybe he could scrape the ticket off with a key. He shouldn't have listened to his coworkers, but they'd scared the shit out of him with "the Valentine's Day rules." If he'd gone to a florist, he wouldn't have stickers on the wrap.

After some effort, he managed to get the dollar figure off. It would have to do. He shook the flowers to try to fluff them and petals dropped. Better leave them alone before all he had left were stems.

He probably should have picked the pink roses. It's not like he was trying to be cheap, but the roses were all budded up and small. The bright, pretty carnations and daisies reminded him of Anne. Besides, giving roses would've broken one of the rules for dating someone only a few weeks before the holiday.

Who knew there were rules? His head hurt when he'd made the mistake of casually asking the women at work what to do for Valentine's Day. Young, female teachers, mostly single, they all had strong opinions. No gifts. Too soon. Don't go anywhere fancy or expensive. Keep it low key and fun. Flowers are okay, but don't go overboard, like a dozen red roses.

Hell, he'd been fine with asking Anne out until he'd talked to the women. By the time they were done, he'd needed to change his drenched shirt into the spare he kept for coffee accidents.

When he'd called Anne, he'd kept it casual, as instructed, by mentioning Valentine's Day was coming up, and why not do something fun together? You know, grab a bite and catch a band or something.

She'd hesitated. He could picture her, biting her lip while she analyzed her options. But in the end, she'd said yes, and he considered that a huge victory after all the coaching from the bleachers.

Turning into her apartment parking lot, he took a deep breath. So far, they'd met for coffee and a casual dinner, but this was an entire night out. Their first real date. Valentine's Day, no less.

Anne greeted him with a smile and an outfit that kicked his already pounding heart up a notch. A white sweater, short black skirt, and heels that showed off her toned, sexy legs. He thrust out the flowers. "They got a little mashed."

Her eyebrows shot to the top of her bangs, but her smile never faltered as she took the bouquet of floppy flowers. "Thanks, I'll get some water and a vase."

He couldn't take his gaze off her as she crossed the carpet to the kitchen, hips swaying. Sexy as hell. He all but lost it when she bent down to check under the cabinets.

"I could have sworn I had a vase under here." Empty-handed, she stood and glanced at the shelf above the refrigerator.

"Want me to check up there?"

"No. I can't reach it, so I wouldn't have put anything there." She pulled a tall glass out of a cabinet, filled it with water, and picked up the flowers. "I'll need some scissors to cut this open."

While Anne rummaged around in the drawer, Wyatt bit the end of the cellophane, tearing it with his teeth. He plopped the flowers into the glass, and they flopped over the rim.

Shit. Where were all his smooth moves? Obviously benched, as always, when it came to Anne. "I think I must have broken the stems when I tried to scrape off the price tag with my key."

"I'm sorry. It's really fine—"

"This sucks." He frowned. "Wait until I get to work on Monday."

"What?" She glanced up from the flowers.

"The advice I…never mind." He stabbed a hand through his hair. That had slipped out. He didn't want her to think he had to phone a friend to plan a date. Amateur hour.

Her eyes softened, and a hint of smile turned up the corners of her mouth.

He reached out and tried to straighten a daisy. Both it and the carnation next to it broke off and fell on the counter.

Anne bent over, covered her face with her hands, and burst out laughing. "I'm sorry."

Wyatt couldn't blame her. "I should've gotten the roses. But then I'd have trailed blood all the way here from the damn thorns."

"Stop." She held up a hand. "I can't take anymore." Her breath came in short spurts as she held her sides. Black mascara smeared under her eyes when she wiped them.

Didn't take away from her beauty. Those adorable dimples and pink cheeks that matched her lips made heat coil in his belly. She stood so close that her sweet scent filled his nostrils. He threaded his fingers into her hair. Soft and silkier than he'd imagined.

She glanced up, but her gaze stalled on his mouth. Her breath turned shallow. Despite their agreement to keep things casual, he knew desire when he saw it. She raised her eyes, and the uncertainty swimming in them gave him pause.

Even though her body sent all the right signals, she wasn't ready for a kiss. He cleared his throat and lowered his hand.

* * *

Anne wiped a palm down her skirt, and Wyatt took a step back. He'd almost kissed her and she'd wanted him to, right until she'd let her brain engage with thoughts of him leaving town. Of course, he'd noticed and backed off. He had to be wondering what he'd gotten himself into.

She picked up the broken flowers from the counter and fiddled with the stems. "Umm…thanks."

"For what?"

"For these." Cop out. She grabbed a small glass, filled it with water, and put the short, broken flowers in it. Her back to him, she sighed. "And for...you know...not pushing. I mean any other guy would—"

"Hey, look at me."

When she turned and faced him, he said in a low tone, "I'm not like any other guy. Let me prove it to you."

She swallowed. His gorgeous green eyes, shining with emotion and honesty, broke down a piece of her defensive wall. She couldn't argue. She'd never met anyone like him. But he might be gone in a few short months.

"I'm starving. You ready to go?" Wyatt asked.

He'd been up front with her about the USC job, and she'd still agreed to go out, so she needed to shake off the negativity. She nodded. "Sure, where we headed?"

"Brady's." He helped her into her coat.

"Never been there, but I've passed it," she said as they walked down the stairwell to the parking lot.

"Where do you live, anyway?" Anne asked as they drove.

"The Oakville apartment complex near the high school. At least for now." He shrugged. "It took a while to sell my mother's house, and I don't want to build or buy until I know about the USC job. So, I'm renting month-to-month."

"That makes sense." Although she'd expected someone famous like him to have one of those huge mansions in the country. For all his notoriety, he sure acted and lived down-to-earth. She glanced at him. "What's this Brady's place like?"

"It's a small pub like Corner Bar. I'm friends with the band that's playing there tonight. The guitar player, Pete, went to Syracuse with me, and we used to jam together. Not that I had a lot of time. Football kept me busy."

"Really?" Anne tipped her head. "What did you play?"

"Guitar. I've played with them a couple of times, but they're serious about music, and I'm not that good. It's a second job for them, playing gigs. I don't have time with teaching and coaching."

"That's for sure." The work didn't end when the kids left for the day.

He stopped for a light and flicked on the turn signal. "This is their first time at Brady's. They're pretty pumped. If they do well, the owner will book them again, and he pays more than most bars."

Wyatt pulled into the parking lot. "Wow, this is a big crowd for here."

"Valentine's Day. Every place is probably packed." Anne zipped her coat as they crossed the lot. "You must be happy to be off the crutches."

"Oh, yeah." He slung an arm around her as they walked. "Cold?"

"A little." And she'd use that excuse to tuck herself against his hard, muscular chest.

They entered the building, and the scent of fried food hit her. The hostess's face lit up when she spotted Wyatt. "Pete said you were coming. I saved a table for you."

"Hey, thanks a lot. I know you don't take reservations," Wyatt said.

"Only for special customers." She winked at him and grabbed two menus. "Follow me."

Anne would have to get used to Wyatt knowing everyone and calm the green beast that reared its head every time another woman flirted with him.

He took her hand and gave it a little squeeze. And just like that, the beast disappeared. He was with *her*.

Unlike the diner, the bar was splashed with cupids and decorations, but not overdone. They ordered a couple of beers and some burgers.

"It's cozy in here. I like it." Anne glanced around. It did remind her of the Corner Bar. Booths lined the perimeter, with wooden high tables scattered around the central bar.

All the tables had condiment caddies next to mason jars filled with pink and red carnations. Most of the guys wore denim or flannel shirts and jeans. Anything went for the women, from dressed up to casual.

"Hey Wyatt." A striking redhead in a black hip-hugging dress stopped on her way past their table. She gave Anne a cursory look and then focused back on Wyatt. In a low voice, she all but purred, "Where've you been hiding?"

Wyatt inched his chair away from her and shrugged. "I haven't been out much."

"Time to rectify that." She leaned over, whispered something in his ear, and then sauntered off toward the bar.

Anne's blood heated. Unbelievable. Did anyone care that he was with her?

"Sorry." Wyatt winced and blew out a breath.

She had a choice to make. Sit there and fume, or let it go and try to have fun. It's not like Wyatt had sought out the redhead. "Don't worry about it."

Their waitress arrived carrying baskets loaded with fries and burgers. Anne leaned back to make room. As they ate, the band came in and started setting up. Wyatt glanced in their direction. "I'll introduce you to them when we're done."

"Okay." Anne drenched a fry in ketchup. "This is pretty good food."

"Glad you like it. And thanks for coming." He covered her hand with his.

Her fingertips tingled under his touch, and she gazed into his deep-green eyes. A girl could get lost in them.

He brought her hand to his lips, keeping eye contact. She swallowed hard.

"Maybe they'll play a slow song, and we can dance?" His breath tickled her fingers.

"I'd like that." More than he could possibly know.

After they finished eating, Wyatt paid the bill and pointed across the room. "You want to meet the band?"

"Okay."

They grabbed their beers and snaked through the place, crossing a small dance floor in front of the stage. When Wyatt walked up, a thin guy in a cowboy hat let his guitar slide down as he held out a hand. Wyatt introduced him as Pete, the drummer as Brian, and the bass player as Dan.

"You got quite a crowd already," Wyatt said.

Pete nodded. "I know. This is a good chance for us."

"I'm sure you can use the money with a baby coming."

A baby? Anne's gaze flew back to Pete. He'd be around Wyatt's age since they'd been in college together.

"How's Sophia doing anyway?" asked Wyatt.

"Great. Big as a house and cranky as a bear." Pete shook his head. "Three weeks to go. I may play a lot of gigs until then."

Dan snorted. "Right. You've checked your phone every five minutes since we got here."

"I better let you get warmed up." Wyatt said. "We'll catch you on your break."

"Sounds good." Pete went back to tuning his guitar, and the other guys gave a quick wave.

"Let's see if we can find some seats." Wyatt led her through the mob, and they stood by the bar for a while until a couple finally left.

Anne sat when he held out the chair. "Pete's wife's having a baby, huh?"

"Yeah. He and Sophia have been married for three years." Wyatt took a swig of beer.

"He looks so young."

"Baby face. We ride him about it."

In three years, Anne would be thirty-five, headed into high-risk pregnancy. Father Time nudged her in the ribs. If she wanted a family, she couldn't afford to waste time with someone who had no interest in one. She glanced at Wyatt.

"You okay?" He leaned over and rested a hand on her knee.

He seemed to read her like a book, missing nothing. The skin-to-skin contact on her bare knee and inhaling his spicy scent wiped her brain clean. "What?"

The band started playing, and Wyatt brought his mouth close to her ear so she could hear him. "You look upset."

His warm breath teased the sensitive spot below her earlobe, and her nipples hardened. Her reactions to him were out of control. She might melt right there on the barstool like soft-serve ice cream on a hot summer day. "I'm, uh, good."

He eased back, and she crossed her arms to cover her breasts. Although she'd like to fan her burning face.

"Are you too warm? We can…" He hitched an eyebrow, and then the tension drained from his face, replaced by a slight twitch of his mouth.

Crap. He must have figured out what was making her so hot. Or rather *who*. "Really, I'm fine."

"Okay, cool." He leaned his elbows on the bar, spreading his shoulders. Not that she noticed.

At all.

They didn't talk much because of the loud music, but Wyatt stayed connected to her, moving a hand to her knee, or her shoulder, while tapping his fingers to the beat. Every contact kept her body in a heightened state of awareness.

Whatever the future held, she might as well enjoy the time tonight with Wyatt. She squeezed his hand and smiled at him.

His eyes lit up. "I think they're playing my song."

"Hey, Anne," a voice called out over the music.

Anne turned. Emily and her friend, Kate, waved frantically, beers in hand.

"Oh my gosh. What are you doing here?" Anne leaped off the barstool and hugged Emily. When she let go, Emily stared pointedly at Wyatt, who had stood.

Anne introduced them, and Kate gaped up at Wyatt, eyes wide. She might faint if she didn't breathe soon. Not that Anne could blame her. He had that effect.

The band announced a break, and the room quieted enough for conversation.

Emily laughed. "We're out for Anti-Valentine's day. Gonna get a ride home later."

Anne had told the girls she was going out with Wyatt, or they would have invited her for sure. After recent breakups, Kate and Emily were taking a rest from dating. But even dressed down in jeans and T-shirts, the perky brunette and redhead still turned heads.

Dan rounded the bar and grabbed Wyatt's arm. "Thank God you're still here."

Wyatt cocked his head. "What's up?"

"We had to cut the set short. Pete left. Sophia's in labor. He's headed to the hospital."

"What?" Wyatt did a double take. "He said she had three weeks."

"I know, but I guess she's early or something. Don't ask me." Dan's shoulders tensed, desperation written all over his face. "You gotta fill in for him. We have a lot riding on this. If we don't finish playing, they'll never have us back."

CHAPTER 11

"Oh, man." Wyatt held up a hand. "I can't—"

"It's okay. Just do it." Anne didn't want Pete's band to lose the gig. Not with him having a baby on the way.

Wyatt rubbed the back of his neck and looked from Anne to Dan.

"Don't worry. She can hang with us." Emily slung an arm around Anne's shoulder.

Dan jumped on the hesitation. "Come on, bro. Brian and I are okay, but Pete told me he needs this gig."

Wyatt glanced at the stage. "This could end up bad, Dan. I haven't played in a long time and never was that good."

"Anything will be better than us bailing," Dan said.

"Really, Wyatt, please don't worry about me. I'm fine." Anne laid a hand on his arm and gave him her best I-mean-it look. Well, as much as she could with his ripped muscles so firm under her fingertips.

"Are you sure? I'll have to be here until they close."

She nudged him away. "I'm sure. Help out your friends."

"I'll make it up to you." His eyes flashed, and her knees went weak.

Emily linked her other arm through Kate's. "Don't worry. Us girls stick together, and we'll have fun."

Wyatt blew out a breath. "Okay."

"Yes." Dan smacked him on the back. "Come strap on Pete's guitar."

As the guys walked away, Emily squeezed Anne's shoulder. "Holy crap. I've seen his car commercials, but he's smoking hot in person."

"Car commercials? Huh. I don't watch much TV, and when I do it's recorded so I can fast forward through the advertisements. I'll have to pay attention."

"Well he's got my attention. Total hottie."

"Yeah, he kinda is, isn't he?" Anne kept her gaze on him as he walked with Dan to the stage.

"Kind of? Look at Kate. He's struck her mute, and she never shuts up."

Kate snorted. "I wouldn't turn him down. Damn that guy is big." She took a sip of her beer, and then choked on it. "I mean, I wouldn't know about *that*, but I mean just in general, he's a big guy."

"And...she's back." Emily play-punched Kate's arm.

Anne shook her head. Now she had *that* to think about. Although, her mind had gone down the naughty path a time or two, noting the size of his hands.

"Now look what you've done." Emily waved at Anne. "Her face is redder than a tomato."

Blah. Enough of this talk. Anne pointed to some people getting up from a table near the stage. "Let's grab that."

The girls rushed over as a server cleared it. Anne eyed Wyatt as they took their seats. Tuning the guitar, he focused on the strings. Dan handed him some sheet music, and Wyatt stared at it with the same intensity Anne's students did when she gave a pop quiz.

Dan snagged the cowboy hat Pete had been wearing and shoved it on Wyatt's head. Wyatt reached up and grabbed the top of the hat as his gaze met Anne's.

Good thing she was seated, because her legs would have buckled. Wearing that cowboy hat, with those vivid green eyes and biceps bulging when his hand grabbed the top of the hat—breathtaking.

He paused and lifted the hat as if about to take it off.

Anne shook her head. Hell no. The hat needed to stay on. Emily snatched Anne's phone from off the table and snapped a picture.

Wyatt settled the hat back on, and Anne nodded. He flashed a smile, and her blood turned to liquid heat.

"Just when I thought he couldn't get hotter." Kate whistled under her breath.

The redhead from earlier approached the band and stopped in front of Wyatt. She held a beer out to him, and he hesitated. Anne's breath froze in her lungs. Wyatt gave a small shake of his head and said something to the woman. She nodded and took a step back, but didn't leave. He glanced at Anne, a slight frown on his face before going back to studying the sheet music.

"Looks like you have some competition," Emily said.

"Yeah. It's a thing." Anne eyed the crowd.

Emily put a hand on her shoulder. "Don't forget he came with you."

At the moment, that wasn't so comforting. Anne shrugged and took a sip of beer.

Brian tapped his drum sticks together three times and the band began playing.

When Wyatt started singing, his voice not quite on pitch, some people stopped talking and craned their necks for a better view. He fumbled with a chord and shot a glance at Dan, who shrugged and nodded.

Anne's chest constricted. Poor Wyatt was struggling, and publicly. It couldn't be easy for someone used to performing well under the spotlight. She checked out the crowd again. A group had formed in front of the band, and people at tables pointed to Wyatt with smiles on their faces. Looked like they recognized him.

Despite his somewhat off-key singing, no one seemed to care. Anne forced out a slow, deliberate breath. He had this.

Emily tugged Anne's hand. "Come on, let's dance and have some fun.

After a set, the band took a break, and the girls returned to their table. Anne peered over Emily's shoulder as two women in cowgirl boots and miniskirts strutted over to the stage. One of them leaned in and said something to Wyatt as he bent down to put his guitar aside. She smiled and handed him a cocktail napkin.

Anne twisted her watch and nibbled her lip. Was she giving him her phone number?

"Now what's going on?" Emily frowned, staring at the women.

The one who'd passed him the cocktail napkin turned to her friend, who dug around in her purse and produced a pen. She handed it to Wyatt.

He glanced at Anne and pressed his lips together. After scribbling on the napkin, he gave it back to the woman and in long strides made his way to Anne.

"They wanted an autograph."

"Come on, Kate. I gotta pee." Emily snagged Kate's arm and dragged her away from the table.

Anne struggled to swallow. Even though she was annoyed, her mouth had gone dry as he'd walked over, still wearing the cowboy hat. "Is it always like this?"

He grimaced. "It won't be for long. Believe me, everyone is going to forget who I even am in no time. And they're harmless. I'm not interested in them."

"They're pretty persistent." Anne glanced at the redhead who loitered near the band.

Wyatt took a step closer and framed her face with his hands. Instant heat blazed under his touch. He locked gazes with her and said in a quiet voice, "You're the only woman in this room I want to be with."

She breathed in his unique scent as waves of warmth radiated from him.

"Correction." He stroked his thumb under her chin. "You're the only woman I want to be with, period."

Her annoyance melted as she stared into his eyes. With his complete attention focused on her, she had to believe him. She gave him a small smile, and he let out a breath as if relieved. He gestured to the stage. "I warned you I wasn't very good. I hope you don't think less of me after that performance."

She gazed up at him. "Believe me, I could never think less of you."

He blinked, and his eyebrows drew together.

"Oh my God. That came out wrong." How did she always jumble her words around him? "I meant I could never think less of you."

His lips twitched at the corners. "Wanna try that again?"

What the hell had she said this time? She couldn't think straight. "What did I say?"

"The same exact thing." He held up two fingers. "Twice insulted."

"Sheesh, Wyatt. I'm sorry. I meant—"

"It's okay. I promise I wasn't fishing for a compliment. I really care what you think and just don't want to embarrass you, since you're here with me."

Him embarrass her? He had it all backwards. She was the no-name date, not the celebrity. Besides, he put himself out there for his friends. "I think you're amazing to do this, and the crowd loves you. You could never embarrass me."

His eyes widened, and she froze. "What did I say now?"

"Nothin', I'm just messing with you." He patted her arm and gave her a wicked grin.

A giggle bubbled up from her chest. "I'm gonna kill you. That's not funny."

"Then why are we both laughing?" His eyes danced with humor, and something stirred inside of her.

Wyatt had a knack for making her feel like a kid again. She'd spent so much of her life taking care of other people and being the responsible one that it felt good to just let loose and be silly. She'd laughed more with him in the last two weeks then she had in the entire time she'd dated either of her "serious" boyfriends.

And the thing about Wyatt was that he didn't expect her to act a certain way or care if things weren't perfect. This night was nothing like they'd planned, and yet she was still having fun. Maybe everything didn't always need to be mapped out in advance.

Anxiety tightened her neck at that thought. She always had a plan. Needed a plan. A plan was what made life safe and predictable. That was her comfort zone.

"Anne?" Wyatt waved a hand in front of her face. "Where'd you go?"

"Sorry, did you ask me something?"

"No, but I have to study the sheet music for the next set, so I better get back to Dan." A small frown tugged his mouth down.

"Hey." She placed a hand on his chest. "You got this."

He touched her cheek, covered her hand with his, and pressed both to his heart. "Thanks."

* * *

After helping the band pack up, Wyatt walked Anne to his car. She sank into the seat and eased back. What a night, and quite the eye-opener. Wyatt wasn't some spoiled celebrity who expected adoration. He'd been nervous, self-effacing, and completely loyal to his friends.

To his credit, he'd brought charisma to the stage, and once his nerves calmed, he'd focused less on playing every chord right and more on drawing in the crowd. It had worked. People seemed to love him because he brought energy and life to the music.

Could she have done it? Put herself out there in front of a ton of people, knowing her talent fell short of the mark. Probably not, because when she took on something new, she dedicated the time until she mastered the craft. Going out on a limb wasn't her style.

Wyatt dropped into the driver's seat, and the car seemed to shrink as he filled the space. His cologne swirled in the air, and she took a deep breath.

"You tired?" He started the engine and drove out of the lot.

"No. I'm kind of wired, actually."

"Me, too."

Anne grabbed her purse and dug around inside. "I had my phone on the table, and I'm not sure I put it away."

"Hold on." Wyatt pulled to the side of the road. He clicked on his hazards and the overhead light.

"Thanks." She fished around in the bottom of the bag, plucked the phone out, and held it up. "Oh, good, it's here."

The corner of his lips turned up, and he nodded. "I got the impression you liked the hat."

What was he talking about? Anne looked at her phone and gasped. The background picture was of Wyatt, up on stage, holding the cowboy hat with one hand. Damn that Emily. She'd saved that picture she'd taken as the background.

"I...didn't know this was on here...Emily—"

"You ever been kissed by a guy in a cowboy hat?" he asked.

Her mouth went dry. "No."

He turned the overhead light off, plunging them into darkness. Anticipation cut off her breath. As her eyes adjusted, the flash of the hazards illuminated the lines of his face, which hovered close to hers. She jumped when he squeezed her knee.

"We'll have to do something about that." He leaned away. "My hat's in the back right now."

He checked the mirrors and pulled onto the road. She caught his mischievous smile in the reflection of the streetlights. He sure knew how to keep her off kilter, in an exciting way.

"Technically, that's not your hat." She pointed to the back seat.

Wyatt shrugged. "Dan wouldn't take it back. Said Pete insisted I'd earned it. Cowboys don't usually share hats you know, so I didn't want to insult him."

"Well, he's right. You did earn it. And now the manager hired them for another four gigs, so you saved the day." She touched his arm.

"They'll just be glad to have Pete back."

Wyatt sure didn't hold himself up on a pedestal. Anne yawned and drew her hand back. "I think the fans would be happy to see you again, too."

He glanced at her. "Thanks."

The car hummed as he drove, and her eyelids turned heavy.

"Anne. We're here."

"Mm…"

A warm hand patted her cheek. She nuzzled against it.

"Anne, wake up."

Her body shook. No, someone was shaking it. She jerked up in the seat. "I'm sorry, I must have drifted off." She rubbed her eyes. "I don't know how. I was so wide awake."

"It's okay. It's really late," he said.

She unbuckled her belt and groped around for her purse.

"No rush. Relax." He reached over and caught her hand in his.

She turned to face him.

"Thanks again, for everything. I know this was kind of a weird Valentine's Day. I'm sorry I didn't get to spend more time with you."

"It's okay. I enjoyed hanging with the girls."

He undid his seatbelt but still didn't turn off the engine. "It's really cold out there, and I don't want you to freeze at the door when I say goodbye."

"You don't have to walk me up. It's—"

"Shh." He placed a finger on her lips. "That's not what I'm talking about. I waited all night to kiss you. There's no way I'm leaving without doing it right."

Her heart thumped in her chest. "Oh."

Lowering his hand, he brought his face slowly closer, as if giving her time to refuse him.

In the dark, her senses heightened to the sound of the whirring heater, Wyatt's tantalizing musky scent, and the electric energy that pulsated between them, drawing her closer.

When his mouth had almost reached hers, he paused. Her pulse throbbed in her neck, and time ground to a halt. His warm breath set her skin on fire, and anticipation squeezed her heart. Unable to wait any longer, she closed the gap and found his lips.

He kissed her, soft and slow. A spark ignited in her chest and blazed a trail to the spot between her legs. When she opened her mouth, he slid his tongue inside. He tasted of mint and promise.

She fisted the front of his coat in her hand, to hold on if nothing else, and moaned. He deepened the kiss, and she pulled herself closer. Flames licked the insides of her core. A low growl came from the base of his throat, and she clung tighter.

He thrust his tongue deeper, and she met it with hers, tasting and exploring. More, she craved more. Desire racked her body like never before. Holding nothing back, she kissed him with all the passion he'd stoked and awakened.

He tore his mouth away from hers, breathing heavy. "I need to stop while I can."

Their chests rose and fell as they both sucked in air. God, the man knew how to kiss.

"Wow." He took her hand and eased back. "I wasn't expecting that."

"Neither was I." She shivered.

He rubbed his thumb under her palm and sighed. "I should get you inside. It's really late."

She had no idea what time it was and didn't care. But he had a point. If she stayed in the car so close to him any longer, she might not be able to control herself. "Yeah, it is."

"I just need a second here." He blew out a breath, glanced at her, and shook his head.

A thrill winged its way through her still-amped body. That kiss had turned him on as much as her.

When he opened her door, the cold wind smacked her face, a harsh wake-up call. They climbed the stairs to her apartment, her teeth chattering.

He leaned down and quickly brushed his lips against hers. "Call you tomorrow?"

"Sure." She stared into his eyes, debating whether to invite him in.

As if he read her mind, he gave a small shake of his head. "It's late and you have to be tired. Go inside before you freeze."

"You're right. Thanks again for the night." She unlocked the door and entered the apartment. Slumping back against the wall, she closed her eyes. The image of Wyatt on stage in the cowboy hat, rocking the place, had every nerve in her body alive again.

She slid to the floor and rested her head on her knees. Wyatt had apologized for not spending more time with her, but he had no idea that bailing out his buddies counted for a lot in her book. He was a true friend, and they were hard to come by.

What she hadn't been prepared for were all the "girl" friends. Women threw themselves at him. Right in front of her, even. And they weren't slouches. Really attractive women, like the redhead who he'd obviously gone out with before. Tough to compete with that crowd. Although he'd certainly reacted to her in the car moments ago.

All logic said she shouldn't see him anymore. He probably would be on the West Coast by summer, and he was in no rush to start a family. She'd built up a good reputation in the school system and had a decent shot at the vice principal job she'd been chasing. If they stayed in a relationship and she eventually moved to California, she'd have to start over as an unknown and get licensed for that state before she could even teach.

She pushed off the floor and paced. Despite all of that, with just a touch he cranked her from zero to sixty. Never mind the way her stomach flipped when he gave her one of his killer smiles. Sometimes emotion trumped logic.

Still, she had a checklist of the qualities she was looking for in a man. A celebrity with no intention of sticking around didn't match up too well. And maybe what scared her most was that she was beginning to question her plan.

CHAPTER 12

DEVON STARTED his car and followed from a safe distance as Pearson drove out of Anne's apartment lot. That was one anemic goodnight kiss at the door. This washed-up jock would soon be out of the picture if that's all he was getting. Coffee and dinner at a chain restaurant for their first two dates. He scoffed. Yeah, this stud really knew how to impress a girl. Probably spent all of twenty bucks.

It had been a miserable night hanging out in the back of the bar, but Devon wanted to see how Anne and Pearson acted together. Turns out there wasn't much to see. Valentine's Day and the guy brought her to a pub, fed her a burger, and then left her while he played in the band. That shouldn't be hard to top.

Devon's mouth twisted. What pitiful losers, Anne and her friends dancing like little whores. Visions of his drunken mother sashaying around the smoky family room with a drink in her hand burned a hole in his stomach.

Maybe Anne was playing the old tempt and tease, leaving the guy with blue balls at the doorstep. Not that it ever happened to Devon, but he knew the type.

Even though he had Pearson's name and address, he followed him home to see where he parked and the security set up. The guy wasn't any kind of threat, but best to keep tabs on him. That would be easy enough once he bugged the apartment. Why Pearson lived there made no sense. He had plenty of money. Most football players had mansions.

Devon hated that time was ticking away, but he couldn't make his move on Anne until he laid the groundwork. And he wouldn't need long to get her to accept a proposal. Once she saw what he brought to the table, it would be a no-brainer for her to want to marry him.

He'd been listening through the bugs in her apartment and overheard her discussing a charity fundraiser. Being a board member at the hospital provided the perfect opportunity. He'd volunteered to act as the liaison between the sponsoring businesses and the school. Everything was coming together.

Time to blow ex-super-jock out of the water. Make room for the man.

CHAPTER 13

ANNE'S CELL phone rang with her sister's tone, "Wild Thing." It fit Maddie perfectly. Anne glanced out the window as the last school bus pulled away.

"Hey, Maddie. How you feeling?"

"Like a blimp. Can't even cough without an adult diaper."

Uh oh. Still a month to go. "I'm sorry."

"Eh, it's okay. I get to eat extra ice cream. Why not? What's another pound at this point?"

"I'm sure you look amazing." Anne bit her lip.

"If you say anything about pregnant women glowing, I swear I'll come through this phone and pummel you."

"Wouldn't dare." Maybe a subject change was in order. "How's Sarah? I haven't talked to her in a couple of weeks."

"Same as always. She has three months to go. I bet she never tops one-ten. So annoying."

"It's in her genes. She got the good ones. Even before she did ballet, she could eat like a sumo wrestler and not gain an ounce."

Maddie sighed. "Sorry, I didn't call to complain. I wanted to know how you and the All-pro are doing?"

"He'd die if he heard you call him that."

"Why? He is. I looked him up, and he's broken a lot of records."

Everyone had looked him up, except Anne. "I don't know much about that, but I do know he doesn't brag."

"So gimme the goods. What base are you guys on, or did he already hit it out of the park?"

Leave it to Maddie to be direct. Anne's face heated. "We are not discussing this."

"Oh hell, you never share. Fine. If you won't tell me how he is in bed, at least give me relationship status."

Wyatt in bed. Anne's stomach knotted. That would be a big step for her. "Well, it's been a month since the Valentine's date, and we've spent some time on the weekends together. So, I guess things are okay, but he's interviewing for a coaching job at USC, so I really don't see this going anywhere."

"Yeah, and my Scott was going to be an undercover DEA agent forever, until he wasn't. Things change. Tell me more. Like if you aren't sleeping with him, what do you do?"

"Seriously? Can we not talk about sex or lack thereof?"

"You wouldn't be so uptight if you were getting some. Just saying." Maddie laughed.

"Okay." Anne blew out a breath. "We watch movies, make dinner, take his dog to the park. You know. Normal stuff."

"Huh."

Anne picked up a stack of papers that needed grading and placed them in her briefcase. "What's that 'huh' for?"

"I'm surprised he has a dog and that you're doing everyday kind of things with him. I mean, there are a lot of flashy pictures of him out on the town with women dressed to the hilt. I figured he lived in some mansion and would be wining and dining you."

A ringlet of anxiety wound around Anne's spine. So far, they'd only gone to local hangouts, and she'd been fine with that because she didn't like flashy or to be the center of attention. If they went some place upscale, that was bound to happen with Wyatt's celebrity status.

He'd offered to take her to that new Baltimore restaurant once, but that was the only time, and he'd been trying to get her to go on a second date. Was he embarrassed to take her out to the nicer places because she didn't measure up? Another log to toss on the fire of doubt. Might not take long for him to think she was boring, too.

"Anne? You still there?"

"Yeah?"

"What's wrong?"

Anne rubbed her neck. "Nothing. How's Scott?"

Maddie sighed. "Okay, subject tabled. I get it. He's fine. Since Sarah and Bruce are having their second baby, Bruce has been giving Scott advice on how to handle a very pregnant wife."

"Ha. Bruce should know." The man had doted on Sarah.

"Scott keeps stocking pickles and chips. I couldn't eat a pickle if it was the last food on earth. But I give him an 'A' for effort. What's going on with work?"

Anne zipped her briefcase. "I have an interview this week for a vice principal job and a meeting tomorrow to kick off a charity fundraiser for leukemia."

"You're so busy already, how will you make time for that?"

"Don't know, but I will." Her heart constricted. "It's important. The school is working with the local hospital. One of my students was recently diagnosed, and we want to do all we can to help his family with the medical bills."

"I'm so sorry. He's lucky to have you as his teacher, and if anyone can do it, you can."

"Thanks, sis. I gotta go. It's been a long day, and I have work to take home."

"Okay. Good to hear your voice. I'll keep you posted on the baby front."

"Make sure you do. I'm so excited for you guys." Tiny bubbles tickled her chest as she hung up.

She glanced at her computer. According to Maddie, there were lots of flashy pictures of Wyatt with women online. Maybe Anne was being naive. So blown away by his charisma and good looks that she didn't want to see anything negative.

With trembling fingers, she typed Wyatt Pearson into the browser. Images of him filled the screen. Some of football games, and others of him with women. Lots of women. Wyatt in a tux, looking hot as hell with a tall brunette hanging on his shoulder. Next a redhead, laughing and clinking a champagne glass to his. More brunettes, more redheads, a few blondes. He didn't seem to have a preference for hair color. The only thing they had in common were glittery, form-fitting dresses.

She shouldn't be surprised. A famous football player drew attention, but he'd sure had his share in the past. She scanned the images and froze. One of Wyatt with a supermodel caught her eye. He had his arm around the woman, whose head touched the side of his, bright smiles on both of their faces. Anne leaned closer to the screen. Valentine's decorations filled the background of the post.

Dated three weeks ago.

Betrayal stole her breath. These weren't all pictures from his glory days. That recent one was taken *after* she and Wyatt started going out.

No. This couldn't be happening. Racking her brain, she ticked back through their conversations. They'd never agreed to be exclusive. He said they'd take things slow and be casual. Did that mean he was seeing other women?

Her gut said no, since they'd spent every weekend together for the last month, but hell, there were plenty of other opportunities if Wyatt wanted them. Technically, it wouldn't be cheating, because she'd never talked to him about the subject.

She shut the computer off and glanced down at her turtleneck sweater with chalk marks across the middle. She closed her eyes and pressed a hand to her forehead.

Who was she kidding? Not even in the same league.

Her stomach queasy, she dusted off her sweater and stood. Emotions threatened to choke her, but she tamped them down. Right now, she needed to focus on getting to her fundraiser meeting.

* * *

Anne circled the hospital's parking lot until she found a spot in the far corner. She'd come during visitor's hours, so the place was packed. She grabbed her briefcase, locked the car, and headed to the information desk in the lobby.

"I'm here for a leukemia fundraiser meeting. Can you tell me what room it's in?"

The receptionist pulled out a paper. "Yes, room six twenty." She handed Anne a guest pass and pointed across the lobby. "Elevators are to the left."

Bright primary colors and animal art greeted Anne when the elevator doors opened to the pediatric wing on the sixth floor. She stopped when she came to an open area with a television, chairs, and a couch. A group of children hooked up to IVs or wearing casts surrounded a man in a dark suit, white shirt, and red tie. The kids laughed and tugged on his pants. "Show us. Show us."

A lump formed in Anne's throat. Poor little things. She took a step to continue past as the man pivoted, and she caught a glimpse of his face. Not just any man. The same man who'd changed her tire. Her pulse sped up. What was the guy's name? She frowned and tried to remember. Devon, that was right.

His hands were fisted in front of him. He opened them, and the children gasped in surprise.

"Where is it?" asked a small girl with a bandaged head and casted leg.

He knelt down to her level, reached behind her ear, and produced a bright, gold coin.

"Why, you had it all the time," he said with a smile.

The children begged to know how the trick worked. He handed the little girl the coin. "Keep this, and next time I'll show you a different trick. I can't tell you how I did it, because magicians always keep their secrets." He put a finger to his mouth. "Shh."

"Do you have to go now?" The little girl pouted.

"I'm afraid so, but I have a surprise for you. The nurses are going to bring ice cream and cookies as a special treat." The children cheered and he turned, still smiling. His eyes grew wide when they met Anne's. "Hi there...Anne, right?"

"Yes. Wow, I'm surprised to run into you again."

"It's a small world." He waved a hand at the kids. "Are you here to visit one of the children?"

"Oh...no...I was just passing by."

The children whispered and giggled.

"Is she your girlfriend?" asked the little girl holding the gold coin.

Devon smiled and patted her on the head. His gaze locked on Anne's. "No such luck."

Heat surged to Anne's face. She tapped her watch. "I better get going, or I'll be late."

"Me too, as a matter of fact. Nice bumping into you." He said goodbye to the children, then turned and walked briskly down the hall.

Huh. People were a constant surprise. With his sporty car and expensive suit, she hadn't expected him to be someone who would kneel down and play games with kids. Maybe she was a bad judge of character. Which brought her right back to thoughts of Wyatt. No. She didn't have time for that. Shaking her head, she checked the room numbers on the wall to figure out which way to go.

She found the conference room and stopped at the sight of Devon standing at the table, pulling papers out of a briefcase. He looked up. "Are you lost?"

"I don't think so. I'm here for a fundraiser meeting. Is this the right room?"

"Yes." He motioned for her to come in. "Oh, Anne...you must be Anne Cooper. I didn't make the connection."

"Yeah...wait, you're the hospital liaison?"

He flashed a smile and nodded, his brown eyes staring deeply into hers. "I guess we'll be working together."

Was she imagining it, or had he emphasized the word "together"? A wisp of unease snuck up her back.

"Please, have a seat." He gestured to the chair across from him. "I'm happy to have you onboard."

The fragrance of his cologne filled the room. The smell was distinctly masculine and nothing she recognized. Probably some expensive European brand. Not unpleasant, but it didn't make her knees weak the way one whiff of Wyatt's clean, male scent did. Raw pain scratched her ribs. She needed to focus.

After sitting, she clicked her pen and opened her notebook. "Have you been the liaison for the walk-a-thon in the past? This is my first time doing this."

"Mine too. I met with the sponsors and other board members earlier."
He shuffled through his papers, then raised his gaze. "I thought it would
be better for us to meet alone."

Again, his eyes bored into hers, and the hint of a smile played on his
lips.

She swallowed and cleared her throat. "I don't understand."

"Oh, I'm sorry." He tapped the folder on the table. "They've
been doing this for years and have all the materials and instructions. I thought since we were both new at this, it made sense to
meet separately to go through the details without disrupting their
day."

So he was being considerate, and she was being paranoid. Her
thoughts about Wyatt were making her suspicious of everyone, damn it.
"Of course. With school, I'm not available during the day, anyway."

Devon handed her a paper. "This outlines the plan for advertising
and promoting the walk-a-thon. Your role is to get as many people as
possible involved at the school. Kids, parents, teachers, anyone who's
interested in helping or participating. I'm open to suggestions and
ideas."

"Great, I'll look everything over and present it to the staff at our
meeting tomorrow."

"Sounds like a good start. I appreciate your help." He held out a business card, his fingers brushing hers as she took it. "I wrote my cell
number on the back in case you need to contact me outside of the
hospital."

She couldn't imagine a fundraiser "emergency" that would require
personal calls, but she didn't trust any of her crazy thoughts at the
moment.

Devon rubbed his hands together. "There's not much else to do right
now. I just wanted to meet you and get things rolling. Why don't we plan
on getting back together in about a week? Next Thursday at the same
time?"

"That's fine. It should be long enough for people to get back to me. At
least the teachers anyway, and we can go from there." She wrote the date
and time in her notebook, entered it in her phone calendar, and returned
both to her bag.

"Perfect." He stood and shut his briefcase. "I'll walk you out. I'm done here for the day."

He placed a hand on the small of her back, guiding her out of the room. She didn't like him touching her, but he dropped it before they passed the children in the open area, where two nurses were handing out ice cream and cookies to the excited crowd.

Devon pressed the down button, and Anne's gaze went to a huge plaque on the wall next to the elevator with "Distinguished Donors" engraved at the top. The first name under it was Devon Blackwood.

Guilt for questioning his every move squeezed her lungs. He must have donated a significant amount to be listed first.

The doors slid open, and Anne entered the elevator. She hit the button for the first floor. Devon stood beside her. Not crowding her, but also not on the other side the way people usually spaced themselves in elevators. Maybe the guy didn't have the same personal bubble that others did.

"You were so good with the children earlier," Anne said.

"I enjoy them. Since I'm on the board here, I see them quite a bit. I like to cheer them up, if I can."

"That's really nice of you, and they sure were happy for the treats."

He smiled. "Some things never change, do they?"

She couldn't argue that. Ice cream was her go-to favorite dessert.

They walked out to the parking lot. Five o-clock and already dark. She'd be so happy when they moved the clocks forward.

"Where did you park?" he asked.

"A country mile off in that direction." She pointed to the far side of the lot.

"I'm right up front here if you'd like a ride to your car."

She glanced at the reserved spaces and spotted his BMW. Being a board member and distinguished donor must merit parking privileges. She'd feel funny getting in his car, though, and would just as soon be done and on her way. "Thanks, but it's not too cold tonight."

"The fresh air feels good. I need to stretch my legs anyway, so I'll come with you. Who knows, you may have another unexpected flat tire, and I've already proven my worth in that situation." He gestured with his hand. "Please, after you."

She didn't want to argue with him, so she started walking. Sheesh. What was it with guys insisting on escorting her to her car? And…right back to Wyatt. Damn it all.

"I really can't thank you enough for helping out with this, especially as busy as you must be," Devon said.

"We're all busy. What do you do?" He clearly had money. Maybe he'd inherited it.

"I'm in the art business and am a collector of sorts."

"That sounds interesting. Do you paint?"

"Not at all. The kids can color better than I do." He laughed. "I'm on the business end of things. I match up buyers and sellers for rare artwork and antiques, mostly overseas. I have a shop just outside of town."

"It sounds fascinating. You must get to see a lot of different things."

"I do from time to time." They reached her car, and she glanced up at him. His dark eyes intensified, and he said in a low tone, "I enjoy finding rare items."

Was he flirting with her? No. Surely not. With his striking good looks and money, he'd have no interest in someone like her. And even if he did, she apparently fell for the green-eyed, athletic type with calloused hands and an arm that could toss a dog toy a mile.

Not sure what to say, she fumbled around in her purse until she found her keys. "I better get going."

"I'm looking forward to working with you," he said as she unlocked the car and got inside. "By the way, how far is the hospital from you?"

"I live about a half hour south."

"Same as me, only I'm a bit farther." He frowned. "You know, it seems silly for us to drive all the way out here next week, especially since we'll both be going back in the same direction, and parking is a bear for you. How about we ditch the sterile environment and meet over at Toni's? Do you know the place?"

"I do." The Italian restaurant was close to her apartment complex and would be more convenient. The carryout section always had empty tables where they could grab a soda and work. It's not like he was asking her out. It was just business.

He must have sensed her hesitation, because he quickly added, "I'm sorry. I don't mean to make you feel uncomfortable. If you'd rather meet here, that's fine. I just thought it might save you some driving."

She nibbled at her bottom lip. No point in making a big deal out of it. The guy was trying to make her life easier. "Sure. It makes more sense."

He smiled. "Great. Since we're meeting at five, we can grab a quick bite while we're there, so you don't have to worry about dinner."

Crap. She hadn't thought he'd meant dinner. Before she could tell him she'd changed her mind, he waved and walked away, calling over his shoulder, "See you next week."

Irritation bit the back of her throat. She wasn't going to yell after him. For God's sake, how had she gotten herself into this situation? She should have gone with her gut when he'd first mentioned Toni's. She needed to be more assertive, and worry less about pleasing everyone, especially if she expected to make a good principal.

Sighing, she started the engine. People had working dinners all the time. She could get through one. She'd insist they meet at the hospital from now on.

Her brain hadn't been functioning right all afternoon. She'd trans-ferred her doubts and fears about Wyatt onto Devon. Not fair.

Everything would be fine.

CHAPTER 14

ANNE HESITATED in front of Wyatt's apartment door. For the last week, she'd been in a funk after seeing all the online pictures. She'd played the "busy" card and kept their conversations short, trying to buy some time to sort out her feelings.

Her birthday was Monday, but Wyatt's lacrosse team had away games then and tomorrow, so he'd insisted on making her dinner tonight at his place. Homemade he'd said. And her heart swelled at that because the guy admitted he couldn't cook for his life. His stack of carryout menus rivaled the size of *War and Peace*.

Avoiding Wyatt wasn't the answer to her insecurities. Besides, she missed him. She took a deep breath and knocked on the door. Goober barked, and the sound of scampering paws was followed by a thud. A giggle escaped. Adorable mutt. Always so excited.

"Hold on," Wyatt called through the door. "Sit."

"No," Anne yelled, stifling a laugh.

"Smart ass." He opened the door and stood back, one hand held up in front of Goober, a treat in the other hand. "Stay."

While his attention was on the dog, Anne indulged in a full head-to-toe gawk. His white polo shirt rode up on his huge biceps and stretched across his ripped chest. A belt cinched the jeans at his tapered waist. A surge of pure lust shot from the souls of her feet to the roots of her hair.

She entered and glanced at Goober, who whined. His legs shook from suppressed excitement, and his tongue hung out of his mouth as he panted.

"Good boy." Wyatt gave him the treat. Goober inhaled the kibble and ran over to Anne.

She bent and hugged him, rubbing under his belly as he licked her cheeks. Pure love. Dogs had no agendas. "He's doing better than the last time I was here."

"I'm working on it. My mother spoiled him, so he needs to learn some manners. The dog walker is training him as well."

"I forgot about him. Probably because we've never met." The guy came on weekdays since Wyatt coached after school. She'd never run into him, which made her wonder who else she might have never run into. Another supermodel on any given night? Her gut churned.

She scratched under Goober's ears, and his eyes rolled back in his head. "Who's the best boy?"

"I'm hoping I am." Wyatt reached down, placed a hand under Anne's elbow, and eased her up.

Oh. Face to face, and so close.

He brushed his lips against hers. "I've missed you."

Her stomach did that flutter-in-a-good-way thing. But then the images of him with all those women popped into her mind.

Goober wedged himself between their legs and whined again.

Wyatt shook his head. "Okay, enough, boy."

Anne forced a smile, and Wyatt's eyebrows raised. "What's wrong?"

"Nothing." She had no clue how to talk to him about it. Besides, they were supposed to be "casual." But they'd spent six weeks together, and it sure felt like anything but casual. To her, anyway.

Wyatt frowned. Before he could ask any more questions, she stepped down the hall and picked up Goober's chew toy. He raced to her, grabbed it from her hands, and ran to the corner of the living room, plopping down on his bed.

"Let me take your coat." Wyatt came up behind her.

When she slipped out of it, his gaze traveled down her body. She'd chosen to wear black leggings and a pastel-blue V-neck sweater.

He laid her coat over the back of a chair and turned to her. Resting one hand on her shoulder, he slid the other around her waist to bring her closer. "You look amazing."

"Thanks." Her voice sounded strained to her own ears. She glanced down to avoid eye contact.

He loosened his hold on her. "I guess I better get to cooking."

She followed him to the kitchen and tried to keep the whole casual thing going. "Whatcha making?"

"Spaghetti marinara."

"Wow. I'm impressed." That wasn't an easy meal to make for someone who didn't cook.

He placed two stemmed glasses on the counter and pointed around the corner to a fully-stocked wine cooler she'd never noticed before. "Do you want white? Or I have red on the shelf."

She blinked and gazed at the bottles. On a good day, she might carry one of each at her apartment. Never such a varied selection. She glanced to the living room, where a huge flat-screen TV hung on the wall. A real-leather sectional and recliner filled the space along with a high-tech stereo surround-sound system.

Their lives couldn't be more different. A weight sunk to the bottom of her stomach.

"Anne? What's up?" He walked over to her and took her hand. "I don't know what's going on, but you haven't been yourself all week. I thought you were just busy, but that's not it. What's wrong?"

She owed him an answer. And she sucked at pretending, so she might as well come clean. "Are we exclusive?"

"What?"

"Exclusive." She cleared her throat. "We never really discussed it."

"Wait, are you saying you want to date other guys?" His brow wrinkled, and hurt flashed in his eyes.

"No." She shook her head. "I'm asking if…you know…you do?"

Relief washed over his face. "No. I do not want to date other guys."

She smiled, but then sobered. "I'm serious, though, because I assumed we were exclusive."

"I don't understand where this is coming from. Have I said or done anything to make you think otherwise?"

She couldn't clam up now. If they had any chance at a relationship, she needed to tell him what was bothering her. "It's just that I...I..."

He leaned in, and his gaze locked on hers.

Her chest tightened. "I googled your name, and a lot of pictures came up. One pretty recent, of you with a supermodel."

He blew out a breath and dragged a hand down his face. "I see."

"I'm sorry. I wish I hadn't, but I can't un-ring that bell or get it out of my head." She lowered her gaze and fiddled with the bottom hem of her sweater.

He crossed the room and picked up a football from the floor in the corner. Tossing it from hand to hand, he paced, the lines on his face taut.

She glanced up at him. Not the reaction she'd expected.

"So, what are you saying?" He squeezed the football and studied the laces. "We're done?"

Her heart sunk like a lead balloon. Sheesh, he'd sure been quick to go there. Maybe he'd been looking for an excuse. She tugged her teeth over her lower lip.

Wyatt twisted the ball in his hands. "I guess that's my answer."

Her throat turned scratchy, and her lungs burned. She must have been a fool to think she could keep the attention of a guy like him. She'd give him the out and leave with what little pride she had left. "If that's what you want."

His gaze shot to her. "I didn't say that. Isn't it what *you* want?"

What the hell was he talking about? This conversation had gone sideways. She shook her head. "No."

His knuckles turned white as he squeezed the football. "I don't understand."

"Can we...sit down or something so we can talk about this? I can't think with you pacing and doing that stuff with the ball."

"Oh. Sorry." He glanced at the football like he didn't even realize he held it, and then tossed it in the corner. A muscle twitched under his jaw. "Talk. Okay, we can...talk."

She took a seat at the table, and he sat across from her.

Throat dry, she swallowed, her pulse beating fast. He looked as uncomfortable as a kid sitting in the principal's office. Might as well spit it out. "I'm not glamorous like the women in those online pictures. And I don't know if you're embarrassed to be with me and only want to take other women out on the town. Either way, I'm not sure I fit into your lifestyle."

He let out a big sigh. "Is that what you think? That I'm embarrassed to be with you?"

"I don't know what else to think."

"Well not *that*. Nothing could be further from the truth." He covered her hand with his. "You're gorgeous. It's all I can do to keep my hands off you. Do you know how many cold showers I've had in the last week alone?"

She glanced at him. His green eyes were wide and intent on hers. Picturing him in the shower sent a hot flame to her face.

"That right there." He touched her cheek. "When you blush, I can barely breathe. So damn beautiful."

The heat in his eyes matched his words and caused her to squirm.

He lowered his hand and held both of hers. "Yes, in my football days I lived in the spotlight and went out a lot. I don't regret it. I was young and enjoyed the excitement. But everything changed when I retired and spent a year with my mother. I grew up a lot in that time."

"It had to be hard. A huge shift of lifestyle."

He shrugged. "I haven't dated much since, and when I have, it's fallen flat. I'm not looking for the same thing anymore. The recent picture you saw must have been the one taken at a Big Brothers Big Sisters event that had been planned for months. I don't personally know that woman. Celebrity shots bring attention to the program, so we posed for a picture. That's all it was."

A sprig of hope took root, and the angst of the last week melted. Wyatt had never mentioned his involvement with the kids.

He scooted his chair closer. "If you want to go out, I'd love to take you. The reason I haven't is because…maybe it's selfish, but I like just being with you. Watching movies, taking walks, cooking dinners. Well, me helping you cook. I've never done that with anyone."

"You haven't?"

"No. I've never dated anyone like you. A lot of the women in my past were interested in my money, or to be seen with a famous football player, or have a glitzy night out. I don't get that from you. In fact, I feel like all the cameras make you uncomfortable, which is the last thing I want." He rubbed her hands. "You're real, and caring, and you don't mind getting down on the floor to hug my mangy mutt."

Her chest expanded, giving her breathing space.

"I'm so sorry if I made you feel bad. And as far as my lifestyle, yeah, I like nice things. But I don't live extravagantly. I've been there and done that." He waved a hand around the apartment. "This is temporary, but it's also fine until I figure out what's next. And even if I get the job at USC, my limelight days are over. There won't be highlights of a sideline coordinator calling in plays."

She swallowed around the lump in her throat. If they were going to move forward, she'd have to accept and deal with his past and his fame. "Okay."

Goober got up and ran over to them as if he'd suddenly realized they were in the same room. He shoved his head between Wyatt and her, tail whipping.

Anne ruffled the fur on Goober's head as Wyatt stood and asked, "We're good?"

Goober barked.

"Not you, ding dong." Wyatt laughed.

Anne gave him a quick nod.

"All right. Now I better get to making dinner. Pick a bottle of wine, and I'll open it."

He headed to the stove, and she checked out his ass on the way. Man, oh man the guy screamed sexy. She followed him and chose a merlot from a shelf. He poured them a glass, and they toasted her upcoming birthday. He'd asked her weeks ago if she had plans for the weekend and she'd told him no. The girls were all busy, and they'd celebrate with her another time.

"You won't give me a clue about what we're going to do Saturday?" She tilted her head.

"You got your clue. Bring a bathing suit. That's all I'll tell you." He motioned to the table. "Go sit down. I'm flying solo tonight."

She took a seat as he walked to the cooking area.

"So how are things going with the walk-a-thon?" Wyatt pulled a small pot out from under the counter, eyed it, then shrugged.

"Good, I guess. I have a dinner meeting with the guy I'm working with tomorrow."

Wyatt turned around to face her. "A dinner meeting for a walk-a-thon fundraiser?"

Crap. So, he found it strange, too? "Yeah. I mean, he suggested it because the restaurant was closer to both of us than the hospital."

Wyatt dusted his hands off and placed them on the counter. Her gaze stalled on his strong forearms, making her mind go to mush.

"I get that you might need to exchange some paperwork or whatever, but how does dinner fit in?"

Hell if she knew. The whole conversation had made her uncomfortable. And now her back was up. "He was being considerate of my time, that's all."

"What's this guy's name?"

Annoyance burned her stomach lining. Wyatt hadn't told her about his charity event picture with the super model, so he had no right to question Anne's volunteer work. "Why does his name matter?"

Wyatt blew out a breath. "It doesn't. I'm sorry. I'm just not used to..."

"What?" She crossed her arms.

He pressed his fingers to his forehead and then straightened. "Nothing."

It wasn't nothing, but she wasn't about to push the issue since she had her own doubts.

"Never mind." He turned back around. "Let's not spoil the night. I promised to make you a nice dinner. This is your night off from cooking."

She took a sip of wine as he picked up a jar of Ragu, spinning it to read the back label. "I hope this turns out okay. I'm following the recipe."

She choked.

His gaze darted to her. "You okay?"

"Mm-hmm." She covered her mouth with a hand to hide the smile.

He cocked his head and gave her an I-don't-know-what's-up look before returning to his "recipe" scrutiny.

Yeah, she didn't know what was up either. But this bad-ass football player who couldn't tell a frying pan from a sauce pot was stepping out of his comfort zone for her. Warmth spread through her. Of course he didn't know how to make a marinara. But it was precious that he was trying so hard and wanted his dinner to turn out just right.

With a frown, he put the jar down. "I guess I'll boil the noodles first so they're ready."

Uh oh. They'd turn into a cold lump of glue. Anne straightened in her chair and suggested, "Maybe warm the sauce first so it can simmer while the noodles are cooking?"

Wyatt paused, holding the tiny pot in his hand. "Okay. I guess I'll at least fill this with water so it's ready."

She eyed the small saucepan. It would boil over when he cooked the pasta and make a huge mess. He'd feel like crap. She got up, went to the cabinet where he kept his cookware, and opened the door. "That's too small. Let me find something bigger for you to use."

"It'll be fine. I'm going to break up the noodles so they fit. Now, go sit down and relax."

"No, you don't understand." She dragged out a larger pot. "You need a lot of water because pasta is a starch and expands when you boil it. If you—"

"What are you doing?" He took the pot from her and shut the door. "Who's making this dinner, me or you?"

She flinched, and heat rushed to her face. "I'm just trying to help because—"

"I think it might be better if you don't finish that sentence." Wyatt raised an eyebrow and shoved a hand on his hip.

Great. Now she'd pissed him off. "I don't know why you're all mad at me. I realize you're not used to cooking and just want to make sure your meal turns out okay."

"Well, you're treating me like one of your students, not an adult. If I want help, I'll ask for it."

He stared down at her, a frown on his face.

"Fine." She stomped back to the table and plopped on the chair. Let him mess up to his heart's delight. He could actually learn something if he listened to her.

Wyatt shot a you-better-stay-put glance in her direction, then filled the saucepan with water and turned the burner on high.

She took a big sip of wine and counted to ten in her head.

He took a packet of ground beef out of the refrigerator and dumped it into the pot she had tried to get him to use for the pasta. With the water boiling, he broke up the spaghetti noodles and tossed them in. Next, he opened the jar of Ragu and poured it over the raw meat.

Her stomach turned. Oh my God, he couldn't be serious. She jumped to her feet. "I'm sorry, but you're not even following the directions now. You don't put—"

"Whoa." Wyatt held up a hand. "Are you kidding me? Even after I told you I didn't want your help, you *still* have to butt in."

"Yeah, because I can't sit here and watch you do this all wrong."

A hissing noise came from the stove as water boiled over from the tiny pot onto the hot burner.

Wyatt whirled around and cursed. He grabbed the handle of the saucepan and moved it to another burner as foam poured all down the sides.

Anne bit her cheek as an I-told-you-so wave of satisfaction rose inside. That's what he got for not listening to her and yelling at her for trying to help.

His back to her, Wyatt gripped the microwave above the stove, taking a deep breath.

She swallowed and regretted the gloating thought.

He slowly turned and faced her. "This wouldn't have happened if you'd let me cook without interrupting."

"That's not true." She shook her head. "I told you before what the problem was, and you refused to listen."

"You know what the problem is?" Wyatt took a step closer so that only the counter stood between them. "Your need for perfection."

"My what?" She jerked her head back.

"You heard me. Things have to be perfect, or you're not happy." He gestured to the stove. "Sometimes things aren't perfect, but so what?"

"I don't—"

"Just listen." He held up a finger. "Some of my longest touchdowns came from botched plays. The quarterback fumbled, or someone fell down, and I got the ball. None of that was planned, but it turned out great. Do you understand what I'm saying?"

Her insides boiled. This had nothing to do with her. "I don't think there's a coach alive who would suggest playing a sport without a plan."

"Damn it. You don't get it. It's not about football." He closed his eyes for a minute, then opened them. "Think about pacemakers and penicillin. Both accidentally discovered."

"Now you're really losing me. How did we get from touchdowns to medicine?"

He looked up at the ceiling and she could swear this time *he* was counting to ten. Finally, he said, "My point is that people learn through their mistakes. If I'd ruined the meal, I'd have figured out a way to fix it and felt a hell of a lot better than with you jumping in and taking over."

Her gaze went to the overflowed pot and the raw meat soaking in Ragu. This was bullshit. She'd only tried to help avoid exactly what had happened, out of concern for his feelings. "Maybe you would have fixed it, but not everyone is as lucky as you. Some of us have to work really hard to be successful and aren't naturally talented at everything they do."

"What?" His eyes widened.

"Look at your life. An only child, a revered jock all through school, and then a superstar athlete. Do you even know what it's like to fail at something? Because I sure do." Tears stung the back of her eyes. "You have talent in spades, and even at the bar, when you were out of your element, you managed to come out on top. What's the hardest thing you've ever had to work at?"

"That's an easy one." Wyatt huffed. "Us."

* * *

Anne gasped and took a step back. "Wh-what?"

Damn he hated the tears shimmering in her eyes, but she'd pushed him to the limit. His pulse pounded in his head. "It's the truth. But for the record, I didn't skate through life. Talent only goes so far. I busted my ass every day to become a successful athlete. So yeah, I do know what it's like to work hard."

She pressed her lips together and gave a quick nod. "I'm sorry. I shouldn't have said that."

"Yes, you should, because you thought it." He rounded the counter and stopped in front of her. "I'm telling you this relationship stuff is harder than all of that. I've never been more clueless."

"About what?"

"You. You're important to me, and I'm scared to death I'm gonna fuck this up because I don't know what I'm doing. If you expect everything to be perfect, we'll never make it."

She placed her hand on his. "I didn't realize I was pressuring you. I try to do the exact opposite by not making demands or expecting special treatment."

"I get that, but I suck at this talking and relationship stuff. I know how to take someone out to a fancy place and impress them, but you don't want that." His gut twisted. "I figured you wanted to break up when you saw my wild-days pictures, not talk about them. Then I got jealous over your charity dinner meeting. What kind of asshole does that make me? I've never been jealous before."

Her eyes softened, and she sniffled. "Me either. That's why the recent picture upset me so much."

He picked up her hand and inched closer. "I wish I could get you to relax. Why is it so important to you that things be a certain way? Can't you just let go a little?"

"It's hard for me because I've always been the responsible one." She gazed up at him. "People depend on me, and I don't want to let them down."

"That's a lot of pressure to put on yourself." He rested a hand on her shoulder. "You don't need to do that around me. I'd love to see you let loose, mess something up, and be able to laugh about it."

"Yeah? That's kind of wacked."

"You don't know what you're missing if you play it safe all the time and never take a chance."

She nodded. "I know you're right. It's just hard for me."

"It doesn't have to be." He pulled her in for a hug and she melted against him, soft and warm. Poor thing tried to carry the weight of the world. If only he could get her to chill.

He eased back. "Can we start this night over?"

"I'd like that." She slid her arms around his neck.

He lowered his head and kissed her. Tenderly at first, but that never lasted long. She kissed him back, pressing closer. He stroked his hands down her sides, flicking his tongue against her teeth. She opened her mouth for him.

God, she tasted good. A unique flavor all her own, sweet and intoxicating. A groan rumbled in his chest, and he dragged his mouth to her neck, trailing kisses down to her shoulder. Her soft, warm skin felt like velvet under his lips. She shivered, goosebumps forming on her arms. The way she reacted to him set his body aflame.

He lifted his head and placed a hand on the side of her face. So beautiful with her cheeks flushed and that slightly out of focus look that meant she'd gotten lost in that kiss. "You mean so much to me. I promise I'll get better at this communication stuff."

"Me, too. And you're right about letting go and taking chances." She leaned her head into his hand.

"It makes life more exciting." His fingers gently massaged her back. "Try this. Think of something that scares the hell out of you, but you really want to do it."

A blush turned her already pink face darker, and her gaze fell to her feet.

"What? Did you think of something?"

"Yeah." Her voice cracked on the word.

He tipped her chin up with his finger and looked her in the eyes. "Can you tell me what it is, and I'll help you do it."

She took a shaky breath.

"Come on, you can do this. Trust me."

"Okay." She stood on her tiptoes, dragged his head down, and whispered in his ear, "I want to spend the *whole* weekend with you."

CHAPTER 15

DEVON TAPPED his fingers on the armrest of the leather recliner in his theater room. His first meeting with Anne had gone well. She'd been clearly touched by his interactions with the brats in the pediatric ward, and she'd agreed to meet with him at Toni's. Good thing. He'd been eating their garbage food and sucking up to them for over a month preparing to make an impression on her. Now he'd have the chance.

He flipped on his new hundred-and-ten-inch television, and the sound of sirens filled the room as reporters stood in front of a burning apartment building. The cameras panned to show firefighters dousing the place with water from the truck hoses as they tried to contain the fire. The female reporter walked over to a couple holding a small child and started asking questions. Devon tuned her out and focused on the flames behind them. He could almost smell the black smoke. Took him right back to the night he'd torched his home.

His family got what they deserved, to die together. If only his mother could see him now. She would regret devoting all of her time and attention to his loser older brother. So what if Owen was an all-star athlete? The trophies, the awards, the constant doting on his every wish still made Devon sick to his stomach. Didn't matter that he was the one with the brains. His parents only cared about sports.

Nothing was worse than the sick smell of whisky always on his father's breath. On good nights, it was only verbal abuse from him. "Why can't you be more like your brother? No boy spends so much time reading. Must be something wrong with you."

At least they paid for it in the end.

Devon had been twelve years old at the time. After he'd snuck out of his friend's house, where he was supposed to be spending the night, he'd slipped back into his own home. Passed out drunk, like always, his parents didn't waken. His pulse raced as he doused the hall carpet with gasoline and tossed a lit match on top.

He left the house and crouched behind bushes at the edge of their property. A rush of adrenaline surged through his body when the dusty old curtains in his parents' bedroom went up in flames.

His gaze darted to his brother's room. Owen, the super athlete, frantically yanked on the window as flames blazed behind him. Wouldn't do any good. Devin had secured it. His gut did a celebration dance, and he grinned.

Time stood still as he held his breath, his gaze riveted on the smoke and orange flares. Glorious in its spreading frenzy, the fire overtook the house. Ashes blew in his face, bringing with them the scent of burning wood, plastic, and chemicals. He'd killed before, but never a person or with fire. Who knew what a high it would be?

When sirens sounded, he dashed back to his friend's home, where everyone was still sound asleep. He wanted to yell or scream to let out the sheer joy of the night. Instead, he curled up in his sleeping bag, having to settle for playing the scene over and over in his head while shivers of delight shook his body.

His parents and brother had all died in the fire, and no one had ever suspected Devon. Why would they? People in rural areas back then didn't lock their doors, and he'd spent the night at a friend's house, which the police verified. He knew enough to cry crocodile tears when he heard about the fire, and the media ate it up. Might be some of the best press he'd ever had.

He flipped off the television and grabbed the keys to his Porsche. A fast drive was in order. He backed the car out and stopped in the driveway, eyeing the five-car garage and his huge Tudor home. Fuck them all, look what he had now. Nobody kept him down. He gunned the engine, swerving around the circular drive, and raced through the gates. He'd shown them.

Wait until Anne saw his mansion. She'd be blown away like all the other women. Money, looks, prestige—he had it all. Anne would hold her hand out and beg for a ring.

Sweet payback to Paul for winning the wager with that bitch Lynn back in college. She'd made a fatal mistake choosing Paul over him. Now there wasn't a woman alive who could resist Devon.

CHAPTER 16

ANNE PULLED into Toni's lot, but her mind was on the upcoming weekend. She didn't have all the answers for the future, and logic said she shouldn't go away with Wyatt, but for once she wanted to color outside the lines. Live a little. Take a chance.

After the marinara mess, they'd ended up ordering a pizza, having some wine, and watching a movie. Wyatt had been right. The night wasn't what they'd planned, but also not a total failure. And he'd actually taught her something. Maybe she was too quick to jump in sometimes and help people, especially her students. She'd keep that in mind and pay more attention in the future.

Anne spotted Devon's BMW parked well away from the other cars in the restaurant lot. He probably didn't want a ding, and she couldn't blame him. The car gleamed under the overhead lights like it had been polished by hand. She grabbed her shoulder bag, got out, and headed toward the entrance.

Devon, standing by the door, waved to her as she approached.

"I hope you haven't been waiting long," Anne said.

"Nope. Just got here. I was about to go in when I saw you." He opened the door for her, and like before, placed his hand on the small of her back as she entered.

The restaurant was busy with people waiting to pick up carryout orders. Patrons took boxes with aluminum-foiled containers and salads from atop a glass case filled with cannoli that made her mouth water.

"Hey, Devon, good to see you," an older man, wearing an apron blotched with tomato sauce, called from behind the counter.

The hostess walked over. "Hi, I have your usual table ready."

Anne followed the hostess as they snaked through the restaurant, squeezing past bussers, servers, and customers. The scent of garlic and tomatoes wafted through the place. Huge plates of steaming pasta and baskets loaded with crusty loaves of bread crowded the small tables.

The hostess led them to the far corner of the restaurant. Devon pulled out a chair for Anne. His gold cufflinks winked under the light of the jar candle on the table. He took the seat next to her instead of across. Strange, but what could she say?

Dressed like a James Bond double in a suit and tie, he drew his share of attention, but Anne couldn't stop thinking about Wyatt's cocky grin and the way his biceps bulged when he squeezed a football. Or the mischievous twinkle in his green eyes when he threw Goober's tug-toy halfway across the park and then kissed Anne senseless until the dog came trotting back with it.

"I doubt you even need this." The hostess gave Devon a menu and turned to Anne, handing her one. "The special tonight is lobster ravioli."

"Thank you." She'd better keep her mind on business and not Wyatt.

The man in the tomato-stained apron came to their table. He clapped Devon on his back. "I see you have a friend here tonight?"

"Yes, Toni. It's a business meeting." Devon introduced Anne.

Toni wiped his hand on his apron and shook hers.

"Nice to meet you." He turned back to Devon. "I gotta tell you, our cappuccino sales are up almost a third since you got us that new machine."

"See? I told you pump was better than steam. How's Donna doing this week?"

"Each chemo is a little harder, but she's hanging in there, and the docs still say she's on track."

"That's encouraging. Tell her I was asking about her."

"Will do. I gotta get back to the kitchen." Toni pointed to Devon and faced Anne. "Maybe if this guy plays his cards right it will be more than business, eh?"

Anne swallowed as the tips of her ears burned. Talk about awkward.

When Toni walked away, Devon shook his head and rested his hand on Anne's, giving it a small squeeze before quickly letting go. "I'm sorry. He can be pushy, but he's a softy and means well."

Now, more than ever, she wished Devon had sat across from her. He hadn't done anything outrageously wrong, but the little intimacies were a bit much for someone she barely knew. A bead of sweat trickled down her back.

"Toni's had it tough. His wife Donna has breast cancer and has been coming to the hospital for treatments. I ran into her a couple of times. Sounds like she's going to be a survivor." Devon's mouth turned up, and he glanced at the kitchen where Toni had disappeared.

"That's really good news." Too many people had to deal with the life-changing diagnosis and side effects of the chemo. "What was he talking about with the cappuccino machine?"

Devon waved a hand and glanced at the specials sheet. "Eh, nothing. Their old one kept breaking. Toni apologized when it wasn't working and said he was going to buy a new one as soon as he paid off the medical bills."

Anne waited, but he didn't say anymore. Curiosity got the best of her. "So, he mentioned that you bought him one?"

Devon glanced up from the menu. "It wasn't a big deal. It actually was a tad self-serving because if there's one thing I enjoy, it's a properly made cappuccino, and I eat here a lot."

Wow. His generosity went beyond caring. He might just be one of those really touchy-feely guys and she'd been reading too much into things.

"It was nothing." He reached for his briefcase. "I don't want to keep you too long, so should we get down to business?"

Relief eased the tension binding her shoulder blades together. A quick bite and she'd be out of there. She nodded and pulled a notebook out of her bag. "I think we're off to a great start with the walk-a-thon. A lot of the teachers want to help."

"That's wonderful." Devon smiled.

A waitress stopped at their table. She placed two wine glasses down and poured from a bottle of red. "Hey Devon, how's it going?"

Oh, no. Anne didn't want dinner with drinks. She glanced at Devon as he held up a hand. "Doing well, but you're too quick, Sophia. We're here for business tonight."

Anne's stomach unclenched. At least she and Devon were on the same page. Just business.

Sophia's saucer-sized earrings swung as she shook her head. "You're not gonna have a glass of wine on your birthday?"

His birthday? Anne's gaze dashed to him.

He wagged a finger back and forth in front of Sophia. "I never should have let that slip when we were talking last week."

Anne eyed the wine. "We could have done this another day, Devon. I didn't know it was your birthday." She gestured to his glass. "You don't have to pass on my account."

Devon frowned. "No, I would feel rude, unless you would join me in one?"

Crap. Now what? It was still early, and she was going to have something to eat. Maybe one glass. "Okay, since you were nice enough to meet with me on your birthday."

Sophia asked, "Did you want the special or some time to decide?"

"I can vouch for the lobster ravioli being really good." Devon tapped the menu.

The sooner they ordered, the sooner they'd be served. Anne nodded. "I'll try it."

"Make it two." Devon handed the menus to Sophia, who took them and left.

Devon picked up his wine glass and held it out for a toast. "To the start of a successful fundraiser."

"Yes, and…happy birthday." Anne clicked her glass to his.

After taking a sip, Devon pulled out some paperwork from his briefcase. "Tell me how the staff meeting went and what ideas the other teachers came up with."

With the focus back on business, Anne heaved a mental sigh of relief.

He took some notes as she rattled off the marketing ideas and thoughts the teachers had passed along.

"The one I like best is to have the kids draw some pictures that we can turn into posters to advertise for the walk-a-thon." Anne drew a star next to the line in her notebook.

"I love it." Devon leaned in and rested an arm near hers on the table. "Maybe make it into a contest or something?"

"That's a great idea." More sweat trailed down her back. Whether he meant to or not, he was invading her personal space. She took a sip of her wine, eased back, and picked up her pen. Keeping her head down, she avoided eye contact and wrote down his comment.

To be fair, he improved upon every idea she suggested. Creative and inventive, no wonder he was so successful.

Sophia brought their dinners, which smelled amazing, and Anne put away her notebook. She glanced at Devon. "I've only been here a few times. You mentioned you come here a lot?"

"Yeah, because it's on my way home from the hospital and the food is so good." A sad frown formed on his face. "They treat me like family."

"That's really nice. Does yours live far away?"

He shook his head and said in a low voice, "No. They all died in a fire when I was twelve."

Her heart caved for him. No wonder he looked so dejected. "Oh my God. That's horrible. I'm so sorry."

He met her gaze and half-smiled. "It was a long time ago. Just sometimes it's still hard, you know, on days like this."

"I'm really sorry." She could only imagine what it would be like to not have her family around on the holidays and special occasions.

"I may not have blood relatives, but I'm thankful for my friends, and that's what's important." He touched her arm and then waved a hand at her plate. "Eat while it's hot. I hope you like it."

Anne took a bite, but she couldn't stop thinking about his loss. She closed her eyes for a second. When she opened them, Devon was smiling at her, his eyes warm.

"Delicious, right?" He ate a piece of ravioli.

She sipped her wine and Devon pointed to her glass. "Please don't feel obligated to finish that."

Thank goodness he understood. She seldom drank on weekdays, and certainly not with men she hardly knew. What would Wyatt think of this cozy dinner-for-two with wine? She let out a slow breath.

"Is something wrong?" Devon asked.

"No." She'd keep the conversation light. "Does your art business require a lot of travel?"

He tilted his head. "Yes and no. I've been all around the world but not necessarily for the art. If I find a piece I really want, I'll make a trip overseas or wherever it might be, but most of the traveling I do is for fun."

He clearly had the money based on his car and clothing. "I'm sure you've been to a lot of exciting places."

"I have." He shrugged and looked up from his plate. "The truth is, I'd enjoy it more if I had someone special with me."

Anne's throat tightened. The way he was staring at her…was he hitting on her?

Sophia and three other servers came to the table, carrying a big piece of chocolate cake with a lit candle on the top. They started singing "Happy Birthday."

Devon opened his mouth as if to protest, but then shut it and smiled.

"Sophia, you really shouldn't have," Devon said as the servers walked away.

"Toni insisted. I'll be right back with a couple cappuccinos."

"Hold on." Devon turned to Anne. "Would you like to get those in to-go cups so I don't keep you out too long?"

"Yes, please. I still have papers to grade tonight." Phew. She had to be wrong about him hitting on her. He was being considerate of her time, and none of this was his fault.

Devon glanced at the cake, then waved to Toni across the room. Blowing out his cheeks, Devon picked up a fork and paused.

"I'm in a bind here. I can't *not* eat this cake now after all that, but I'm full. Any chance you can help me with it?"

Her gaze darted back to Toni, who was still watching them.

"Sure." She was stuffed, too, but the cake did look good. Not wanting anyone's feelings hurt, she took a small bite.

Devon took a forkful of cake off the same side. He slid it into his mouth and gave the thumbs up to Toni, who finally walked back into the kitchen. "Thanks, I owe you."

Why had he taken a bite from the same spot she had when the other side of the cake was untouched? Seemed like an intimate thing to do. Then again, she probably was reading too much into everything since the night had sort of imploded.

Sophia brought over the cappuccinos and the check. "Let me know if you need anything else. Happy Birthday."

They both took another sizeable bite of cake, then Devon put his fork down and picked up the check.

"These guys are too much. This says, "Happy Birthday," with no charge."

"That's awfully sweet of them." But it posed a problem for her. She couldn't pay half of nothing. Reaching for her shoulder bag, she said, "I'll leave the tip."

Devon tossed some bills down on the table and stood up. "No, but thanks."

Another generous act. She couldn't help but notice he'd left enough money to pay for the entire meal.

When they got outside, Devon turned to her. "I had no idea they were doing all this tonight. I'm sorry if it made you feel uncomfortable."

It had, but it's not like he'd asked for it. "It's okay. I'm glad you weren't alone on your birthday, and I enjoyed the food."

After they reached her car, he waited until she opened the door and got in. Since he was still standing there, she rolled down the window. He leaned over, placing his arms on the ledge. "So, next week do you want to try this again?"

Hell no. They needed to get back on solid, safe ground with no cake sharing or wine. Nerves bounced in her stomach, but she couldn't agree to another dinner. "I think it might be better if we met at the hospital."

He nodded. "That's fine."

She started the car, but he didn't move from the door.

"Thanks for tonight," he said in a soft tone.

"No problem."

"I really mean it." Devon's sad half-smile appeared again. "You know, this was probably the nicest birthday I've had in years."

Now she felt like a jerk. All she'd done the whole night was analyze his intentions. Meanwhile, he'd spent his best birthday with a stranger doing charity work. A piece of her heart melted. "Well, happy birthday, again."

"See you next week." He patted her shoulder, and took a step back.

Anne frowned as she drove. Devon was full of surprises. With his stunning good looks and charm, he had to have women falling all over him. Yet he'd commented on wishing he had someone special to take on trips. As generous and kind as he was, the right woman would come along. He deserved as much for buying a cappuccino machine to help out a man struggling with medical debts. Who did that?

She had to be wrong about him flirting with her. He was a stand-up guy who cared about people. Next week they'd meet at the hospital, and everything would be fine.

* * *

Wyatt pulled out of the away-game parking lot, his brain still frozen since last night when Anne had told him she wanted to spend the whole weekend together. Even during the lacrosse match tonight, his mind had wandered. Tomorrow, unless he fucked something up, they'd have sex. He'd fantasized about it for over a month. Hell, pretty much from the first time he'd laid eyes on her.

But now that he'd gotten to know her, he wanted her even more, if that were possible. It went beyond lust or attraction. They'd really connected after the whole spaghetti fight, and even though he knew she was scared of taking this next step, she was doing it.

It meant a lot that she didn't care about his money or his fame, only about *him*. But that complicated things, too. In the past, women had drifted in and out of his life. There was something to be said for having a good time and moving on. No sticky conversations or discussions of feelings. His lungs pressed against his ribs. He'd never committed to anyone before and could be offered that USC job, which meant he'd leave.

He hit the brakes for a stop light. This whole thing could turn into a big, ugly mess with Anne getting hurt. That would kill him. But he had to look out for his future and hadn't even known her for very long or made any promises.

Still, they'd been getting closer, and she stirred up all kinds of new emotions. She might not be the only one who got hurt in the end. He wouldn't back out now, but he needed to protect himself as well.

He hit the accelerator and called, using the speaker phone. On the fourth ring, she finally answered.

"Hey, Wyatt. How'd the match go?"

"We won, but it was close. I'm headed home now. Everything okay with the fundraiser meeting?"

"Umm...yeah. Devon is really pumped about having a poster contest and came up with some other great ideas."

So, the mysterious person was Devon. First time she'd mentioned his name. "Good. You get your papers graded?"

"Not yet. I...uh...just left Toni's."

Wyatt's eyes cut to the time display on the radio. "Wasn't your meeting at five?"

"Yeah, but dinner took longer because of some weird stuff. Doesn't matter, I'm headed home now."

The hairs on the back of Wyatt's neck stood up. He turned into a convenience store parking lot so he could pay full attention to the conversation. "What weird stuff?"

Anne cleared her throat. "It turns out it was Devon's birthday today, and apparently he goes to this restaurant a lot, so they kinda, you know, made a fuss over it."

Nothing strange about that. Time to throw the challenge flag. "What do you mean by them making a fuss?"

She didn't answer right away, and each second of delay ratcheted his heartrate higher.

"There were just some awkward things like the waitress brought out wine for us. Devon tried to explain that we were working, but she said it was his birthday and she'd already poured it."

Wyatt inhaled and waited.

"We didn't want to be rude, so I had some with him."

What bullshit. A person didn't have to drink something they never ordered. "Sorry, Anne, but that's lame. You don't have any trouble speaking your mind with me. Why didn't you say you didn't want to drink?"

She sighed. "I felt bad for him spending his birthday with a stranger. His entire family died when he was twelve."

What the fuck?

Wyatt squeezed the steering wheel hard. "How do you know that?"

"Well, he looked so sad when the waitress commented he was like family there. I felt horrible when he told me they all had died."

Yup. She would. Wore her heart on her sleeve. Sure, it was sad, but no guy dumped emotional shit like that on someone he just met unless he had an ulterior motive. Wyatt's blood heated to a slow boil.

"So, there he was, stuck with me on his birthday," she said.

Uh huh. Stuck with her. A gorgeous, adorable blonde with a killer body who didn't seem to have a clue about it. The gut instinct he'd had about this dinner meeting reared its ugly head again.

Before he flew off the handle, he'd better find out more information. That's what communication was all about. Or at least that's what he'd read in the article online. It said to repeat back what his partner said and ask for clarification. He counted to five. That's all he had. Ten was a stretch.

"You said there were awkward 'things.' What else happened?"

"Umm…the waitress brought over a big piece of birthday cake."

Wyatt closed his eyes and leaned his head back. She'd had this business meeting that somehow ended up at a restaurant, drinking wine and eating cake. His pulse throbbed in his throat.

"He asked me if I could take a couple of bites because Toni was watching us, like waiting to see if he liked it, so I didn't want to say no."

"Wait, who's Toni?"

"The owner."

Now she was on a first name basis with the staff? This was so like her. Never wanting to upset anyone. Even at her own expense.

"It seems like this Devon guy took advantage of the situation."

"None of it was his fault." Her tone took on an edge. "He apologized and agreed to meet next week back at the hospital. He had no idea any of that was going to happen."

"I'm sure."

"What's that supposed to mean?"

Wyatt thumped his palm against the steering wheel and blew out a frustrated breath. "Maybe I don't like my girlfriend going on dinner dates with other men. What happened to exclusive?"

"That was not a dinner date."

"Really? Because it sure sounds like it. And by the way, how did they even know it was his birthday?"

She huffed into the phone. "I don't appreciate the inquisition. I didn't have to tell you any of this."

"Oh, so now we're going to start lying to each other?" Heat flared through Wyatt's body. "This whole thing spun out of control, and don't tell me it was nothing."

She didn't say anything for a couple of seconds. After a sniffle, she said, "I think we should reconsider this weekend. I don't want to spend it with someone who doesn't trust me."

Shit. It wasn't *her* he didn't trust. "Look, it's not—"

"I have to go. Goodbye." The line went dead.

What the hell? Wyatt blew out a long breath. Yeah, he was jealous, but damn it she'd been so defensive. Devon didn't know the waitress would bring wine. Devon was too polite to hurt the owner's feelings and asked her to please share the cake. Devon was happy to meet back at the hospital next week. Yes, he sounded like the perfect gentleman.

Then why did it feel like the perfect storm?

Wyatt shook his head. From that sniffle and the way her voice broke, she might be crying. His heart pinched in his chest. Anne may not have handled the situation the way he'd liked, but one of the things he loved about her was her concern for others. Maybe he'd been too hard on her. Jesus, this relationship shit was complicated.

Only one thing to do. He pulled out of the parking lot and headed to her apartment.

CHAPTER 17

WYATT TEXTED Anne that he was at her door. He didn't want to scare her since she probably wasn't expecting anyone. Hell, she might ignore him for all he knew. He waited a minute, but she didn't respond to his text, so he knocked.

A muscle ticked in his neck. He hated arguing with her, but the whole "dinner charade" had been ridiculous. The more she'd told him, the worse it had gotten. Maybe this Devon dude was a complete wuss and afraid of his own shadow. If he didn't have the backbone to say he didn't order drinks for a business dinner, he shouldn't have pressured Anne to play along.

Period.

Wyatt didn't really care about whether she had a drink. It was the fact she'd done something she didn't want to that bothered him.

He knocked again and tapped an impatient foot on the concrete. At last the knob jiggled and the door opened. Anne, dressed in a pink robe cinched tight at the waist, crossed her arms and thrust her chin up. "Why did you come here?"

Her puffy eyes and red nose meant she'd been crying. Shit. Guilt shrank his heart. "To talk to you. Can I come in, please?"

She sniffled but stepped aside, opening the door wider.

He entered, and she shut the door, taking her time to turn around. "I really wish you could have given me the benefit of the doubt tonight. You weren't there. I told you everything that happened. I don't know what else you want from me."

"I'm sorry." He stepped closer, but didn't reach out to touch her. "I got upset. I do trust you, but put yourself in my shoes. How do you think it all sounded?"'

She rubbed the back of her neck. "Well, to be honest, I guess pretty suspicious. I mean, it's just one thing happened after another, and I didn't know what to do without insulting someone or hurting their feelings. And then I told you everything, and you got mad at me."

He sighed. She had told him about the entire night and how uncomfortable she'd been. "I wasn't mad at you. I was annoyed he put you in that situation and you went along with him. Do you understand the difference?"

She bit her lip and slowly nodded. "Yeah. I'm sure part of the reason I got so upset is that you hit a nerve. I wanted to please everyone and not make any waves."

"I've noticed that." Wyatt pulled out a chair and they both sat at the kitchen table. He took her hand. "You're the most giving person I've ever known, but you don't always stand up for yourself."

"I know, and I'm nervous because I've got to change that if I intend on being a principal one day. I can't make everyone happy in that job."

She had a point but was overlooking her major strength. "That's true, but you'll be good at it because you'll be making decisions that are for the best of your students and school. There's no way you'd back down from the tough ones in that scenario."

She cocked her head, and her brows wrinkled. "You're right. I wouldn't hesitate a second to make a hard call if I knew it was the right one for someone."

"Exactly." He squeezed her hand. "You'll go to the mat for anyone else, just not always for yourself."

"I never thought of it that way." Her eyes sharpened, and she nodded. "I feel so much better about this now that I see it in perspective. I can't tell you how grateful I am to you for pointing this out."

A wave of pride washed over him. He'd actually talked to her about feelings and insecurities. He, the rookie at communication, had helped *her*. "I told you I'd get better at this talking stuff."

"Well, I would give that an A plus." She kissed him on the cheek, and his heart soared.

"Hey, I'd be happy to just get some A."

She slapped his hand and grinned. "You're so bad."

"Just sayin'." He shrugged.

Her smile fell. "Seriously, though. I'm sorry I transferred this onto you earlier. And don't hold this against Devon. I think he felt as awkward as I did."

Wyatt doubted that, but maybe he was still caught up in jealousy. The most important thing was that Anne had opened up to him.

She stood and he pulled her onto his lap. Wrapping his arms around her, he breathed in the sweet scent of her hair. They fit together. Perfectly.

So much for that "protecting himself" plan. He'd just dove in deeper with her.

"Thanks for coming over." She kissed him. "If I can take back what I said earlier, I'm still up for the weekend."

CHAPTER 18

ANNE ZIPPED HER SUITCASE, anxiety tightening the walls of her chest.

A knock sounded, and she jumped. Sheesh. She needed to get a grip.

When she opened the door, Wyatt stood in the hall, hands in his pockets. He cleared his throat. "Hey."

"Hi." Oh, shit. She didn't realize how awkward it was going to be. He usually greeted her with a hug and kiss. Now they faced each other like kids with spin-the-bottle pointed at them.

"Come in. I just need to turn out some lights and get my bag." The one that had black-and-pink lacy lingerie packed inside. She'd bought the outfit a week ago on a whim to have in case she decided to let things go to the next level. A wave of heat surged to her face.

Wyatt entered, leaving an all-male, spicy scent in his wake as he passed. His pine-green T-shirt stretched across his chiseled pecs, and he wore the jeans she liked best on him. Not that he knew it. They fit him like a lover's hand, hugging all the right places. He caught her staring when he turned around, and grinned.

Crap.

"I'll grab my suitcase. Be right back." She hurried past him to the bedroom. A glance in the mirror confirmed what she suspected. Her cheeks were bright red. How was she going to get through this?

"Need any help?" Wyatt called.

"No, I got it, thanks." She brought the bag out and stopped in front of him.

He glanced down at the suitcase and swallowed. Awkward silence again. Spiking a hand through his hair, he sighed. "This is ridiculous."

She frowned. "I know it's kind of big, but I fit everything inside so I'd only have one thing to carry."

Wyatt waved at it. "No, not the suitcase. Me."

"You? I don't understand."

He paced to the door and back. "I'm not used to...not knowing what to say or do."

So she wasn't the only one. "Just be yourself. What are you worried about?"

He held her hands and stepped closer. "Messing up. I've never wanted anything more than I want you, and I'm afraid I'm going to blow it."

"Well that makes two of us." She squeezed his hands and gazed up at him. "If anyone's going to blow anything, it's going to be me."

Wyatt's mouth twitched.

She blinked. Crud, that had come out *way* wrong. "I mean..."

"You're priceless." He laughed, a deep, guttural sound that vibrated through her body.

He let go of her hands, wrapped his arms around her, and lowered his head to kiss her. As always, his warm mouth worked its magic. She melted into the kiss and crawled her hands up his chest, massaging the defined, hard muscles. He pulled back and touched his forehead to hers. "Tell you what. Let's put the bag in the trunk and forget about it for the day."

She nodded. "Okay."

"I want us to have fun and not worry about what happens later." He raised his head and held her gaze. "And when the time comes, if you change your mind, that's fine. I'm here for you, however you want me."

The tenderness in his tone wrapped around her like a warm blanket. "Believe me, Wyatt"—she rested a hand on the side of his face—"I want you."

His eyes flashed, and he smiled the cocky grin that made her knees wobble. Picking up her bag, he jerked his head in the direction of the door. "Let's go then."

As they drove, a smile stayed plastered on his face. He'd managed to keep their destination a secret, but now he looked like an overfilled helium balloon about to burst at any second.

She tapped his arm. "Enough mystery, where are we headed?"

"Ocean City." He glanced at her. "I figured off-season it wouldn't be crowded."

"Really? I love the beach." She rolled down the window and stuck her hand out. "And this is the perfect day. We don't usually hit the seventies in March."

"I know. Next month I have another Big Brothers Big Sisters event on the beach. I'm supposed to sign a bunch of footballs and camp out with the kids. It's the biggest fundraiser of the year for the organization, and they're really hyping it. I hope the weather is good. It's a crap shoot in April with the rain."

She glanced at him, and her heart softened. He really cared about the kids. "That sounds like fun. They're lucky to have your support."

He shrugged. "They're not so lucky, but I do what I can."

"It's not seventies yet. My fingers are freezing now." She held the button to close the window and touched his arm.

A wicked smile formed on his face. "I have a place where you can warm them up."

Oh hell no. Now that thought would get stuck in her head. Like he needed to give her any ideas. "Not while you're driving."

He raised an eyebrow. "Is that a challenge?"

"Stop it." She play-slapped his arm.

As they approached the boardwalk, bright pink marathon signs lined the streets. Police officers stood in front of roads with cones blocking access.

"Are you kidding me?" Wyatt frowned. "I never thought to check for any events because it's off-season."

"Don't worry about it." Even with the race, it couldn't be as packed as any day in the summer.

Wyatt parked in the crowded lot at the end of the boardwalk. When Anne got out, the cool, salty ocean breeze blew her hair. The scents of cotton candy, fried dough, and popcorn wafted over, making her stomach rumble.

They navigated between groups of people gathered at various mile markers on the boardwalk.

"How about some lunch?" Wyatt asked. "It's almost noon."

"You read my mind. What should we get?"

"We're at the boardwalk. Gotta start with a big tub of salt and vinegar fries." He steered her over to the stand.

They sat on a bench overlooking the water while they ate. Seagulls screeched, diving and fighting over dropped food from tourists.

"These are so good." Anne wiped her mouth with a napkin and took another bite of a French fry.

Wyatt leaned over and kissed her. "Yum. You're more delicious than the food. Salty and sweet."

She wasn't going to last the day. Her brain ceased functioning when his lips moved over hers like that. What would it be like when they were on her breasts?

"Mommy, Mommy can we get ice cream?" A little girl's voice rang out.

Wyatt pulled back and sighed. He traced a hand down her neck to where her pulse was erratically beating, and she shivered.

A ghost of a smile formed on his face.

He knew the effect he was having on her, all right. And damn if she didn't love it.

A man wearing a Ravens jersey walked past with a woman. He glanced in their direction, stumbled, and stopped. "Wyatt Pearson?"

Wyatt nodded, and the man hurried to their bench, followed by the woman. "I'm a huge fan. Any chance I could get a picture with you?"

"Sure." Wyatt stood, and the woman pulled her phone out of her purse and snapped a shot of them.

Another group of people passing by stopped and pointed to Wyatt, whispering to each other. After the man thanked Wyatt and left, the others approached, also wanting pictures.

He glanced at Anne as more fans gathered, a worried frown on his face. Is this what would happen whenever they went to public places? No more stealing kisses on the bench. Her heart sighed.

She stood and moved to avoid being stepped on by the fans. He posed for several more pictures, and the crowd kept growing. This was getting out of control. A thread of annoyance wove between her ribs. This was supposed to be their special day together. But he'd told her before that he hated to disappoint anyone and appreciated his fans. She couldn't blame him for caring about them.

Once again, though, she'd been nudged to the outskirts of the group.

A whiff of coconut oil and suntan lotion floated from a sundry shop she now stood near. Wyatt's gaze darted across the people in front of him until he met hers. His cheeks puffed and he blew out a breath.

He didn't look too happy about the situation, but the fans were so excited that Anne didn't want to make him feel bad. She touched a finger to her chest and pointed to the store before entering. She'd kill some time in there away from the mob.

The tiny shop was jam-packed with beach toys, towels, and souvenirs. She picked up a big conch shell with a bright painting of a dolphin jumping through the waves and "Ocean City, Maryland" written across the bottom. She held it up to her ear to "hear the ocean" like she'd always done as a child.

A large, warm hand covered hers over the shell, and Wyatt's clean, fresh scent surrounded her.

"I'm sorry about that." He brought his other hand around her waist and pulled her back against his chest. "It seems like all I do is apologize to you when we go out."

The timbre of his deep voice against her ear made her insides quiver. She lowered the shell and spun around in his arms. "It's kinda hard, is all, with no privacy and fans always flocking you. I'm starting to think you need a disguise like the Hollywood actors. What did you say to the people out there?"

He stroked his thumb over her knuckles. "I told them I was flattered and wished I could take pictures with everyone, but I was here with someone special and needed to get back to her."

Warmth flooded her chest. He'd put her first.

"How about if we drive up north to the less crowded beach?" he asked.

That sounded way better. She nodded, and he let go of her hand. "This is a huge conch."

"And you women say size doesn't matter."

For the love of God, she always said something suggestive around him. Maybe because he screamed sexy, and her brain fixated there. Then again, he sure never missed a chance to jump on it, so his mind had to be in the same place.

He snatched the shell and headed toward the register. "Gotta get it now. A souvenir from our weekend."

They snagged a slice of pizza to eat on the way to the car, and thankfully, no one interrupted them.

When they reached the quieter beach, Wyatt dropped her off at the bath house so she could change into her bathing suit and told her to meet him down by the water. The sun, high in the sky, had brought the temps to the promised mid-seventies.

She slipped on a black halter-top bikini she'd bought for the trip. Sexy in its simplicity, or at least she hoped. Then again, he'd been with super models who probably wore Sports Illustrated special-edition bathing suits. Her stomach twisted.

She shook her head. Comparing herself to other women served no purpose. She slid her arms into a white mesh cover-up, leaving it unbuttoned. After grabbing her beach bag, she climbed the fence-lined slope leading to the beach. Her flip-flops dug into the sand, spitting it up against her calves after every step. When she got to the top of the hill, the fresh, salty ocean breeze hit her face. Heaven…

Wasn't hard to find Wyatt on the almost deserted beach. Her jaw dropped at the sight of him, bent over, twisting the umbrella holder into the sand. The sun beat down on his shirtless, muscular body. His arms flexed as he twisted the pole deeper. It was one thing to feel his muscles rippling under his shirt, but quite another to feast her eyes on them. She didn't move for a moment, enjoying the view.

She kicked off her shoes and grabbed them with one hand. Her feet sank into the sand, warm on the top, cool underneath as she walked.

As if he sensed her presence, he glanced up and then slowly straightened. He stood frozen in place as she made her way toward him. She couldn't see his eyes behind his sunglasses, but there was no doubt his focus was completely on her. Her insides quaked, but she tried to strut down the beach with complete confidence.

When she reached him, she dropped her bag on the blanket and her flip-flops on the sand. "I can't believe how warm it is."

Wyatt stepped over to her. "That's an understatement. Holy smoking-hot."

His voice sounded strained, and she tried to look up at him, but her gaze didn't make it past his chest. Bulging, hard muscles flexed as he ran his hands down her sides, settling them on her hips.

"You're freaking gorgeous." He drew her closer until her breasts pressed against the granite surface of his abs. Another plane she'd like to explore.

With her tongue.

She shivered.

He wrapped his arms around her. "You cold?"

"Not even close." This time she did gaze up at him, but her face reflected in his sunglasses. Her pupils were huge and her eyes wide. If not for the breeze, her breath would fog his shades. Is that what she looked like aroused? She glanced back down to hide a certain blush.

He chuckled, and his chest vibrated against her cheek, causing more shivers. "I don't think you look in the mirror much, which is why you have no idea how sexy you are."

All that mattered to her was that he thought so.

He gave her a squeeze. "What do you like to do at the beach?"

"Read." The word came out before she even had a chance to think.

He smiled down at her. "Let me rephrase that. What would you like to do *today* at the beach, unless you brought a book?"

If she had, it would've been the Kama Sutra. What the hell? Now she was picturing erotic positions with him on the beach blanket. His naked body over her, under her, twisted around her. Her thighs tightened.

"Did you?"

"Huh?" Focus. What had he even asked her?

"Bring a book?" An eyebrow peeked over the top of his shades.

"Oh, no. Let's ah…take a walk. Cool down a little and maybe look for shells."

A bemused grin on his face, he took her hand. "Sure. Cool down. Didn't realize how hot you were."

Damn Wyatt. He knew exactly what he did to her. And now his warm hand caressed hers with every swing of her arm. Kinda nice. Contact with no sexual agenda. Except what went on in her dirty little mind.

She glanced at the ocean as they walked. The waves rhythmically rolled in, crashing and receding. Creamy foam eased across the beach, stranding tiny clams that flipped sideways and dug down into the sand.

Wyatt glanced at her. "How's your student? The one with leukemia?"

"As good as can be expected. He's been doing the chemo, but it's tough on him." An ache gnawed in her chest. "I'm going to be tutoring him from here on out at his home."

"Wow, I guess I never thought of that. He would be too sick to go to school." Wyatt shook his head. "All the medical expenses, parents' time off work, private tutors, it's gotta be financially crippling."

"Oh, I'm not charging anything." She couldn't imagine adding to their burden. "They have four kids. The mom's a bus driver, and the dad's an EMT. They're hurting."

Wyatt stopped, his hand jerking her to a halt.

"Something wrong?" She faced him.

He slid his sunglasses to the top of his head and cupped her chin with a hand. "Do you know how special you are?"

He stared down at her, the ocean reflecting in his eyes, turning them almost blue. She squirmed under the intensity of his gaze. "It's the least I can do. He's my student, and I don't want him to have to repeat the year and lose all his friends."

Wyatt tucked her hair back and held his hand there. "This is what I'm talking about. As busy as you are, you're making time for him and not even charging for it."

Her scalp tingled under the heat of his hand. Comforting and warm. "I just hope we can raise enough money through the walk-a-thon to make a difference."

"You're one determined lady. I'm sure you will." He slid his sunglasses back down. Taking her hand again, he resumed walking. "Heard any more from your interview?"

"Only that it's down to me and one other candidate. I should know soon. I'm hopeful." If she got the position, she'd be grounded in Maryland. A knot formed in her stomach.

Wyatt squeezed her hand. "By the way, my lacrosse team thinks you're the bomb now."

She rolled her eyes. "Please, that was such a flub-up. Bringing dirt pudding cups with gummy bears to high school boys? I don't know what I was thinking."

"They loved them. Those guys all try to be tough, but inside they're still kids." He shook his head. "Of course, I had to confiscate the extras when they started flinging the worms at each other."

Anne laughed and stepped over a clump of seaweed. "I didn't see that."

"They saved it for the locker room." Wyatt bent and studied a shell, then tossed it. "Not much on the beach with the tide so high right now."

"That's okay, you already got me a shell today."

He snorted. "Real quality piece of work."

"Well, I like it."

"Then that's all that matters."

They walked a few more beach blocks and then turned back. Being with Wyatt away from the crowds was heaven. He seemed like any normal person when they were alone. She could relax around him and be herself. But out in public? She'd rather moderate standardized tests than deal with the paparazzi.

When they reached their blanket, Wyatt waved to the ocean. "You managed to stay on the sand, but we can't get this close without putting our feet in."

Before she could answer, he tugged her closer to the ocean, stopping at the edge.

She wasn't excited about freezing, but she didn't want to dampen the huge grin on his face.

They both took a step in.

"No. This is crazy cold." Arctic water froze her toes. He dropped her hand and laughed as he plunged ahead to knee-deep.

"Wimp. Come on."

She scampered backwards until her feet were clear of the surf. "Not in a blue moon."

"Ha, you wanna see a blue moon? I'll give you one." He sprinted out of the waves toward her.

"Oh, no. Don't you dare!" She took off at a run. No way was she going to be one of those girls that got tossed into the surf by her boyfriend.

He grabbed her by the arms, hoisted her, and faked a move to the ocean. When she squealed in protest, he whirled around and carried her back to the blanket, dropping her gently down.

"I may be a Neanderthal, but I ain't stupid." He lowered his head and kissed her.

Sensations flooded her. His mouth hot, his legs cool and damp against hers. Both their hearts pounding from the jaunt back. The umbrella shaded their heads while the heat of the sun warmed their bodies. The kiss was salty, breathless, and tasted like the sea.

Liquid fire speared through her body. He skimmed his hand over her bikini top, teasing her nipple through the thin fabric. She moaned when he dragged his mouth away and seared her neck with hot kisses. His hand slid from her breast, to her stomach.

The sputter and hum of one of those low-flying airplanes dragging an advertisement sign grew louder.

Wyatt drew his head back. "Damn, I forgot where we were."

She gazed up at him. His jade eyes were shades darker with desire, and her breath stalled. He slid his hand from her stomach and eased to his side.

The sun disappeared behind clouds, and the wind kicked up. She glanced at the incoming front. Foreboding. A sliver of anxiety stole air from her lungs.

"Looks like we might get some rain." He eyed the sky.

Her heart continued to thump hard. Decision time was coming.

"We should get going." He rested a hand on her arm.

"Yeah, we should pack up."

But neither of them moved.

He blew out a breath and lightly stroked her skin. "This day didn't turn out anything like I had planned. I mean, the race, the fans…now the rain."

"You can't control Mother Nature." Her voice came out higher than usual in her effort to sound casual.

Wyatt shook his head. "I know, and I can't change any of it, so here we are." He met her gaze. "I meant what I said earlier today. No pressure."

She swallowed, uncertainty swirling in her head.

With a resigned sigh, Wyatt eased back, giving her space. "So, do you want to stay or go home?"

CHAPTER 19

POURING A SCOTCH ON THE ROCKS, Devon recounted the events of the day. After hearing the conversation between Anne and the ex-jock on her apartment bug, he knew they'd be gone for the weekend. Devon's "birthday" dinner had caused some friction. Perfect. He intended to cause a lot more.

He'd entered her place and made copies of the spare key she kept to Pearson's apartment. Easy work, as organized-Anne had it labeled in a drawer no less. Next, Devon had planted bugs in Pearson's apartment.

Things were getting way too cozy between Anne and the pigskin player. Devon needed to eliminate the competition. The muscles in his upper body stiffened. He wouldn't lose another bet over a woman to Paul, of all people. No fucking way.

Women always went for powerful, strong, successful men. Devon had to take Pearson down a notch. Make him look weak and lame. Show him up.

A plan started to form. Yes. Devon narrowed his eyes. He took a drink and sat in his recliner. The scotch burned down his throat and swished in his belly, warming his insides. This could work. In fact, if he played it right, he would come out the hero. He'd have to enlist the help of some of his old buddies, but that shouldn't be a problem. They'd whore out their own mothers for the right price.

Time for the gloves to come off.

CHAPTER 20

WAVES CRASHED ON THE SHORE, pounding as hard as Wyatt's heart while he waited for Anne's answer. Resisting the strong urge to touch her, he stared into her eyes and steeled himself for a negative response.

Instead, she eased closer and looped an arm around his neck. "I want to stay."

A mix of relief and anticipation tightened his belly. He pulled her close and kissed her. She molded her body to his, pressing her soft breasts to his bare chest, and kissed him back.

Hard.

Okay, time to go some place more private. He tore his mouth away from hers, and she gazed up at him. Stroking her cheek, he struggled to keep his voice steady. "I know this is a big step. It means a lot that you trust me." He touched his lips to hers. "Ready to leave?"

She traced a finger down his abs and teased him with a naughty smile. "How fast does that Lexus of yours go?"

Hot damn. They were so out of here. He jumped to his feet and made quick work of yanking out the umbrella. Couldn't help staring at her gorgeous ass as she bent down to pick up the blanket and shake it out, causing his dick to twitch. Christ, at this rate he wouldn't make it to the place he'd rented.

Wanting complete privacy, he'd found a whole-house rental for the night. Anne would be more comfortable not traipsing back and forth in front of other people in a hotel lobby. And he sure didn't want to be stopped for pictures again. Still, he'd only stayed at hotels in the past and had no idea what to expect.

He grabbed the beach bag and followed her back to the car. Nice view that only added to the intensity of his already raging hard-on.

On the way to the house, a million thoughts spun in his head. For the first time, he found himself nervous before sex. What if he couldn't control himself long enough for foreplay? A real possibility with as long as it had been and as excited as Anne got him. She wasn't like any other woman he'd known. He didn't want to go too fast or intimidate her with his size.

He winced. Not *that* size. His overall size. Who had highjacked his brain? He was thinking crazy stuff.

"What's wrong?" Anne placed a hand on his thigh.

A spark shot up his leg, and he jumped at the contact. "Huh?"

"You're…so quiet. Are you having second thoughts?"

Second thoughts? She had to be kidding. He'd been having a billion thoughts of little else for the last month and a half. His chest rumbled with a laugh he couldn't stop.

Anne drew her hand back. "Why are you laughing at me?"

Shit. He shook his head and glanced at her. "I'm not laughing at you. I promise."

"Well, then what's so funny?" She crossed her arms, a small pout on her pretty pink lips.

He couldn't tell her that a guy's second, third, and most every thought was about sex without sounding like a horndog. Which he was at the moment.

Thanks to her.

But he wanted to ease her mind. "Honestly, I'm kinda unnerved."

"What? You?" Her voice rang with disbelief. "Why?"

He stole a glance in her direction. "Because you matter. I don't want to disappoint you."

"*You* disappoint me?" She swallowed and her eyes widened. "I'm so scared of…"

"Wait." He pulled the car into a spot against the curb. Turning to face her, he placed a hand over hers, which felt cold to the touch. "What are you scared of?"

She nibbled her lip and let out a breath before raising her gaze to his. "Measuring up. I don't have much experience with…well…you know."

He blinked. This beautiful woman had no idea what she did to him. Maybe that was his fault for not telling her enough. But he hadn't wanted to pressure her. He brought her hand to his lips and kissed her fingers. "You have nothing to worry about. No one has ever made me feel the way you do."

"Yeah?" Her tentative smile inflated his heart.

"For sure." He glanced at the GPS. "We're almost at the house. I'll prove it to you there."

She nodded and squeezed his hand. "House?"

"Yeah, I wanted some privacy so I rented a beach cottage." He drove back onto the road.

Anne sighed. "That is such a relief. I admit I was a little nervous about people snapping shots of us together at a hotel."

He patted her leg. "I might be a slow learner, but I'm figuring you out."

The GPS announced their arrival, and Wyatt parked the car in the short driveway of a two-story, bright-blue house.

"This place is so cute." Anne perked up in the seat next to him. "Look at the shell-lined walkway and the painted, wooden dolphin on the door. I love it."

A thrill shot through Wyatt. He'd nailed it. Of course, he could have afforded something bigger and glitzier, but he'd gone with his gut and apparently chosen right.

He grabbed their bags from the trunk and punched in the access code on the door lock. When they entered, his gaze went to a plate of muffins and a note on the kitchen table that read, "Welcome to the shore." Nice touch.

Anne scouted out the rooms while he hauled their bags up the stairs to the master bedroom.

"Oh my gosh, there's a rooftop deck with an ocean view," she called from above.

Hell yeah, he hoped to make use of it after dark. The excitement in her voice sent a ripple of pride through him. He'd made her happy.

She came busting into the bedroom, a big grin on her face. "This is amazing. But what if I'd said I wanted to go home? I'd have felt horrible after you'd found such a nice, private place."

He smiled and shook his head. "You never would have known."

She squeezed her eyes shut and tapped her fingers to her forehead. "Oh, right. I swear, I don't think straight around you."

"I don't want you to think at all." He threaded his fingers through her hair and brought his lips closer to hers, a mere breath away. "I want you to feel."

She shivered and stilled. Her eyes grew large, and her breath turned shallow. In a husky voice, she said, "Give me a sec to freshen up?"

"Hurry," he whispered against her neck, nipping her ear lightly with his teeth.

She snatched her bag and headed to the bathroom. "Be right back."

The image of Anne in the black bikini flashed in his head and kept the blood supply flowing south as he pulled down the sheets of the bed and tossed some condoms on the nightstand.

Anne cleared her throat, and he glanced up. She stood in the doorway wearing a hot-pink, lacy sheer bra and a tiny black triangle bottom with a small pink bow on the front.

His mouth went dry, and he sucked in a breath. Sweet Jesus.

From the swell of her breasts, to the curve of her hips, to the flat plane of her stomach, she screamed sexy. She did a slow, tentative pirouette showing him her firm little ass framed by the thong straps.

"I wanted something special to wear. Do you like it?" The little hitch in her voice turned him on even more. She'd stepped out of her comfort zone for him.

Somehow, he managed to cross the room, but his gaze continued to rake up and down her gorgeous figure. When at last he met her eyes, electricity surged between them. Palpable energy that caused his cock to throb.

"You are so beautiful." He choked the words out of his parched throat.

She wet her lips and took a step closer, staring up at him. Her soft, sweet scent filled his head as she splayed her hands across his chest. Not breaking eye contact, she kneaded the muscles, heating his body with her touch.

He ran his hands down her exposed sides, over the flare of her hips, and back up to rest at her waist. Her muscles trembled under his palms.

She stood on her tiptoes, and he leaned down to kiss her. Slowly at first, he pressed his lips to hers, barely touching them, teasing until she strained higher for more contact. Her breasts pressed against him, and her hard nipples scraped through the fabric. His blood heated to molten lava, burning through his veins.

Anne wrapped her arms around his neck and pulled herself up to deepen the kiss. Her tongue mated with his, twisting and dancing in his mouth as a small moan came from deep inside her. Fisting a hand in his hair, she rocked her hips against his raging hard-on.

She nipped his lower lip, kissing him with a fierce hunger that took his breath away. Thunder pounded in his ears, and a primal need to be inside of her consumed him. He'd never reacted to a woman like this. It was Anne, all Anne. Time to slow things down before he lost it.

He scooped her up, carried her to the bed, and gently laid her down. When she reached for him, he eased back and stroked her hair. "Not so fast. I want to worship every inch of your gorgeous body."

Her eyes, glazed with desire, followed his finger as he traced it down her neck to the edge of her lacy bra. With the lightest touch, he rubbed the fabric over her breast, causing the nipple to pucker even more. He brought his mouth down to suckle it. Anne arched her back, filling his greedy mouth with her breast.

* * *

Wyatt's hot tongue did wicked things to torture her through the lace of her bra. He slipped a strap down her arm, then followed it with open-mouthed kisses that set her skin on fire. An ache grew at the delta of her legs, begging for attention.

She rested her hands on his broad shoulders when he focused on her breasts again, sliding the lace down to suckle her bare nipple. He flicked, then licked it repeatedly until she thought she'd levitate off the bed. Tiny sparks lit in her belly. Dear God, the man knew how to arouse every cell of her body.

The stubble of his chin scraped and tickled her ribcage. He blew warm air across her wet peak, and then licked it again. His mouth devoured her. Possessive one second, and gentle the next. His unique, all-Wyatt scent intoxicated her.

She dug her fingers into the hard muscles of his shoulders and whimpered. A guttural sound of satisfaction that came from somewhere deep inside him vibrated through her. She pressed her hands harder, nudging him down to the source of her longing.

He moved lower, blazing a path with his tongue until he reached the top of her thong. Sliding a finger under the material, he found her engorged nub and traced small circles around it. Desire coiled tighter and tighter in her belly, causing her to pant and writhe.

Wyatt nipped at the elastic strap with his teeth, sending a ripple of pleasure to her core. He slid the thong down her legs and positioned his face between them. Licking and teasing the soft flesh of her inner thighs, he slipped a finger inside her.

Her leg muscles quivered, and she opened farther for him. He withdrew his finger and sucked it. "Mm."

The growl in his voice made her toes curl. He gazed up at her, emerald-green eyes raw with lust. The room blurred behind him, filling her vision with nothing but the pure passion in his face. Her heart lurched at the strength of her feelings for him. He cared more about her than himself, making sure he pleased her first. She'd been right to trust him and let go.

He gave her a sinful smile full of promise, and lowered his head, at last placing that hot, wet mouth on her center, and then she couldn't think at all. She squeezed her eyes shut as pressure built, each brush of his tongue bringing her closer and closer. Her senses spun, drowning in anticipation.

She tangled her fingers in his hair, pressing his head harder against her.

"Wyatt...oh Wyatt." She held her breath as he took her over the final crest. A kaleidoscope of lights exploded behind her eyes. She cried out in release, her body pulsing, riding each wave of ecstasy. He continued sucking and teasing her, drawing the orgasm out until her bones melted, and she shuddered.

A sigh escaped as she floated back down to reality.

The bed sagged beside her, and Wyatt's warm breath tickled her neck. He nuzzled the top of her collarbone as she blinked several times and the room came back into focus.

"Oh my God." She shuddered again. "I've never…"

He brought his lips to hers in a soft kiss, but his erection pressing into her side was anything but soft. "You have me so hot, I'm ready to explode."

"We better take care of that." She eased up on her elbow and tugged at the waistband of his swim suit. It barely budged, and she tugged harder.

"That's not going to work with me lying on the bed." He shook his head and stood up. With a quick yank, the suit hit the floor, and he sprang free.

She dropped her jaw. His cock was proportionate to the rest of him.

And he was a very big man.

He must have noticed her expression, because he placed a finger under her chin and tipped her head up. His eyes gazed down at her, the lines on the edges laced with concern. "I'd never hurt you."

"I know." The last thing she wanted was for him to worry. She had to remember that everything about Wyatt was larger than life, and he'd just proven it in delicious ways that she would relive for a long time.

She scooted to the side of the bed and closed a hand around his cock. He flinched and sucked in a breath. A thrill ripped her apart, knowing her touch did that to him.

Lowering her head, she used her tongue to tease him. She started at the base, and licked her way to his tip, sucking the head in and out of her mouth. He made a strangled sound, followed by a guttural moan that only spurred her on.

Her abdomen tightened as her own need built again, fueled by the excitement of feeling him grow even harder. In a bold move, she grabbed his ass and took him deep into her throat, inch by inch.

The muscles in his buttocks turned to rock, and he gripped her head and held it steady. "Don't move. I want this to last." His chest heaved, and for a long moment he stood stock-still. "I can't wait. Now."

He snagged a condom from the nightstand and unrolled it over his length.

Taking a short breath, she gazed up at him. The lines on his face taut, his pure arousal made her dizzy with power. She'd never turned on a man like this. The scent of sex swirled in the room, and she fed on the unleashed desire in his eyes.

She slid back on the bed and he positioned himself above her, braced on his elbows.

His shaft pressed against her entrance, right below the tight bundle of nerves at her sex.

He penetrated her slowly, stretching her until he filled her completely. She wrapped her legs around him, and his eyes flashed. Gripping his back, she dug her fingers into the hard muscles as he began to thrust in and out.

Yes. Wyatt inside of her. Nothing had ever felt more right. She clung to him and matched his rhythm as he increased the pace. Giving all of herself, she held nothing back. Caught up in a whirlwind of pleasure, their moans mixed, and the room spun around her. Pure heat consumed her body, and all that existed was her connection to Wyatt. At one with him.

Her climax came hard and strong, like when two fronts clashed in a high-powered storm. She clutched him, and he went rigid, threw his head back, and let out a deep groan at his own release. Her insides rhythmically squeezed his fullness as she catapulted into another realm.

Wyatt hugged her to him and spun over to lie on his back. They both sucked in air, chests thumping against each other.

Her limp body melded on top of his as she collapsed into a sated puddle. Good God, she never knew sex could be like that. She could spend the rest of her life exploring the options.

The rest of her life?

She closed her eyes as Wyatt's heartbeat blended with hers. Caring, strong, and giving, he was everything she'd ever hoped for in a partner. She hadn't meant to fall in love, but it had snuck up on her, and now the reality struck her. She was in deep.

Her body still tingled, and her brain only functioned at half-speed, but the way he'd looked at her when they'd made love gave her hope. If he felt anywhere near the emotions she did, they'd somehow work things out. She snuggled against him as he stroked her hair and rubbed her back.

"So, you like that rooftop deck, huh?" Wyatt shifted, propping his head on his elbow.

She gave a quick nod. "I bet you can see a million stars from up there."

He nuzzled her neck and tugged at the blanket. "How about we take this up there and I'll make you see a million stars...with your eyes shut."

Like she could say no to that.

* * *

Anne blinked at the sunlight streaming through the crack of the bedroom curtains. With her head on Wyatt's shoulder and a leg across his stomach, she couldn't get any closer to him. Heat radiated from his body, all muscles and hard planes. Her thigh tingled against his skin, reminding her that his every touch sent her into orbit.

"Hey sleepyhead." He stroked her back and kissed the top of her head. "I didn't want to wake you, but we have to get going."

"Hmm..." She'd rather stay wrapped in his arms. "Does this weekend ever have to end?"

He squeezed her and laughed. "Not on my account. We can pick this up back at home."

"Now that sounds nice." He might be turning her into a sex fiend. They'd made love multiple times, and she still wanted him again.

"I have to admit, you surprised me."

She gazed up at him. "How?"

"I thought you might be shy, but you were nothing short of amazing."

Her heart expanded, and his words boosted her confidence. "It's all you, Wyatt. I've never felt like this before."

"Well it works for me." He rubbed his thumb along her chin.

His erection pressed into her leg, and she arched an eyebrow. "Oh? Are we—"

"We don't have time." Regret laced his voice. He dropped his hand and eased away. "It's close to checkout. But we *will* pick this up later."

The spark in his eye turned her knees soft. "Well, alrighty then."

After they packed up, Wyatt unplugged his phone from the charger and paused, staring down at it.

"What's wrong?" Anne asked.

"I missed a call last night." A ghost of a frown outlined his mouth.

"Was it important?"

He raised his eyes to hers and sucked in a breath. "I'll know in a minute."

CHAPTER 21

HOLDING the phone to his ear, Wyatt played the voicemail message.

"Hey, Pearson. Callahan here. We need a tight end, and I'm looking for someone who knows the system. I want to talk to you about coming back. Give me a call."

A bolt of adrenaline spiked through Wyatt. He hadn't heard from anyone on the team for over a year and had never expected this.

"What is it?" Anne stepped closer.

He shook his head and shrugged. "That was the Ravens' coach. He wants me to play again."

Anne blinked.

Twice.

"What?"

"This is a shock." Wyatt shut his eyes and pinched the bridge of his nose. A million thoughts zipped around in his brain. Did he want to play again? He hadn't considered it because he'd retired. But hell, players came back all the time.

"What are you thinking?"

"I don't know." He opened his eyes and blew out a breath. "I should at least talk to him. Find out what he's offering."

Anne's shoulders hitched and her lips drew into a thin line. "You'd have your old life back."

His chest tingled as a twinge of excitement laced his ribs. He missed the game, which is why he wanted the USC job. College raised the level of competition to a new height. But even that came nowhere close to playing in the NFL.

He glanced at Anne, and his heart squeezed. So much had changed in the last two months since he'd met her. For the first time, he was emotionally invested in a relationship. He could get really used to waking up with her next to him, snuggled against his body.

That wouldn't happen if he moved to California. But playing for the Ravens wouldn't be much better. He'd spend a lot of time on the road and be back in the limelight. And like it or not, as his girlfriend, she'd be thrust into it as well.

She smoothed a hand down the leg of her jeans. "We should get going."

"Anne."

"Hmm?" She raised her chin and tilted her head, as if they'd discussed the price of a hotdog at the stadium instead of his future career and how it might affect their relationship.

He put down his phone. "I'm just going to explore the option."

"Uh huh." She headed to the bedroom. "I'll grab my suitcase."

Damn it. He didn't want to upset her, but he had to find out more about the offer. Surely, she could understand that.

She came out of the bedroom carrying her bag. "Ready?"

Tension hung in the air thicker than fog on the Golden Gate bridge. He opened his mouth, but he had nothing to say that would comfort her. He sighed and nodded. "Let's go."

Anne stared out the passenger window and remained silent during the drive for a long time. At last, she turned to him. "It's just that you said you were done with being the center of attention and wanted to be on the sidelines."

"Well, that's when I thought my only chance to be around the game was as a coach." He switched lanes and frowned. "It's not the spotlight I miss, it's the thrill of catching the ball and scoring points. Every new set of downs is a challenge. What defense will they bring? Can I get open? It's...fun and exciting. Do you understand what I mean?"

She gave him a slow nod and faced the window again.

His stomach balled into a knot. Words couldn't convey the excitement he felt when he played. It killed him to see her so sad, but he had to at least talk to the Ravens. "I'm just going to see what they're offering. Doesn't mean I'm going to take it."

"I know you don't need the money, so what does it matter what they pay you?"

Shit. She had a point.

Her phone rang as they pulled into her apartment complex, and she answered. "Hey, Emily."

After a pause, she said, "Yeah, we were at the boardwalk, why?" Her voice pitched higher. "No, I haven't seen it. What went viral?"

Uh oh. The word "viral" never led to anything good. Wyatt's nerves stretched thin.

"Okay. Send it." Anne hung up and stared at the phone. A second later it beeped with a message. Her eyes widened and her hand flew to her mouth. "No. Oh God, no."

CHAPTER 22

ANNE GAPED at the images on her phone. Her chest hitched, and a wave of nausea rose from her stomach. Why? Why would anyone post those?

Two pictures, side by side, filled the screen. One of Wyatt with a supermodel draped over his arm, and the other of him and Anne, coming out of the souvenir shop on the boardwalk. The caption below the pictures read, "From supermodels and super-pro, to high school coach and plain Jane Doe."

"What is it?" Alarm in his voice, Wyatt parked in her apartment complex lot and placed a hand on her shoulder.

She shook her head hard, hot tears burning her eyes, and thrust the phone at him for him to see. Emily said the images had gone viral. Anne's phone dinged with a text, then another, then another.

"What the fuck?" Wyatt squeezed her shoulder. "This is messed up. People are always taking pictures and splashing them over the tabloids and media. Don't pay attention to it."

"Not of me, Wyatt." She covered her face with her hands. *Plain Jane Doe.* They were right. She was a no-name school teacher. Wyatt had told her the publicity would all calm down. Now he was thinking about playing again. Nothing would calm down.

Is this what her life would be if they stayed together? Public humiliation and constant judgement? She'd worked hard to build a solid reputa-tion, and if she wanted to be a principal, she couldn't have pictures of her with demeaning captions blowing up on social media.

"I'm sorry. This is so wrong. So untrue." He placed a hand on her thigh and rubbed her shoulder. "You're beautiful, and real, and the only woman I want to be with. Please, don't let this get in your head."

Ding.

Ding.

Ding.

More texts. Wyatt's words floated around in her mind, but the pictures had burned into her brain. Feeling nauseous, she needed air and space.

She opened the car door and stepped out. Wyatt was at her side in a second.

"I'll bring your bag up and stay with you tonight." He grabbed her suitcase.

She drew in a long breath and exhaled. The air cooled her lungs and helped clear her head. She needed some time to process and think. The last twenty-four hours had been a whirlwind. From the realization that she loved Wyatt, to the shock of the Ravens' call, to the social media nightmare, she'd had enough

Publicly red-penned, she just wanted to tuck herself away, safe in her apartment, where no cameras would snap secret photos, and she had her privacy back.

She inhaled another breath of the cool air. "Thanks, and I'm sorry, but not tonight. It's been too much."

He gazed down at her with concern in his eyes, jaw set. "I don't want to leave you like this."

"I appreciate that, but I need some time alone." She touched her hand to his, and he squeezed hers, like he'd been waiting for a sign of hope.

"I wanted this weekend to be so special. I don't know how to fix this."

The honest emotion in his face softened her heart. Their connection was real, and he didn't seem the least bit worried what anyone thought about him dating a *plain Jane Doe*. That said something.

More dings on her phone.

She toggled it to vibrate. "The photos aren't your fault. I get that, but I need some time to deal with everything going on right now."

Wyatt frowned and glanced at her cell. "Don't engage. Ignore the gossip. The less you say, the quicker it's forgotten."

She didn't doubt him, but it was a lesson she'd rather not have to learn. "Okay."

He stroked a finger down the side of her face and slowly leaned in for a kiss. Her insides quaked with emotion as their lips touched.

He drew back, not pressing. "I'll call you tomorrow?"

"Okay."

After she entered her apartment, the number of texts overwhelmed her. Friends, coworkers, Maddie, Sarah...the list went on. She shot a quick response to her sisters and Emily, telling them that she was okay. Everyone else would have to wait.

Her stomach flip-flopped, and sweat chilled her body. She wasn't cut out for this kind of "attention."

But then where did that leave her with Wyatt?

CHAPTER 23

DEVON TOOK a seat at the conference room table and added a reminder in his calendar to call Paul. Devon had another shipment to process and a wired payment coming.

He glanced up when Anne tapped on the open door and entered. *"Plain Jane Doe"* fit her attire. Khaki pants and a loose-fitting sweater. She tried to cover up, but she had curves worth exploring. Couldn't be soon enough in his book. The bet stipulated no other women until the wager ended, and he was used to getting some on a regular basis.

He noted the dark circles under Anne's eyes and the tense way she held her head. Sure signs of the strain she'd been under the last couple of days. An extra shot of confidence spiraled through his chest. Today, he'd make his move on her.

Someone had done him a big favor, shaming her on social media. He'd listened to her over the bugs at her place. Her phone hadn't stopped ringing. She'd talked to Emily about her embarrassment and how much she hated the publicity. And apparently, the Ravens wanted to talk to Pearson about playing again. Anne hadn't been happy about that at all. Another strike against Pearson.

The conversations he'd overheard between the jock and Anne the last couple of days had been stilted. For all his smooth moves on the field, the guy face-planted when it came to relationship talks.

Anne pulled out a notebook. "I brought a list of questions."

Devon chose his words carefully, seeing if he could get her to bring up the social media debacle so he could use it to his advantage. "Before we get started, I want to apologize for the situation you were put in."

Her face flushed. "It certainly wasn't your fault."

"Well I didn't plan it, but I still feel responsible."

"Why would you feel responsible?" Her eyes widened, and she scooted the chair back. "Oh my God. Did *you* take the picture?"

Perfect. Almost laughable. His pulse picked up pace. He gave her his best confused expression, followed by one of distress, jerking his head back. "No. You misunderstood. I meant the situation at Toni's."

Her face turned redder, and she pressed her fingers to her forehead. "Toni's?" She grunted. "Believe me, that's not even on my radar anymore."

He reached across the table and placed a hand on her arm. "I'm sorry. I saw that horrible post. And whoever wrote that caption is blind."

She let out a weary breath and met his eyes. "It's so humiliating. So many people have come out of the woodwork, pretending to be sympathetic, but all they really want is to gossip, you know?"

His stomach jumped. Making progress. She was opening up to him. He gave her arm a squeeze. "Yes. Everyone loves drama, and at times like these you find out who your real friends are."

"Right? It's so nice to talk to someone who understands."

Ah. The weak link. Being famous, Pearson was probably used to sloughing off bad press. It went with the territory. News of a possible offer for him to return to the Ravens had boosted the already viral post. Telling Anne to ignore it did nothing to get her out of the unwanted spotlight, and he seemed clueless about how to assuage her feelings.

Devon keyed in or what he hoped would hit home. "I understand. The worst part is the damage it can do to your hard-earned reputation. Something you have to always protect."

She pressed her lips together and nodded. "I know. And I'm a candidate for a vice principal's job. I'm worried this will affect the decision."

He arched a brow. Of course he knew about the position, but this presented another opportunity for him. "It's a valid concern. Where did you apply?"

"Kirby's Mill." She squinted and rubbed her chin. "Do you think they'll factor this into their choice?"

Well, well. As complete and together he'd thought her to be, self-doubts loomed under the surface. Ones he could capitalize on. A sliver of anticipation slinked up his spine.

"I really don't know." He drew his hand back and tapped his chin. "I'm friends with the superintendent in that district, though. I'd be more than happy to put in a good word for you."

She quickly shook her head. "No. I need to do this on my own, but thank you."

"Okay, but if you change your mind, let me know. Damage control can be difficult, and I'm more than happy to help." Might as well hype the fear. He didn't miss the grateful look in her eyes. Mission achieved. "You're sure there isn't anything I can do?"

"No, I'm sorry. I didn't mean to get into all of that. Not your problem, and I shouldn't have brought it up." She opened her notebook. "Let's get to this list of questions."

He took his time addressing all of the issues, trying to put her at ease. The confident, reliable source that she could count on. When they finished, Anne packed up. "I think this is all coming together."

"Thanks to your hard work." He stood. "I'll walk you out."

"Thanks, but that's not necessary."

"Maybe not, but it's my pleasure. I'm leaving for a while, anyway." Flicking the light switch, he followed her out.

He'd timed his meeting with her, knowing that the pediatric brats would be in the open area, and the gifts he'd sent would be delivered that day. Sure enough, as he passed by the children flocked to him.

"Mr. Blackwood, thank you." The little girl that he'd given the gold coin to before, whatever her name was, held up a magic book. "I've been practicing. I know how to do some tricks now."

He winked at her and placed a finger on her lips. "Shh. Don't tell anyone how you do them. Remember, magicians never reveal their secrets."

She hugged his leg and the other children gathered around, each holding up their gifts. He had no idea what half of them were, but he'd googled the best toys for kids their ages and ordered some. Seemed to be a success, but nowhere near the reward he got from Anne's expression.

Ka-ching. Big winner.

He said goodbye to the mob and headed to the elevator.

"You're so generous." Anne glanced back at the horde.

"I try to help where I can." Now to pull the ace from his sleeve. As they passed an office, he paused at the door. "Sorry, I need to check something. Hold on a sec."

He ducked his head in. "Hey, Mary. Is the cuddle orientation at seven or eight tonight? I have two different times in my calendar."

"Seven. I'll see you there?"

"Wouldn't miss it." He gave her a wave and continued down the hall.

When they stopped at the elevator, Anne gazed up at him, a faint smile on her lips. "I've heard about that program. Are you training to hold the NICU babies?"

And…the house takes the hand. He gave himself a virtual high-five at the excitement in her voice. "Yeah. I'm taking my second class."

She nodded. "That's fantastic. It's something I want to do, but I don't have time right now. I love babies."

"Me, too. I can't wait to have my own one day." The elevator door opened and she entered. Her smile had faded, replaced by a worry line. Another score for him. Now he had her thinking. He'd heard her tell Emily that Pearson didn't want children. Devon had only signed up for the orientations to impress Anne. Since he'd made his point with her, he wouldn't even go anymore. He had zero interest in holding a wailing sack of poop.

"I'm sure you'll make a great father as good as you are with the kids." She pressed the lobby button and stepped back.

"I hope so." He warmed his tone and looked her in the eyes. "I just need to find the right woman first."

She stared back at him for a second, then gazed at the elevator numbers, a hint of pink creeping up her neck. "I'm sure you will."

The doors opened and they walked out to the parking lot. Anne stopped. "Have fun tonight. I'll see you next week."

Time to make his move. "Actually, I'd like to see you sooner."

"Sooner?" She glanced up at him.

"Yes." He held her gaze. "How about going to dinner with me, unrelated to the walk-a-thon."

"Oh." She looked away. "I'm sorry, I'm seeing someone."

Shit. Irritation burned his stomach. The wedge between her and Pearson wasn't big enough yet. "The ex-football player in the picture?"

"Yeah." Red spots blotted her cheeks.

"I wasn't sure if you were still together. I mean, you don't have a ring on your finger, and I know how disturbing all that social media was to you."

"It is, but..." She shrugged.

He squared his shoulders. "May I be direct?"

"Yes?"

"I think you and I have a lot in common. We work well together. If you were dating me, you'd never have to worry about your reputation or being trashed on social media."

The flicker in her eyes told him he'd made a direct hit. He placed a hand on her shoulder. "I care about you. You touch me like no one else has. I'd like to see what we might have together."

She shuffled her feet. "You're a wonderful person, but like I said, I'm in a relationship."

He drew his arm back and nodded. "I understand, but I didn't get to where I am in life by stepping away from a challenge. Some things are worth the effort and wait." He smiled at her. "I won't pressure you, but know I'm not giving up hope."

She shook her head. "I don't want you to waste your time. Really, I'm flattered but—"

"I have nothing but time. Trust me, you're worth the wait." He touched her cheek, and then stepped back. "Have a good night, and I'll see you next week."

She nibbled her lower lip. "You, too."

He narrowed his eyes, devouring her perfect little ass as she walked to her car. Couldn't wait to get some of that. He'd definitely made progress, but now he needed to up the ante and make Pearson fold.

CHAPTER 24

SLIPPING ON A PAIR OF EARRINGS, Anne pondered the conversations she'd had with Devon yesterday. He'd caught her completely off guard when he'd asked her out. As far as she knew, she hadn't said or done anything to encourage him. And she didn't want him waiting around for her. Despite his good looks, she had no chemistry with him and no desire to have a relationship outside of the walk-a-thon event.

Wyatt was the only one who'd ever brought her senses to life. His touch, his scent, the way his eyes twinkled when he teased her. She loved him and hated the awkwardness between them since the media blowup.

A knock sounded, and she hurried to the door because she couldn't wait to see him. The tiny peephole did nothing to dwarf his frame or stop her breath from catching. It had only been a few days since the beach, but she'd missed the hell out of him.

She opened the door and inhaled the fragrance of his cologne blown in by the crisp, cool night air.

He thrust a box out to her. "I hope you're not allergic to these."

She took the white carton with a cellophane cut out, containing humongous chocolate-covered strawberries. Her mouth watered. "Oh my."

"You like it?"

She glanced up, her gaze traveling from his sexy-as-sin leather jacket to his deep-green eyes. A wave of pure lust rocked her body.

Double yum. "What's not to like?"

She swallowed, and he waved a hand at that box. "I feel bad about everything and figured with my lousy flower selection skills, I'd try something different."

Her body choked with emotion. Actions spoke louder than words. Words they'd both struggled with the last few days.

"I've missed you," they both blurted out.

She stepped back and placed the box on the table. When she turned, he wrapped his arms around her, bringing his mouth to hers in a crushing kiss that sucked the air from her lungs. She came away breathless.

He framed her face with his hands. "Are you okay? I know this all has been a lot to deal with."

She took a deep breath. "I'm managing."

"I haven't been able to think about anything but you." He stroked her cheek. "I wish I could make the media go away."

Regret reflected in the depths of his eyes. Yeah, this was her Wyatt. He might suck at phone conversations, but in person he launched her into another orbit. "It wasn't your fault."

"Doesn't matter. I never want to see you hurt." He pressed his lips to hers, then pulled back, keeping his arms around her. "I talked to the Ravens coach today."

Her stomach dropped. "And?"

"It's a decent offer. One worth considering."

"I see." She couldn't keep the disappointment out of her voice even though she'd expected as much.

"Hey." He ran a hand through her hair. "I didn't say yes. It's just on the table for now."

"Okay." Handling change and uncertainty weren't her long suits, but she had no choice in this matter except to break up with him or wait it out.

"You sure you're still up for going to Baltimore?" he asked.

"Yes. I'm not going to hide from the world. Besides, since we're catching a late dinner before the movie, the restaurant shouldn't be crowded." She snatched her purse and locked the door on the way out.

They managed to find a quiet booth at their favorite Italian place, and the waitress who'd served them several times before didn't mention social media. Anne relaxed, finishing off her glass of chianti as Wyatt paid the check.

"Do you want to walk to the theater like we planned, or would you rather drive?" He slid out of the booth and stood.

"It's not super cold, and I have my coat. Let's walk."

He took her hand as they strolled along the sidewalk lined with groups of small, older townhouses separated by alleys. She frowned at an unlit lamppost they had to pass. Cloudy skies hid the moon and any light it might shine. She picked up the pace a little, her heart beating faster.

"What's wrong?" Wyatt tugged on her hand to slow her down.

"I don't—"

Suddenly, a figure emerged from an alley. A man grabbed her arm and yanked her away from Wyatt. Before she could react, a large hand clamped over her mouth while he dragged her into the alleyway.

"Hey, let go of her," Wyatt yelled as three guys emerged from the shadows and pounced on him.

Huge, muscled arms held Anne in a vise-like grip. She struggled to no avail. The other men hauled Wyatt deeper into the alley. He got several punches in before two of them managed to pin his arms. Three against one—despite Wyatt's size, he didn't stand a chance.

Anne's stomach churned at the sickening sound of punches thudding into him. She wrenched and jerked to get free. She had to do something. With all her strength she slammed a foot down on her captor's, bit his hand, and tasted blood.

He jerked away, freeing her mouth. "Fucking bitch."

"Help!" she screamed and ran toward the men attacking Wyatt. She was snatched from behind before she could get to them. The man spun her around and slapped her viciously across the face, knocking her to the ground. Her temple slammed on the concrete followed by searing pain.

Didn't matter. She had to get to Wyatt.

She scrambled up, whipped her leg out, and tripped her captor. He landed with a thud followed by a string of profanities.

Anne lunged at the guy punching Wyatt. She grabbed his arm and jabbed at his eyes but she was yanked back by her hair and once again pinned against her captor's body. She reached behind and clawed at his face, her gaze still rivetted on Wyatt, as much as she could see in the dark.

Wyatt twisted from side to side, but couldn't escape.

"Stop." Another man came running into the alley from the street.

Thank God. Someone to help. She struggled even harder to get free.

The stranger moved quickly, landing a roundhouse kick over Anne's head to her captor's temple, causing him to release her and fall to the ground. The stranger pivoted and turned his attention to the guys beating Wyatt. The one punching him stopped.

The man from the street was on him in a second, connecting his fist with the guy's chin, then whirling around to deliver a crushing kick to the other man's kidneys. Both men fell to the ground, writhing in obvious pain. The third thug released Wyatt and took off running.

Blood pounded in Anne's ears, and her heart threatened to explode. Her attacker pushed up to his feet and stumbled out of the alley. The stranger took a quick step toward the other two men, who scurried after their friend.

Wyatt laid limp on the ground, silent and motionless.

"Oh, no." Anne staggered over to him as fast as she could manage.

"Anne, is that you? It's Devon."

Devon? What was he doing there? Her brain couldn't process that right now. She dropped to her knees beside Wyatt and tried to wake him up, lifting his head. He moaned and slumped back down. Her hands shook, and fear sliced her lungs. "He's not moving. Call nine-one-one."

Pinprick points of light appeared before her eyes. Then everything went black.

* * *

Anne cracked her eyelids open and winced.

"Good. You're waking up. I'll beep the doctor," a male voice said.

Where was she? She tried again to open her eyes, squinting enough to see this time.

A man wearing scrubs peered down at her. "You're at the hospital. I'm your nurse and need to ask you some questions. Can you tell me your name?"

Her head throbbed. She reached up and touched an ice pack.

Oh my God...the assault...Wyatt. Her blood pressure soared. The machine beside the bed pinged, and panic gripped her throat. "I need to know if my boyfriend is okay. Wyatt Pearson?"

The nurse eyed the beeping monitor. "Let's focus on you right now. What's your name?"

"Anne Cooper."

"What day is it?"

"Friday."

Her chest ached, and her breath came in short bursts, making her lightheaded. God, she couldn't breathe. She needed to know about Wyatt. Why was the nurse asking all these stupid questions? "Please, where's Wyatt?"

The nurse raised the bed higher and placed a hand on her shoulder. "Take some deep breaths. You're hyperventilating."

After she did, he continued questioning her. Maybe if she answered enough of them, he'd ask someone about Wyatt. She told him everything she could remember to the point of blacking out, and then he entered her personal information into their system.

Bells, beeps, and someone calling out codes on a speaker sounded. She flinched at the hospital noises that rang in her ears, causing her head to ache even more. Everything was so loud. She glanced down at the hospital gown she wore. "What happened to my clothes?"

The nurse pointed to a clear bag on the seat beside her that contained the remnants of her outfit and purse. "You were unconscious, so the EMT's had to cut them off to assess your injuries."

Oh no. People she didn't know had seen her naked. Her face grew hot.

A doctor came in and examined her. He flashed a light in her eyes and tested her reflexes while asking about the events before she'd passed out. She couldn't recall what had happened between the time she struck the ground and when she reached Wyatt. She felt like she was in a fog, floating in and out as the doctor finished the exam.

He said in a low voice, "You have a concussion, and it's normal to have some memory gaps." He turned to the nurse. "Order a CT scan."

A concussion. No wonder her head hurt so much. Probably nothing compared to Wyatt's injuries. Worry tethered a leash to her heart, dragging it down. "Please, doctor, have you seen my boyfriend? Wyatt Pearson?"

"I'm really sorry, but we aren't allowed to share any medical information with non-family members." He gave her the same sad look the nurse had. "There's an officer who wants to ask some questions. Are you feeling up to it?"

"Yes. Anything to help find whoever did this to us."

The doctor left, and a policeman entered. For what seemed like the millionth time, Anne recounted the story, answering his questions to the best of her ability. Her body shook as she relived the nightmare, and the nurse covered her with a blanket.

The cop handed her a business card. "I have all I need for now. Call me if you think of anything else."

"I'm sorry, I know I wasn't much help. It was so dark and—"

"You did great. Don't worry." He nodded. "We're questioning everyone and will do our best to find these guys."

He stepped aside as yet another nurse came to take her for the scan. No sign of Wyatt in any of the halls or rooms she'd passed. Was he in the ICU? Her pulse sped up again.

As she waited for the results, all she could think about was the gut-wrenching sounds of fists thumping into Wyatt. She nibbled on some crackers, hoping to settle her queasy stomach.

The doctor finally returned. "Good news. The scan was negative, so we can discharge you, but you shouldn't be alone for the next six hours."

Ugh. Tension tightened her neck. Emily left for work super early and wouldn't be able to stay with Anne. She might have to call Sarah, who didn't need to be upset so late in her pregnancy.

"I'm going to take you out to the waiting area because we need this room." The nurse held up a pair of lightweight pants with a drawstring. "Do you want these to wear, or is someone bringing you clothes?"

"I'll put those on for now." She hadn't thought that far ahead yet. A female nurse entered to help Anne put on the pants and sit in the wheelchair. When the other nurse returned, he handed her the bag containing her belongings. "I'll get your discharge papers together. Do you have a ride home?"

She pressed a finger to her sore temple. "I'll call someone."

He wheeled her to the waiting room, spoke to the receptionist, and secured her in a corner out of the way. She closed her eyes, and a tear slid down her cheek. Why had this happened? What were they doing to Wyatt?

Someone touched her shoulder, and she jumped.

"I'm sorry. I didn't mean to startle you."

She gazed up at Devon. Surprise turned to concern. "Oh, no. Are you hurt too?"

"I'm fine. I came to check on you. I would have come sooner, but they took me to the station for questioning."

Relief flooded her system. Maybe he could get some information. Everyone knew him at the hospital.

His is eyes narrowed as he stared at her face. "They messed you up."

"I'll be okay." She twisted her hands in her lap. "It's Wyatt I'm worried about."

A vein bulged in Devon's forehead, and the tips of his ears turned red. "Someone is going to pay."

"Can you find anything out about him?" She grabbed his hand and squeezed it. "I can't stand not knowing."

"I can try, but first, how are you? What did the doctor say?"

"I have a concussion." She still felt like she was in a fog, and took a deep breath.

Devon's mouth twisted. "This never should have happened."

"Please, see if anyone will talk to you?" She squeezed his hand harder. He was her only hope.

"Okay, I'll be back." He strode toward the elevator, looked back, and shook his head.

She hugged her arms around herself, warding off a chill. The hospital probably wouldn't release her until she had a ride home, but she wasn't going to leave until she could see Wyatt.

Devon returned and said quietly, "I found out that he's here and staying at least overnight. That's all I know."

"It must be bad if they aren't letting him go home." Fresh tears filled her eyes.

"Not necessarily. Sometimes they keep people for observation."

"Do you think they'd let me see him?" She swiped at her wet cheeks.

Devon frowned. "No. I asked. Not tonight."

The walls of her chest deflated. She fumbled to open the bag that held her phone and purse.

"Please, let me help." Devon slid the seal open for her.

"Thank you. I need to call my sister. I don't think they'll discharge me without a ride."

He checked his watch. "It's three o'clock. I'm headed home and have plenty of space in my house. Why don't you stay with me, and I'll bring you back first thing in the morning? I have an early meeting anyway."

"That's nice of you, but you've done enough already."

"It's so late. It would only be for a few hours to catch some rest and not worry your family. I promise, it's just a friend trying to help out, nothing more."

The room turned blurry for a second, and she blinked a couple of times. His offer made sense, but the awkward conversation with Devon about him "waiting for her" reared its head. "Thanks, but I should probably call my sister. I hate to drag her out of bed, though. She's pregnant and lives an hour away."

"I could take you to her house if you want."

"Really?"

He nodded. "You've had a traumatic night and need to feel safe. I'm happy to help however I can."

She rubbed the back of her neck. That was a generous offer. He had to be exhausted after the incident and spending hours at the police station. If he took her to Sarah's it would mean a two-hour round-trip drive for him. Plus, Anne wanted to be back first thing in the morning, which wasn't that long from now.

The throbbing in her head made it hard to think. What was she so worried about? Everyone at the hospital respected and held him in high esteem. Never mind that he'd risked his own life to save her and Wyatt.

Anne's nurse came out holding some papers. He stopped in front of her. "Hello, Mr. Blackwood. Nice to see you."

Devon nodded. "You, too."

The nurse addressed Anne. "Your discharge instructions are ready. Do you have a ride?"

Anne bit her lip and gazed up at Devon.

CHAPTER 25

DEVON WAITED, confident that he'd played his cards right and Anne would agree to stay with him.

Letting out a sigh, she nodded. "I really don't want to upset and disturb anyone at this hour. If you don't mind, I'll take you up on your offer."

He ran a victory lap in his head. Now he'd have a chance to win her over, showing off his mansion and toys.

As the nurse wheeled Anne out to the sidewalk, he went to get his car.

She dropped into the passenger seat and closed her eyes for a brief second, then checked her phone again.

The sight of her bandages enraged him. He'd paid Moe Dog and his goons a hell of a lot of money to do a simple job. And his instructions had been clear. Don't hurt the woman.

Louie had it coming. Anne would be hideous to look at for weeks. Devon ground his molars. And not once had she thanked him for saving the jock's and her pitiful asses. Of course, he'd paid the thugs to take a hit and run away, making him look good.

Still, his performance had been impeccable. The bugs had allowed him to overhear Anne and Pearson's plans. He'd seized the opportunity he'd been waiting for to show up that loser. His guys had knocked the light out in front of the alley and positioned themselves where he'd told them to hide. Pure perfection.

Anne tapped the phone. "No messages. I wonder if he's still unconscious. He could be in a coma or something."

Her whining grated worse than the jackpot bell at the casino. "He might be drugged up on pain meds."

Devon stopped at a set of gates and punched in a code. They slowly opened. Low lights on both sides illuminated the long driveway.

Fixated on her phone, Anne paid no attention to his huge, Tudor mansion. He drove past the elaborate, stained-glass front door with gold trim showcased by a white spotlight. She still didn't look up. He hit a button that opened one of the doors to his five-car garage.

The muscles under his clenched jaw quivered. How could she be so fucking oblivious? She should be blown away by the place.

"I wish I knew what his injuries were." She covered her face, rubbing her temple.

Devon parked and punched the remote button hard, shutting the garage. With her hands over her eyes, she wasn't going to even see the other cars inside. He'd paid good money to have the Corvette and Porsche detailed. Women drooled over them.

Feigning concern, he patted her arm. "Come on, let's go inside. You've had a long night."

When they entered the house, she stared straight ahead, saying nothing about the granite countertops, marble floors, or brushed stainless steel appliances as they walked through his high-end kitchen.

The ugly hospital gown and pants made him want to puke. "Would you like to change?"

She glanced down. "Yes, but they cut up my clothes, and there's blood on them…"

"I have something you can wear. Might be baggy, but clean at least."

She nodded and swayed a little. "Okay, thanks."

He sucked in a breath. No point trying to impress her tonight. His best move would be to play nursemaid and follow the doctor's instructions to earn some points. Maybe in the morning she'd be more lucid.

Blood pounded in his ears. Louie would pay for fucking her up so badly that she couldn't even see straight.

After leading her to the first-floor guest room, he pulled some clothes out from the dresser and handed them to her. He pointed to the adjoining bathroom. "If you want to wash up or just change, I'll be right here. "

"Thanks, but I'll be okay." She nodded and walked stiffly into the bathroom, shutting the door behind her. When she came back out her face had more color. His grey T-shirt sleeves came down to her elbows and she'd rolled up the bottom of the sweats. If her face wasn't such a nightmare, she might even look cute.

"How about if I heat up some soup? You have to be hungry." Devon said.

"I'm fine, but thank you." She kept checking her phone.

Even so, Devon led her to the kitchen and slid out a high bar stool. Six of them flanked one side of the L-shaped counter, overlooking a center island with a stovetop. She hoisted herself up and frowned at her phone as he heated up a bowl of chicken rice soup. "Maybe Wyatt lost his cell in the scuffle, or the hospital has it in a bag that he can't reach."

Devon's chest blazed. Enough already about Pearson.

She raised her gaze to his. "Thank God you saw us in that alley and helped."

About fucking time. "Yeah, that was lucky."

"Way more than lucky." The corner of her mouth turned down. "What you did...how did you do that?"

That was more like it. Finally, some admiration. He took the bowl of soup from the microwave and set it in front of her. "I've had training. And please, have this soup."

"Okay, thanks." She picked up a spoon, shook her head, and winced. "But there were four of them, and they were big. I mean, Wyatt couldn't even handle them, and he's huge."

Vindication uncurled in Devon's belly. Perfect. He'd shown up Pearson all right. "In martial arts size doesn't matter. It's all in the technique."

"Are you a black belt or something?" She sipped a spoonful of the broth.

"I earned my fifth degree a while back."

Her eyebrows shot up, and she winced again. "Fifth degree? No wonder."

Going for humble, he shrugged. "Just glad to help."

"Why were you there?" she asked between spoonfuls.

He'd expected the question and had set up Paul as an excuse. "I was supposed to meet a friend at a nearby bar but had to park on the street and walk a few blocks because the lot was full."

"That was a good thing for us." She finished the soup and closed her eyes, pressing her fingers to her forehead.

"Why don't you come sit on the couch for a bit? You have to be exhausted, and I'll keep an eye on you for a while."

She nodded. "Okay. I'll admit my head is a bit fuzzy."

He came around the counter and helped her from the chair to the sofa. A fire blazed to life when he hit the remote. Clutching her phone, she sat and fell asleep within minutes. He took a seat beside her, placing his arm around her.

With a small whimper, she shifted and leaned against him, her head on his shoulder. Drawing her in, he took the phone from her limp hand and stuffed it down between the cushions. Now she wouldn't hear if it rang and would stay the night.

The tables had turned. Heat from the fire and her body warmed him. He gloated over the success of his scheme. Not only had he impressed her, she was sleeping in his arms and wearing *his* clothes.

Without a doubt, this should lead to more trouble for her and Pearson tomorrow.

CHAPTER 26

AT THE SCENT of fresh brewed coffee, Anne opened her eyes. She glanced around the unfamiliar room. Her stomach knotted as memories of the nightmare flooded back. That's right, she'd gone to Devon's. But wait, why was she in the guest bedroom? Her fuzzy brain couldn't keep track of what had happened. All that really mattered was that she needed to see Wyatt.

She scanned the room, searching for her phone. Nowhere in sight. She hurried down the hall to the kitchen.

"Good morning. Would you like a muffin or some coffee?" Devon sat at the kitchen counter, holding a steaming cup, his laptop open in front of him. In a suit and tie, he clearly had been up for a while.

"No, thanks. What time is it? I have to get over to the hospital." She squinted to read the clock and winced as the tape from her bandage pulled at her temple.

"It's seven. I was going to wake you if you didn't get up soon, but I knew you were exhausted. I checked on you several times throughout the night, and you were sleeping soundly."

"Thanks for doing that. I can't believe I slept at all. I'm sure you didn't get much rest." She frowned. "I don't even remember going to the bedroom."

"You didn't. You fell asleep on the couch. I carried you there," he said matter-of-factly as he stood and shut the laptop.

What? He'd carried her? A creepy sensation crawled up her back. "I would have been fine on the sofa."

Devon shrugged "I wanted you to be comfortable, and you were sort of…leaning on me."

She cringed as it came back to her that she'd cuddled up against him, thinking he was Wyatt. "I'm sorry. I hope you didn't think—"

"What I think is that you were very tired and confused." With a gentle touch, he placed a hand on her shoulder. "I'm glad I could be there for you. You're always safe with me."

"Thanks." She took a step back and glanced around the kitchen. All she could think about was getting to Wyatt. "Do you know where my phone is?"

He frowned. "No idea."

"It wasn't in the bedroom." She crossed to the family room, checking the end tables. "Can you call my number?"

"Sure, but I need to warn you about something."

"Warn me? What?"

"The press reported the assault last night. It's all over the news." He shook his head. "I want to prepare you. There are rumors and speculation about Wyatt's injuries and whether the Ravens will want him back."

A weight dragged down her shoulders. More publicity. Poor Wyatt. They never left him alone. The ache in her head sharpened. "I really need to find my phone."

"I'll call it." Devon tapped his screen, and a muffled ringtone came from somewhere near the couch. She followed the sound until she stood in front of the sofa. Bending down, she moved the pillows, and the ringing grew louder. She ran a hand between the cushions and pulled her phone out. "Oh no. I never would have heard this from the bedroom."

"You must have dropped it in your sleep."

Her hand trembled as she pressed her finger on the screen to unlock it. Cripes. Tons of missed calls and texts from her family and friends. She scrolled through and found three from Wyatt. "Oh my God, he tried to call me, and I didn't hear it."

She dropped onto the couch and clicked on the texts. He had to be living the same nightmare as her, with no way to get in touch and fearing the worst.

Are you ok? Where are you?

Call me ASAP. I'm panicked.

I'm out of my mind now. No one will tell me anything. Please call.

Her hands turned clammy, and sweat slicked her back. He hadn't said anything about his condition in the texts.

"Is everything okay?" Devon sat beside her and touched her arm.

"I…I don't know." She called Wyatt, not wanting to waste a second listening to the voicemails.

He answered on the first ring, and her heart leaped.

"Anne? Are you okay?"

The sound of his voice brought tears to her eyes. "Yes. Are you?"

"Oh, thank God. Where are you? I've been going crazy." He wheezed. "No one would tell me anything."

"You don't sound okay. What did they say is wrong?"

"I have a fractured sternum and a cracked rib. There's some internal bleeding, so they're observing me for now. I'm going to be fine. Don't worry."

"Internal bleeding?" Adrenaline rushed through her body. That was serious. "Will they need to operate?"

"They hope not."

She brought a hand to her chest and took a shaky breath. Breaking down wouldn't help. "I'm coming right over."

"Don't rush. I'll be here. I thought maybe you were admitted, too. Scared the hell out of me."

Her head throbbed. No point in worrying him over the concussion. "They checked me out in ER and released me last night. I'll be there soon."

"Okay. John's on his way over to interview me."

"John?" That's right, he was a Baltimore police detective.

"Yeah, this happened in his precinct. He'll be working the case."

"Well that's good." It couldn't hurt to have a friend on the force who cared about the outcome. "See you as soon as I can."

She hung up and let out the tears she'd held in check. Devon rubbed her back. "I'm sure he'll be all right."

"I don't know. Internal bleeding? That's bad. And he has a cracked rib and sternum." She took a deep breath and exhaled slowly. "Could you please take me to the hospital?"

"Do you want to go to your apartment first?"

"No. I don't want to waste the time. I'll ask Emily to run some clothes over to me on her lunch break or something. She has a key to my place."

"Whatever I can do to help." He stood, and she followed him to the kitchen.

He packed up his laptop and opened the door to the garage. "Which one do you want to ride in?"

"What?" She glanced at the row of cars gleaming under the light. Last night she hadn't even noticed them. Who needed that many?

"I...I really don't care. Whichever one has the least chance of breaking down. That seems to happen to me." Much as she hated heights, she'd take a helicopter if it got her to Wyatt faster.

Devon's eyes flashed. He snatched a set of keys from the hooks on the wall. "Every one of these is in perfect shape, so that should never happen. We'll take the Porsche."

On the ride to the hospital, a million "what ifs" badgered her brain. None of them good. She gripped the arm rest and forced herself to breathe.

"The seat and backrest are independently adjustable if you aren't comfortable in that position," Devon said. "That's one of the nice features of a Porsche."

"It's really fine. But thanks." She sent a group text to let people know she was okay, telling them she'd call from the hospital after she saw Wyatt. Her empty stomach gurgled, and a headache made her queasy.

After what felt like forever, they reached the hospital. Devon parked in his reserved spot, and they got out of the car. When they neared the entrance, a woman and man, both holding microphones, raced up to Anne.

"Ms. Cooper, can you tell us what happened last night? What's the status on Wyatt Pearson? Is it true that his injuries might prevent him from going back to the Ravens?"

Cameras snapped, and Anne's heart rate soared off the charts. This couldn't be happening.

Devon held a hand up and slung a protective arm around her. "No comment."

Oh, God no. Now they had pictures of her wearing Devon's shirt and sweats, her bandaged face pressed against his chest, while presumably on her way to see Wyatt.

The press was going to have a field day.

CHAPTER 27

WYATT HUNG up the phone and closed his eyes. Thank God Anne was okay. He sighed, and pain ripped a route from under his cracked rib to his fractured sternum. Holy shit, he'd forgotten from his football days how much injuries hurt.

Last night had been nothing short of a living hell, not knowing Anne's condition. He'd never been so scared in his life. When that bastard dragged her into the alley, Wyatt's world exploded. He'd been crazed to get to her, but couldn't overpower three men. Worst of all, he'd failed to protect her. His stomach sank, defeat dragging it down. Not a feeling he had much. Then again, nothing but saving her had ever mattered more.

All morning his phone had been blowing up from people who'd seen the breaking news. Poor Anne, for the second time, thrown into the spotlight.

"I've seen red-assed baboon butts that looked better than you," John's voice rang out as he entered the room.

"Guess you spend a lot of time looking in the mirror, huh?"

John snorted. "Not enough pain meds if you can still make wise cracks."

"Nah, I just have super powers when it comes to insulting you."

Wyatt hit the button to raise the back of the bed. He grimaced and caught his breath.

"Seriously, bro, are you okay? Cuz you look like hell."

"I'll be fine. The Steelers have done worse damage." Well, maybe not. The image of Anne, leaning over him, her face bloody, singed his insides. He met John's eyes, all kidding aside. "Tell me you're gonna find the fuckers."

John nodded and approached. "Damn straight. Let's get to it." He pulled out an iPad and tapped the screen. "I read over the statements taken last night from Anne and Devon Blackwood. They matched."

Wyatt blinked and shook his head. "Blackwood? What does he have to do with this?"

"He's the Good Samaritan who came to the rescue and called nine-one-one."

A vague image of a man entering the alley and kicking a guy flashed in Wyatt's mind.

"They questioned him at the police station. According to the report, he fought three of them, and then they all fled the scene."

Wyatt's lungs collapsed. "Are you kidding me? Those assholes were big. *I* couldn't take them, and believe me, I was motivated."

John shrugged. "Just reading the report, which Anne corroborated. I checked out Blackwood, and his record is clean as a whistle. He had a valid reason to be in the area at the time. Do you have any cause to suspect him?"

Other than he irritated the jealous hell out of Wyatt, no. He'd never even met the guy and clearly owed him a debt of gratitude. "No."

"Try again." John arched a brow. "Know that look."

Wyatt set his jaw.

"Come on, this is important. Spit it out." John straightened, all cop-mode.

"It pisses me off I wasn't able to handle the situation. And knowing he did, well—"

"Cut yourself a break. He's a fifth-degree black belt. Different skills. Put him on the field and see how well he blocks and catches."

"Yeah, whatever." That hadn't been too helpful in the alley.

John waved a hand. "Moving on. Can you describe any of the attackers?"

"It was dark, but I did get a look at a couple of them," Wyatt said. "The guy punching me was about six foot, muscular, and had an acne-scarred face. He wore a bandana." Wyatt angled his head and squinted. "I really didn't see the two holding me."

"What about Anne's assailant?"

"Bigger dude. Not fat, but large."

"Her statement said he had a lot of tattoos on his arms. Anything else distinguishing? Scars, jewelry?"

"There was something." Wyatt nodded slowly. "Yeah, he had some sort of earring. I can't tell you what it was, though. I saw it flash really quick, and then we were in the alley."

John scrolled down the tablet. "This all matches what Anne and Blackwood reported." He scratched his head. "These goons ask for any money, wallets, keys?"

"No. Nothing."

"Anne said her attacker didn't make any sexual threats, but we don't know what might have happened if Blackwood hadn't broken up the party."

Wyatt's heart hardened, and ice ran through his veins. With him unconscious, they could have done anything they wanted to Anne.

"Stop that train of thought. It goes nowhere good." John tapped the bed's sidebar. "I'm trying to figure out a motive."

Wyatt waited while John paced the room. "They didn't ask for or take anything. I can't rule out rape, but why pick a woman walking with a guy your size? Too hard. Wondering if someone had it in for you or Anne. Any enemies you know of?"

Sometimes things got scrappy on the field, but Wyatt hadn't played in over a year, and he'd never had a fight. "No one comes to mind."

John came back to the bed. "What about an old flame?"

"But the attackers were men."

"Someone could have hired them to do the job." John shrugged. "I've seen a lot, and that wouldn't be anywhere near the craziest."

"There was that thing with Victoria, but that was five years ago, and I haven't seen or talked to her since." Wyatt frowned. She was an up-and-coming model who craved camera time with a football star. They'd gone out twice, and she'd started talking serious relationship shit, so he'd told her he wasn't interested. She came unhinged and made a huge deal out of nothing, gossiping to the tabloids about their "big break up," only he'd barely known her.

"I remember that. She was a wack job, but why wait so long?"

"All she cared about was money and fame. Mostly money." Wyatt's eyelids grew heavy, and he blinked. "Damn meds make me groggy. I want out of here and off them."

"I hear that." John ran a hand across his chin. "Something's not right about this. You know I have a family full of cops, so I'll send these descriptions out to all of them, and they'll pass them along to their friends. That's a lot of territory covered. We'll get these guys."

John was like a pit bull with a big bone; he wouldn't give it up. He lowered the tablet and sighed. "What do you need help with while you're in here?"

"The dog walker is taking care of Goober, but my car is still parked at Luigi's in Little Italy."

"Gimme your keys, and I'll bring it here."

Wyatt pointed to a bag on the windowsill. "They're in that."

John fished them out. "You need some clothes, pretty boy, or do you like wearing dresses?"

"My exhibition days are over. Grab something from my apartment. Key's on the ring."

"Got it. Call me if you think of anything else."

"Thanks, man. I owe you."

"Get some shut-eye, baboon butt." John tapped the bedrail again, and left.

A nurse came in and checked Wyatt's IV. "Time for your pain meds."

"I'd rather not take them." He gritted his teeth, shifting again. Damn hospital gown. He couldn't wait to be in normal clothes and back at his place.

"I understand, Mr. Pearson, but the doctor's orders are—"

"It's okay." He shook his head. "I'm sorry. Not your fault."

Relief eased her face, and she tipped the pill into his hand and gave him a cup of water.

He swallowed the med and sank back into the bed, cringing.

The nurse bustled out, passing Anne, who appeared in the doorway. His breath stalled in his lungs. She had a bandaged head, bruised face, and dark circles under her eyes. "Holy shit, Anne." His voice cracked, right along with his heart. "You said you were okay."

"Wyatt." She rushed to his side. Grabbing his hand, her gaze raked over him. "I was so scared that you...that I might not see you...that—"

"Shh, I'm okay, baby." He squeezed her hand. *She* wasn't okay. A deep-seated need for revenge made his blood boil. "What happened to you?"

She blinked repeatedly and squeezed his fingers. "I have a concussion, but I'm doing better. It's you I'm worried about with internal bleeding."

A concussion? His blood went from a boil to molten lava. Whoever did this had better end up in a cage with rats. "They ran tests last night and found some bleeding under the ribs. Wanted to keep me for observation. The doctor came by after I talked to you this morning. She said I'm stable and should be able to go home tonight. How are you feeling?"

"Better today. I have a headache, but the CT scan was negative, so I'll be all right." She let out a huge breath and reached across the bedrail to hug him, but stopped short, planting a kiss on his forehead instead. "I don't want to hurt you."

Her oversized T-shirt caught his attention. "What are you wearing?"

She drew back and glanced down. He eyed the baggy sweats that couldn't be hers.

"Everything was insane last night. The EMT's cut my clothes off, and I didn't have anything to wear. I went to Devon's house to catch a few hours of sleep, and he gave me these. Emily's going to bring me my clothes later. I didn't want to waste time going to my place before I came here."

"Wait." Wyatt fought to focus through his drug-fogged brain. "You slept at Blackwood's? I thought they took him to the police station and you went to the ER?"

"He came to the hospital to check on us, and...it was three in the morning by then. They wouldn't release me without a ride home." She shrugged. "He offered to take me to Sarah's, but she lives so far, and I knew I was coming back here soon. So I stayed at his place. It was actually very generous of him."

Generous, yeah, that's the word Wyatt would use. Both of their phones dinged with messages, but they could wait. He took a breath. Still pissed at himself for failing to protect her, he probably was projecting that onto Blackwood. "I guess there's nothing wrong with crashing on his couch for a couple of hours."

She rubbed the base of her neck and shuffled her feet.

His internal radar went up. She wasn't telling him something. "What is it?"

"Nothing." She cleared her throat.

"Come on. I know you better than that. Tell me."

"I fell asleep on the couch, but woke up in the guest room. I didn't remember going there." Her nose crinkled and she tilted her head. "He said he carried me to it, but I didn't remember that either."

A stink bomb exploded in Wyatt's gut. Carried her to bed? That crossed a line. "What did you say to him about that?"

Touching her temple, she closed her eyes. "Nothing. I thought it was kind of weird, but really, he'd been so nice to me. He said he wanted me to be comfortable."

"And you don't remember anything?"

"No. I was pretty exhausted and still kind of in a fog."

Agitation burned his stomach. That would make it damn easy for someone to take advantage of her. "Could anything else have happened that you might not remember?"

Her eyes widened, and she took a step back. "I can't believe you'd ask that. Devon risked his life for us in that alley and helped me when no one else was around."

Ouch. That stung. Now he'd made her mad. But damn it, couldn't she see how wrong that was? She and Blackwood had only had two business meetings together and weren't even friends. No way he should be picking her up, especially if she wasn't awake. And taking her to a bed? No. Just no.

A man wearing an apron and hair net entered, holding a tray with muffins, fruit cups, juice, and coffee. He turned to Anne. "Are you Ms. Cooper?"

"Yes."

"Mr. Blackwood said to tell you he was concerned that you hadn't eaten this morning and hoped you would enjoy this."

Wyatt snorted. Perfect. Just perfect.

The food-service man set the tray on the stand next to the bed.

"Thank you," Anne said as he left.

Wyatt's phone dinged repeatedly as more texts came in. He snagged it and tapped the screen. His blood pressure sky-rocketed, and fire scorched the back of his eyes.

What the fuck?

CHAPTER 28

Gripping the phone, Wyatt's fingers turned white as he checked the picture message from John.

This is fucked, but thought you should know. He'd attached a press link with an image of Anne, head burrowed into Blackwood's chest, his arm around her. The caption read, "Pearson's girlfriend has a new hero."

A red haze blurred Wyatt's vision. He'd always been the strong one. The one no one could take down. The one who ran twenty yards after the catch, dragging three defensive players with him.

"What is it?" Anne leaned closer, her face pale.

He held the phone out, and she gasped. "Oh my God. I'm so sorry. The press took all these pictures when Devon brought me here. I forgot about them because I was so worried about you."

Wyatt's ego took a hard hit, rattling his brain. He'd just had a taste of what she must have felt like with the "Jane Doe" social media blowup. This time, he was on the receiving end, and it sucked. And as much as Anne hated the attention, she'd endured the paparazzi to be with him.

She shook her head and placed a hand on his shoulder. "Those vultures are horrible. They have no idea what you went through in that alley. Don't believe a word of this garbage." Tears shimmered in her eyes. "I'm so sorry if I've embarrassed you. I just wanted to see you as soon as possible, so I didn't even think about what I was wearing. I'm not used to being chased by the press."

What the hell was he doing? He knew better than to let the media get to him. He'd spent the last night frantic, fearing the worst. Now Anne had a bandaged head, a concussion, and pictures of her splashed across the press wearing God-awful clothes because she'd rushed to his bedside. She must have been out of her mind with worry for him. Meanwhile, he was thinking like a jealous asshole. He didn't know how to deal with jealousy, because he'd never been in love before.

Bam.

A high-speed pass whacked him in the chest, knocking the wind out of him. In love? Yeah. He loved her. Until they'd met, his life had been a series of plays and players. Growing up, his whole life had been sports. Travel teams, competitions, skills training, cheerleaders. Fun at the time, but he never knew what he was missing—a deep connection with someone real who wore her heart on her sleeve and gave to everyone she touched.

He and Anne took walks in the rain because she liked the sound drumming on the umbrella, with her nestled against his body. She brought homemade dog treats to dense-and-dumb Goober, giving him belly rubs even when he was wet and covered in mud. And Wyatt didn't have sex with Anne, they made love. Huge difference.

Before he'd blacked out in the alley, his last thought was he might never see her again. It had paralyzed him, shredding his heart. He swore if they got through the night, he'd never let her go.

He took her hand, lacing his fingers through hers. "None of this is your fault. You don't ever embarrass me."

She pressed her lips together and gave a quick nod.

He squeezed her hand. "We'll get through this. Just like we have before. But if it's too much for you, I understand."

Her eyes softened, and she bent down and kissed him. "I can handle anything with you by my side. You're worth it."

His heart rolled in his chest, and his body relaxed for the first time since the fight in the alley. "Goober will be happy to see you again."

Anne jerked. "Oh my God, Goober. I almost forgot all about him."

She grabbed her phone. "Poor thing has to be starving. I'll get a ride so I can go feed him."

"He's fine."

"But no, he needs—"

"Nothing. He's taken care of. I called the dog walker."

"Phew, Okay." Anne let out a breath.

"Thanks for caring." Wyatt squeezed her hand. "About him and about me." He shut his eyes and frowned. "I'm so sorry I didn't protect you."

"Stop it. You had no chance." She rubbed his arm. "It happened so fast, and there were four of them."

Yeah, well, that hadn't stopped Blackwood. Wyatt tamped down the irritation because he should be grateful.

"Please, let it go. All that matters is that we'll be okay." She lowered the bedrail, sat in a chair, and rested her head against his shoulder.

He stroked her hair and held her hand. Yeah, he loved her. Warmth spread in his chest as nerves tensed his shoulders. What the hell was he going to do about USC and the Ravens?

CHAPTER 29

PAUL STRAIGHTENED HIS TIE, smoothed back what was left of his hair, and adjusted his glasses. Small spasms squeezed his stomach as he stood in the foyer of the Hilton. Lynn might be at the reunion. The only reason he'd come. No idea what he'd say to her, but maybe he'd find out why she'd disappeared before graduation.

He walked down the carpeted hall and past the bathrooms with glittering, gold-plated door handles. Following the signs for the reunion, he stopped in front of a banquet room and pulled out a handkerchief to dab the sweat from his forehead.

He scanned the place, searching for Lynn. People milled around buffet tables loaded with appetizers, and a band played soft music in the background. No sign of her. His shoulders fell. He ordered a drink and sipped it next to the bar. Just like in college, no one bothered to talk to him. He might as well be invisible.

His pulse jumped when he spotted Becky, Lynn's old roommate and best friend. Becky swayed and waved her hands, engaged in a vivid conversation with a man he didn't recognize. The guy took a step back and glanced around like he was looking for an excuse to get away. Sure enough, as soon as Becky turned her back to him and picked up her drink, the man bolted.

Paul approached her. "Becky?"

Her eyes widened, and her mouth twisted in disgust. "You?" She poked a finger into his chest and wobbled. "You have the nerve to show up here after what you did?"

"What are you talking about?"

"Lynn would still be alive today if it weren't for you." Becky's red-rimmed eyes glared at him.

"What do you mean?" His mouth went dry. "She's not—"

"You don't know? She died years ago, and it's your fault, you bastard."

All the blood drained from his head, numbing his brain. This couldn't be true. "She d-died? How? When?"

Becky waved her drink in the air. "Right after graduation. In a fire at her apartment complex in Virginia. She took the first job she could find to get away after you broke her heart."

Paul blinked several times, his head spinning. He broke *her* heart? She was the one who'd deserted him. "What do you mean? She left without a word. I never understood why."

"She found out about your little bet"—Becky's eyes narrowed to slits —"and realized that all she meant to you was winning some stupid wager."

Paul flinched as if struck. He swallowed around the baseball-sized lump in his throat. Only he and Devon knew about their bets. If Lynn found out, Devon had to have told her.

Becky poked a finger into his chest again. "She wouldn't have been there if not for you. It's your fault. Now get out of my face." She shoved him and stormed off toward the bar.

All the air left his lungs. He set his drink down and grabbed the back of a chair for support. Lynn hadn't left him because she didn't love him. What they'd had was real. And now she was dead, and he could never tell her the truth.

The scent of fried food turned his stomach. Loud, drunken laughter hurt his ears, and he fumbled his way out to the parking lot. He got in the car, took off his glasses, and lowered his head in his hands. Sobs wracked his body. Lynn died believing he didn't love her.

Pain carved a hole in his heart as he pictured her beautiful, sweet face. Why? Why had Devon done that? Paul took a shaky breath and slid his glasses back on. He straightened his spine and pursed his lips.

Devon had mentioned he'd be working late at the shop. Paul checked the time. Not even seven yet, he should be able to catch Devon there. And he'd better have some answers.

* * *

Paul entered the antique store, letting the door swing shut on its own, his heart beating a staccato.

Devon glanced up from his seat at the desk. "I wasn't expecting you tonight, but since you're here, I have the tax files ready." He tapped a stack of papers. "Do your magic and make my hospital donations offset my 'other income' so it passes Uncle Sam's scrutiny."

Not giving a shit about business at the moment, Paul stalked across the room. "I just came from the reunion."

Devon snorted. "Don't know why you bothered to go. Bunch of losers. Everyone fat and ugly?"

Paul's body stiffened at the disdainful question. He'd been bullied his whole life, which is why he'd latched onto the friendship with Devon in college. By association, people had at last included Paul, and he'd been freed of the nerdy geek stigma. But at what cost? He had to know. "I ran into Becky. Do you remember her?"

"Can't say I do." Devon shrugged.

"She told me something about Lynn. You remember her?"

Devon's eyes narrowed, and his nostrils flared. "Ah yes. The one bet I lost." He spun his chair around to the file cabinet behind him and yanked the drawer open, his back stiff.

No denying Devon's angry reaction. Paul fought the turmoil inside to keep his voice calm. "She wasn't a bet; she was a person. Did you know she died?"

"No. I didn't keep tabs on her." Devon spun back around and punched some numbers into a calculator.

"You don't seem surprised or upset."

Devon looked up. "Why would I be upset? I barely knew the girl."

The girl. The one bet I lost. Not Lynn. Not the sweetheart who'd stolen

Paul's heart. Not the woman who never had a chance to live out her life. Paul's blood pounded in his ears.

"What's your problem? I really don't have time for games." Devon stood.

Despite the fact that Devon towered over him, Paul met his gaze. "Why did you do it?"

For just a second, Devon's eyes widened. If Paul hadn't been looking for a reaction, he would have missed it.

"Do what?" Devon asked.

"Tell Lynn about the bet."

"Oh, that." Relief flickered in Devon's eyes. Again, it was fast and subtle. He waved a hand. "I did it for you."

"What do you mean, you did that for me?" Paul's body quaked with pent-up anger. "You made her think I didn't care about her. She left town and died not knowing the truth."

"You didn't see it then, and you're blind to it now. She was all wrong for you." Devon shook his head. "I tried to spare you from getting crushed when she dumped you. Someone had to save you from yourself."

Paul balled his hands into fists. Devon couldn't be serious. "You honestly thought you were doing me a favor?"

"Yes." Devon nodded. "I don't mean to be harsh, but take a look in the mirror. She was out of your league. The longer you dated her, the more it would hurt when she cut you lose."

The truth kicked Paul in the gut, and his shoulders slumped. Devon was right. Lynn could have done a lot better. Guys asked her out all the time. But she'd turned them down for him and might be alive today if she hadn't left town.

Devon grabbed his coat and shrugged it on. "Hey, sometimes people get what they deserve. I'm sorry she died that way, but you were her little puppet, and when she snipped the strings, you were gonna crash. I had your back the whole time."

Paul couldn't think, his brain so overloaded.

"I'm done here. Tell me if I missed anything." Devon headed toward the entrance. "I may have a buyer for that glass lamp. I'll let you know if it goes through so you can handle the sale."

The door banged shut behind him.

Paul sucked in a sharp breath. Devon had said, "I'm sorry she died *that way.*"

But Paul never told Devon that Lynn had died in a fire. The tiny hairs under Paul's collar raised. Come to think of it, Devon's family had died the same way.

No. Had to be a coincidence.

Paul tried to shake the suspicion off, but a sick feeling twisted his gut.

Where there was smoke...there was fire...

CHAPTER 30

ANNE DABBED concealer over the cut on her temple. It had been a week since the attack, but she still needed makeup to cover the spot. She and Wyatt had planned a hike through the woods to see the rapids. She'd wanted to climb up to the waterfall, but with both of them on the mend, they'd decided to take the short, flat trail and save that for another time.

A thread of worry knitted around Anne's heart. Wyatt had been offered the USC job, and she'd also gotten the call for the vice principal position. He had to realize that if she took it, she'd be grounded in Maryland. What future could they have together if he went to California?

She shook off the negativity. His enthusiasm when she'd told him about her offer had been genuine. He knew how much it meant to her.

Her phone rang, and she glanced at the screen.

Devon.

He'd called three times in the last week, making sure she was okay after the assault and the news-splash photos of them. Nice of him, but she just wanted to put the whole thing behind her. Considering he'd expressed feelings for her prior to the attack, she would rather limit their interactions strictly to business.

She frowned. Actually, he'd said he was interested in her, not that he had feelings for her. Regardless, she didn't want to be rude, so she answered.

"Hi, Devon. What's up?"

"I called to congratulate you on the job offer."

"Thanks, but how did you know—"

"Larry Edmonson and I golf together, and he told me about it. In fact, we're having dinner on Thursday. Would you like to join us? It might be a good opportunity for you to talk to the superintendent in a casual setting and get onboard."

A tick of annoyance tracked up her spine. She'd earned the job and had told Devon before that she didn't want to use his connections. She forced a polite response, because he probably meant well. "Thanks, but I'm going to do this on my own."

After a pause, Devon responded. "Of course, I understand. Congratulations."

He hung up, and she shook her head. Something in his voice...

Her phone dinged in her hand. A text from Scott. Maddie had gone into labor hours ago, and he'd promised to keep Anne updated. She tapped the screen and a picture of Maddie holding a baby wearing a pink beanie popped up with the caption, "*It's a girl. Zoey Ella. 7 lbs 13 oz.*"

A thrill rushed through Anne's body. She typed a quick congratulations and zoomed in on the image. The grin on Maddie's tired face said it all. Anne stared at the baby, and her heart twinged with longing. She wasn't getting any younger, and Wyatt had been clear about not wanting kids.

With a sigh, she opened the refrigerator and pulled out the fruit, cheese, and sandwiches she'd prepared for their lunch. She packed everything into the picnic basket she'd found at a thrift store. That day she'd felt like she'd won a free vacation. She had a thing for old-fashioned picnic baskets and had been looking for one for a long time. This basket had called to her with a pretty pink ribbon woven around the sides and matching bow on the front. Of course, she could have bought a new basket, but she liked to support the charity that ran the store.

She drove to Wyatt's place since it was on the way to the park. When she knocked, Goober barked, and like the last time, *thumped* against the door. A giggle tickled her throat. So much for the training.

Wyatt opened the door and Goober bounded out to Anne, tail whipping. He whined as she bent to hug him, and Wyatt gave her an apologetic smile. "I haven't been consistent, and I don't get many visitors, so…"

"It's okay. He's probably just excited to go, aren't you, boy?" She ruffled the fur behind his ears.

"What? Did you think he was coming with us?" Wyatt's smile fell.

"Of course. He'll love it." She scratched his side, and his leg started thumping a staccato rhythm on the floor. "It's so funny when he does this."

"I don't think it's a good idea to bring him today." Wyatt stared down at Goober with a slight frown.

"But I made him those special dog biscuits he likes, and he's come before. Why not today?" Anne stood.

Wyatt shrugged. "Just…I don't know…he might get into trouble."

"Trouble?" What was he worried about? Goober wasn't aggressive and got along with other dogs.

Her phone dinged, and she jerked. "Oh my gosh. I didn't tell you. Maddie had her baby. That's probably Scott."

"Everything okay?" Wyatt cocked his head.

"Yeah." Anne picked up her phone and clicked on a selfie of Scott, his arm around Maddie and the baby. A lump formed in Anne's throat. "Precious."

She held the phone out so Wyatt could see the picture. His Adam's apple bobbed, and the corners of his mouth turned up. "They look so happy."

"Yeah." Anne sent a heart emoji and tamped down the longing in her own heart.

Wyatt opened the door wider and stepped inside. She followed him, and Goober raced to his bed and returned to Anne with a tug toy in his mouth.

"Aww. He loves this game." She yanked the other end and he pulled back, play growling and thrashing his head from side to side.

"I'm ready to go when you are." Wyatt snatched his keys off the counter.

"Okay." Anne let go of the toy, and Goober pranced around with it in his mouth, showing off his victory prize.

When Wyatt opened the door, Goober dropped the toy and beelined to Wyatt.

"We'll go for a walk when I get back, buddy. Be good."

Goober whined and nudged Anne's hand with his nose.

"Look at that face." She rubbed his snout. "He's here alone all week. We need to bring him. I can't leave with those pleading eyes staring at me."

Wyatt blew out a breath. "All right. We'll take the truck."

He didn't look too happy, which made no sense because it wasn't super-hot, and they took Goober to the parks on weekends all the time. "What's going on with you today?"

"What do you mean?" He whipped his head around as he grabbed a leash from the closet.

"You're not acting like yourself. Is something wrong?"

"No. I'm just...hungry."

More like grumpy. She wasn't buying it, but okay. "Well then, we can eat as soon as we get there. I brought a blanket and lunch."

He took Goober to the truck while Anne brought over the picnic basket from her car.

Wyatt hitched an eyebrow and pointed to it. "What's that?"

She held it up. "My picnic basket. Remember I told you about it?"

"I guess. I didn't realize it would look like that." He shoved a hand on his hip. "Am I supposed to carry that thing around in the park?"

Oh, this was more fun than she'd dreamed. "I don't see why not."

He gazed at it, a sour expression on his face like he'd just sucked a lemon. "Stay here for a minute, and I'll get a cooler. You can hide...I mean put that flowery blanket in the basket and I'll carry the cooler with the food."

She bit her tongue to keep from laughing and had to wait a second to respond. "But I have it all packed up right."

"It's not china. I'm sure we can just throw it in the cooler." He turned and took a step away.

"I bet Tarzan would have carried this picnic basket through the jungle for Jane," she called out to him.

He stopped and pivoted. "What are you talking about?"

"I'm just saying. I think Tarzan was secure enough in his manhood to carry this."

Wyatt's eyes narrowed and he came back over to her. "Yeah, and he was surrounded by nothing but monkeys. Are you trying to make me crazy?"

She let out the laugh she'd been stifling and set the basket down. "I'm just messing with you. I'll carry it. It's not heavy." She pressed a hand to his cheek. "You're wound tight today for some reason, and I wanted to lighten the mood."

He snorted. "So torturing me is your answer to that?"

"Yup." She lowered her hand. "I think sitting on the rocks by the water is the perfect thing for us to do today."

He kissed her forehead and gave her a hug. "All right. Sounds good."

When they reached the park, they drove past a crowded picnic area. If someone recognized him, that would be the end of their privacy. She glanced around and pointed across the lot. "Let's go near the woods away from everyone. I see a spot where we can put the blanket."

"I'm down with that." Wyatt parked in the farthest space and opened the door for Goober.

Anne carried the basket over to the grass and spread the blanket out. The sun warmed the top of her head and a soft breeze blew. Couldn't ask for better weather.

Goober bounded over to Anne, and she gave him the biscuits she'd made. He plopped down and chomped them while she set up the picnic.

"I brought his bone to keep him busy while we eat." Wyatt tossed it on the ground next to the dog.

"Aren't these cool? I found these little plates with the dip holder in the middle so you can put the fruit around it and have your own dish." Anne plopped a spoonful of peanut butter in the center of the cut-up apples.

Wyatt stood at the edge of the blanket and wiped his palms on his jeans.

He didn't look like he'd even heard her. "Wyatt?"

"Huh?" He swallowed. "Sorry, did you ask me something?"

"Nothing important. Are you going to sit down and eat?" She slid over to make room for him. What the heck was going on?

"Oh, right." He dropped to the blanket and wiped his brow.

Anne's stomach tightened. He was sweating and it wasn't that hot. Maybe he had a fever. "Are you not feeling well?"

"I'm fine." He tugged at the neckline of his T-shirt. "Just a little warm."

"We can move into the shade if you—"

"No. I'm good." He gave her a not-so-convincing smile.

She frowned, finished setting out the food, and handed him a cold water. "Drink this. It might help."

He downed half the bottle.

Good thing she'd brought a bunch more. They hadn't even started the hike. She dipped an apple slice in peanut butter and took a bite.

Wyatt shifted so that he faced her. "Anne?"

"Yeah?" She munched on the fruit.

"There's something I've been wanting to ask you." He wiped his brow again.

"Sure, what?" Her shoulders pinched with tension. Maybe he'd made his decision about the jobs.

"I've been thinking, and…"

A squirrel emerged from the woods, scampering next to them. Goober bolted up and trampled through the middle of the blanket, giving chase. He launched himself on the picnic basket, smashing the lid down and busting the sides out. His paws stomped on the food, and he knocked over their water bottles.

Anne jumped back to get out of the way, but a piece of watermelon flew up, smacked her in the chest, and slid down her shirt, leaving a pink streak.

"Goober, stop." Wyatt leaped to his feet.

The dog slid to a halt and barked under a tree the squirrel had climbed.

So much for the picnic. The carnage was epic. Wyatt's sandwich had landed in the grass, watermelon littered the blanket, and the plates were upside down.

Anne pulled the front of her shirt out as the sticky, cold goo from the watermelon trickled down into her bra. Wyatt dragged Goober back to his bone and snapped the leash on his collar. His gaze went to the destroyed picnic basket, and his mouth firmed. "This is exactly what I meant by him causing trouble."

"It's not his fault. It's their nature to chase squirrels." Anne opened a water bottle, poured some on a napkin, and stuck it down her shirt to wipe up the stickiness.

Wyatt's gaze went to her breasts, following her movements, and then he sucked in a breath and knelt. He picked up squashed pieces of melon and tossed them into the trash bag Anne had brought. "I told you I didn't want to bring him today."

Her blood pressure spiked. She grabbed the overturned plates and waved them at Wyatt. "It's our fault for not controlling him. And for the record, it's not me who's freaking out this time because of botched plans. It's *you*."

Wyatt tossed more food into the bag.

Harder.

Goober chewed on his bone, his tail slowly wagging like nothing had happened. What she wouldn't give to be a dog sometimes with a short-term memory.

Anne continued to clean up the mess, refusing to look at Wyatt. She did shoot a glance at her picnic basket, all broken apart. Her heart sank. She'd been so happy to find it. Oh well. "Why don't we just go home? You're in a mood, and I have plenty of work to do."

Wyatt sat back on his heels and scrubbed a hand down his face. "I'm sorry. You're right. Let's go to the water like we'd planned."

She eyed him, not sure what to think anymore. "I guess we can."

They rolled up the blanket and put everything back in the truck. Goober trotted along aside them like he didn't have a care in the world. Anne couldn't help but smile.

Wyatt shut the truck door and faced her like a big annoyed grizzly bear. "Why are you smiling at him? He just crushed your prize basket, ruined our lunch, and probably destroyed your blanket and shirt."

Anne glanced at the pink splotch on her blouse. She raised her gaze to his and held it. "Because this really amazing guy told me that I shouldn't get caught up in expectations and outcomes. That I shouldn't worry about perfection and learn from experience. That I should let things go and realize it's not the end of the world if I have to wash a shirt or buy a burger from the snack bar when my picnic lunch went to hell in a handbasket. No pun intended."

The tension lines in Wyatt's face smoothed. He stepped closer and placed his hands on her shoulders. "You're right. This is a big leap for you."

"I'm working on it."

He lowered his head and kissed her, soft and gentle. "I'm proud of you."

"Then don't make it so hard. Why did this outing matter so much?"

He stiffened and pulled her closer. "No reason. My bad."

She rested her head against his chest and let the tension ease out of her muscles. The day wasn't lost. They just needed to chill. "How about if I go to that general store by the picnic area and get us something to eat? You stay with Goober, and I'll be right back."

"Okay. I'd rather keep a low profile." He let go of her and pointed to the interior of the truck. "My wallet's in the glove box."

"I got this. Thanks." She walked to the store and bought a couple of hot dogs. Not her first choice, but with slim pickings, they'd have to do.

After they ate, Wyatt tugged on Goober's leash. "This stays on for the walk. It reaches twenty feet, so he'll have plenty of space to roam with it on."

Anne grinned. "The squirrels thank you."

As they hiked through the forest, she glanced at Wyatt. He'd stopped sweating, and his face was no longer blood red. But that reminded her that he'd been interrupted earlier when he wanted to ask her something. Anxiety squeezed her lungs. He might have been about to tell her his job decision.

Goober paused to sniff a bush, and she touched Wyatt's arm. "What was it you wanted to say to me earlier?"

Wyatt froze and then stared at the ground. His knuckles turned white on the leash handle.

Shit. That must be it. He was going to tell her he'd decided to take the USC job. "Please, whatever it is, can you spit it out? I'm imagining a lot of things."

"Right." He took a deep breath and faced her. "This isn't how I wanted to—"

"Oh my God, no," she yelled as a startled skunk sprang from a bush, sprayed Goober, and ran away.

The strong, foul odor burned her nostrils and made her eyes water. She covered her mouth and coughed. "Ew. Ew. Ew."

"Fuck." Wyatt shook his head and shuddered. "You've gotta be kidding me."

Goober sneezed and blinked. Poor thing didn't understand what had happened.

Wyatt yanked on the leash. "We better take him home and scrub him down or something."

"Wait, let me check his eyes. I think it only got his side, though." Gagging, she bent down to make sure he didn't have any spray in his eyes. "He's good. Let's go."

They took off at a fast pace. No stopping to smell any bushes on this walk.

"God, my truck is gonna reek." Wyatt huffed. "I'm going to have to get it professionally defumigated."

"I think you mean fumigated. Defumigated isn't—"

"Are you serious? You're correcting my grammar at this moment?" He shot her a sidelong look.

She closed her mouth. He had a point.

He cinched the leash, and Goober stopped. "Why don't you go ahead of us. No sense in both of us smelling this stench the whole way."

"Good idea, thanks. I'll look up what to clean him with when I get to the truck."

He tossed her the keys and then covered his nose.

She hurried back to the truck and googled what to use on skunk spray. Glancing at the carpet and upholstered seats, she frowned. If Goober rode home inside, it might never smell the same again, professional fumigation or not. She snatched a couple of towels from behind the seat and rounded the truck.

Wyatt approached as she tossed them into the bed. "What are you doing with those?"

"I'm gonna ride in the back with him so he doesn't destroy your truck. It's not that far, and if you go slow, I can hold him so he doesn't try to jump out."

"I can't ask you to do that. I'll just take it somewhere to get the smell out."

She shrugged. "You didn't ask me. I offered. My aunt paid to have a car that she'd bought from a smoker professionally fumigated. The smell came back. It's not worth chancing."

Wyatt looked down at Goober. "Well, then you drive, and I'll ride with him."

"No way. This truck is huge. I'm not comfortable behind the wheel. Let's just go already."

Wyatt scratched his head, and finally nodded. "All right. Thanks."

He dragged the pet steps over to the tailgate and Goober climbed them and got into the bed. Anne covered him with a towel. Probably wouldn't be enough to keep the stink from getting on her, but better than nothing. She gripped his collar, keeping her head as far away as possible and breathing through her mouth.

"We need to stop for apple cider vinegar, dish detergent, baking soda, and rubber gloves," she said as Wyatt passed her.

He cringed. "They're gonna love me in the store. Bet no one asks for my picture with them this time."

When they got back to Wyatt's condo, he pulled into the car wash area. Anne's throat burned, and her eyes still watered from the fumes, but they'd made it in one piece, and at least Goober hadn't been bitten in the attack.

Wyatt grabbed a bucket and used the hose to mix water in with the vinegar. Anne read off the instructions she'd found online and they both worked, saturating and scrubbing the dog. He shook, and she held up an arm and shut her eyes. Now the scent of vinegar filled her head.

"You okay?" Wyatt placed a hand on her arm.

"Yeah." She blinked and nodded. "We got this."

After another round of scrubbing with the dish detergent, Wyatt hosed down Goober and dropped his bone onto the grass next to the concrete. The dog shook again three more times, flopped to the ground, and laid his head on his paws. He had to be bushed.

Anne hoisted herself up on the open tailgate and let out a long breath. This might have been the craziest day of her life. Her arms ached, her butt was sore from sitting on the hard bed of the truck, and she had a bag full of squashed food and dirty plates still to clean.

Wyatt slowly approached, stopping in front of her at eye level. He rested his hands on the gate, one on each side of her. Raising his head, he hitched an eyebrow. "For the record, will you concede that Goober did in fact get into some trouble?"

She glanced down at her shirt because it killed her to admit he'd been right.

"Uh huh. Nothing to say?" He tapped her on the nose. "To quote my favorite movie line, 'You can't handle the truth.'"

She smiled and then tugged her blouse out for a closer look. Ha. All the dog washing had removed the watermelon stain. The insanity of the day bubbled up in her mind, and she couldn't stop the eruption of laughter. A deep, belly-gut release that took her breath away.

"What's so funny?"

"M-my shirt. It's clean. We saved it." She held her stomach and doubled over with laughter.

Wyatt's chest rumbled, and he shook his head. "This day stank."

She swiped the corners of her eyes. "I can't breathe. Quit it. No jokes."

"Okay, no more jokes." He grabbed her hands, met her gaze, and blurted out, "Marry me?"

"Stop it. I said no more kidding." She tried to pull her hands back, but he held them steady.

"I'm not kidding. I've been trying to ask you all day."

Her heart somersaulted, and the little breath she had left caught in her throat. He couldn't be serious.

"What?"

"This is nothing like I'd planned, but what the hell?" He glanced at her soaked shirt. "You're drenched. You're beat. You rode in the back of my truck holding my skunked dog, and you've never looked more beautiful to me."

She cocked her head as blood pounded in her ears. "But—"

"I'm messing this up and doing it all backwards, because there are some things I need to tell you." He brought her hand to his chest. "I'm turning down the USC job."

"But what would you do then?"

He squeezed her fingers. "I didn't want to say anything until I was sure, but I've been talking to University of Maryland, and they offered me an offensive coordinator job."

Her pulse picked up its pace. "When did you talk to them?"

"This week. They aren't as big as USC, but that doesn't matter. Maryland has a great program. I really connected with the head coach, and he's excited about bringing me onboard."

A spark of hope ignited in her chest. "What about the Ravens? I mean, you'll heal up. Don't they still want you?"

He shook his head. "I'm done playing. The sport is brutal, and I don't want to be so messed up that I can't throw a pass to my kid someday."

A shockwave rocked her body. His kid? "Wait, are you saying—"

"Until you, I never thought about having a family." He placed a hand on her cheek, and his eyes turned soft. "But then something changed."

His gentle touch sent shivers down her neck. "What?"

He stared at her, his eyes full of emotion. "I fell in love."

Anne's heart rolled, and her stomach did a free fall. He loved her? She'd hoped he would one day, but she never expected to hear the words so soon. Especially after all they'd been through. Then again, overcoming adversity had bonded them. Anyone could get through good times. The true test was when the road got rocky.

"In that alley, when I got knocked out, my last thought was I might never see you again." His thumb stroked her chin. "When I came to, and no one could tell me if you were okay, I panicked. I couldn't imagine my life without you."

She knew the feeling. That night had been the longest in her life, being sick with worry over him. But she had no idea it had affected him so much. "I felt the same way."

Stunned by his revelations, her brain fought to keep up. The job, the desire for a family, and he loved her. The enormity of it all had her head spinning. "These are a lot of big, life-changing decisions that you've come to kind of fast. Are you sure about them?"

"I know we haven't been dating long, but I've never been surer of anything in my life." He slowly dropped to one knee, not breaking eye contact, and pulled out a ring box from his pocket.

Everything surrounding Wyatt blurred as she gazed into his eyes, her pulse racing to the point of making her dizzy.

"I've lived in a fantasy world, experiencing everything on the surface, with nothing solid in my life. You're my anchor. You've shown me what it means to be grounded and real. You make me...feel." He patted his chest. "That picture of Maddie and Scott? I want that for us."

Anne's breath hitched, and tears misted her vision.

"When we first met, you told me you wanted to take things slow. There's no rush, but I'm ready to commit." Wyatt opened the box lid and held it out. "I've probably blindsided you, but I love you and want to know this is where we're headed. Will you marry me?"

His eyes reflected pure love, and heat radiated from her heart. She gazed at the huge pear-shaped diamond, sparkling in the sunlight. They hadn't talked about this. They hadn't planned this. They hadn't mapped out this future.

And for the first time, she didn't care. She'd throw caution to the wind to be with him. Yes, she wanted this man in her life. He stumbled and bumbled through relationship stuff, but he never gave up. Always coming back to try again. For her.

She constantly sold herself short, thinking she wasn't good enough. What she and Wyatt had was special. He accepted her for who she was and appreciated her, making no demands. That was love.

The box in Wyatt's strong hand shook ever so slightly. "Anne?"

Too many thoughts whirled in her head, but she shoved them to the backseat. Not trusting her voice to speak, she nodded.

His eyes widened. "Yeah?"

"Yes. I love you." She smiled through tears.

Letting out a huge breath, with a smile brighter than the sun, he drew the ring out from the box. She held up a trembling hand, and he slipped the ring on her finger. He tugged her down from the tailgate and wrapped his arms around her.

"I love you so much." He stroked her back.

And at that moment, it didn't matter that she was exhausted, wet, and emotionally drained. Everything in her world was right.

Their troubles had to be over.

CHAPTER 31

SITTING AT THE KITCHEN COUNTER, Devon checked his emails. A message confirmed the purchase of the glass lamp he'd mentioned to Paul earlier. Paul had almost tripped him up at the antique shop. He'd thought Paul was asking him why he'd killed Lynn, not why he'd told her about the bet.

Crisis averted. He'd talked his way out of it as usual, and Paul was none the wiser. The guy still held a torch for that bitch back in college and had even gone to the reunion. Pitiful. It would be satisfying to rub another loss in his face. Always felt good to come out on top.

Devon frowned. Time to check his recordings. Anne and Pearson had gone on some hike, another cheapskate date. He pressed a button and listened to Anne on her phone excitedly telling Emily about Pearson's proposal.

Proposal? A red haze clouded Devon's vision, and he fisted his hands. He pounded one on the kitchen counter and knocked a bar stool to the ground.

Engaged? They'd fucking gotten engaged?

Devon clenched his jaw and stalked to the wet bar. He poured a drink, downed it, and refilled the tumbler. He'd never expected this and had no tip-off because Pearson hadn't discussed it with anyone at his condo.

In two gulps, Devon finished the second drink and slammed the glass on the counter, cracking the thick glass of the tumbler. He paced the room, panting and fuming.

Why would the bitch have accepted the offer from a loser who couldn't even hold his own in a fight? Didn't make any sense. Devon had showed him up, big time. Even the press had heralded him as the new hero. He was the hands-down winner.

He'd gone out of his way to hit all of Anne's hot spots. Good with children, wanted a family, charitable, and well respected in the community. She should be chasing him, not turning down offers for dinner with him and the superintendent.

Pearson still rode on the coat tails of his former fame, but Devon was rich, connected and powerful. A much better prospect. Anne wasn't even worthy of him. Stupid, ignorant whore. He had a list a mile long of women who'd marry him in a heartbeat.

He would not lose another wager over one. No fucking way. The liquor burned in his belly, and his head throbbed. He knocked another chair to the ground, then took a deep breath.

Focus. This game wasn't over. He paced again. Proving his superior strength and ability hadn't impressed Anne enough. Devon needed to take Pearson out of the picture.

His fingers itched to do to Pearson what he'd done to Louie, that incompetent goon who'd messed up Anne's face. After Devon had killed him, he'd ripped the earring out of the moron's ear and added it to the memento collection in the secret room beneath the antique store. A reminder of what happened to people who crossed him. Pearson's Super Bowl ring would be another trophy. No doubt, the conceited asswipe wore it all the time.

Devon rubbed a hand across his chin and narrowed his eyes. Much as he'd love to kill the meathead, it wouldn't work. Anne would mourn the bastard, and time would run out. Devon needed to discredit Pearson in such a way that Anne would break the engagement.

The raging hot blood in Devon's veins cooled as he conjured up a scenario. He twisted his lips as a plan formed. Yes. This would definitely break them up, and when her world came crashing down, guess who would conveniently be there to pick up the pieces?

CHAPTER 32

PAUL TOSSED his coat onto the kitchen chair and grabbed a bottle of bourbon. Sipping merlot was more his style, but the last twenty-four hours had been pure insanity, and he needed something stronger. He poured a shot and knocked it back. His throat scorched, and sweat slicked his brow.

Lynn, dead.

Devon admitting he'd sabotaged Paul's relationship with her.

The fatal fires.

He swiped a hand across his forehead and poured another shot. Crazy as it sounded, he had to find out if Devon might be responsible for them.

Paul's wife entered the kitchen and stopped short. "Oh, you're home earlier than I'd expected."

He glanced up as her gaze went from his coat thrown on the chair to the shot glass.

"What's going on?" she asked, alarm in her voice.

He'd never mentioned the reunion, blaming business meetings for an expected late night. Didn't matter. All they talked about was the weather, news, and where to go to dinner next. He'd stepped into the Twilight

Zone now. No way he'd discuss a possibly murdered past love and potentially psycho friend.

After gulping the bourbon, he plopped the shot glass down on the countertop. His lenses fogged as the liquor flushed his face.

"Paul? You're scaring me. What's wrong?" His wife took a step closer.

She deserved an answer, but his muddled brain couldn't give one. He had to get to his computer to find out more about the fires. "Nothing. I'm sorry…I need to look into something."

He walked to the study and shut the door behind him. His ready-to-explode head rendered him incapable of niceties. Her footsteps approached the door, stopped for a second, then faded away down the hall.

Tapping the mouse to life, he sat at his computer and googled apartment fires in Virginia. When he typed in the year Lynn died, several articles popped up. His stomach in knots, he scanned the information from multiple newspapers.

The stories named three people, including Lynn, who were killed in the apartment fire, with several others treated for burns and smoke inhalation. The blaze, which had started around two a.m., originated on the first floor and rapidly spread.

Investigators found evidence of an accelerant used and ruled it arson. Paul's heart seized, and his hands shook. So, it hadn't been an accident. At the time, there were no known suspects, and a number was listed to call if anyone had information.

For the next hour, he read every article he could find on the fire, but none of them identified any suspects or arrests. He took off his glasses and sat back, rubbing his eyes. The bourbon rolled around in his stomach, threatening to come up. No motive was ever uncovered for the fire. He knew someone with a motive all right. Sure as hell not enough of one for any normal person, but an arsonist didn't fall into that category.

He shuddered. Earlier, when he'd mentioned Lynn to Devon, his reaction had been barely controlled anger. Flared nostrils, narrowed eyes, and the way he'd turned his back, yanking out a file from the cabinet. Way over the top for a bet he'd lost back in college.

Paul tilted his head and squinted. He'd seen Devon angry several times throughout the years, but never sad, upset, or even happy for that matter. Sure, he gloated when he won a wager, or laughed at a joke, but that wasn't the same as expressing feelings. Was he capable of having them? Paul shook his head, put his glasses back on, and started a new search.

He knew Devon had grown up in Finksburg, Alabama, and was twelve at the time of his family's death. After doing some quick math to figure out the year, Paul found an article about the house fire. The piece stated that Devon's parents and brother had died of smoke inhalation and severe burns. An investigation revealed gasoline had been dumped in the second story hall between the bedrooms to accelerate the fire. Owen Blackwood, an aspiring young athlete, had died trapped in his bedroom, unable to escape due to a tampered-with window.

Paul gasped. Tampered with? Someone wanted to make sure that kid didn't survive. Devon had never mentioned anything about arson or his brother dying that way.

The back of Paul's neck prickled. Just like with Lynn's fire, no suspects or motives were ever discovered. He needed to find out more about Devon's brother. A search on "Finksburg and Owen Blackwood" brought up some links.

Owen had been some sort of small-town hero athlete. Paul zoomed in on a picture of Devon's parents next to a coach with Owen between them holding a huge trophy. Devon appeared in the far corner of the shot, almost out of the frame. His thin, pale body a huge contrast to the muscular build of his older brother. In the picture Devon's mouth was pursed, his eyes squinted, and face contorted with what could only be contempt. Another motive?

This time the bourbon in Paul's gut made its way partly up, choking him. Sweat poured down his back as his heart raced out of control.

Devon did it. Deep in every cell of his body, Paul knew it. Devon had murdered his family and Lynn. That's why his eyes had flashed with alarm for the briefest second when Paul had asked him, "Why did you do it?" Devon thought Paul was asking why he'd killed Lynn, not why he'd told her about the wager. Now it all made sense.

The man was a total psychopath, incapable of feelings or remorse. Smart enough to create a persona beyond reproach—the philanthropist who cared about children and donated to the hospital. Only Paul knew his secrets now. How had he never seen the signs?

He ran a shaky hand through his balding hair. No point in calling the police without proof. And crimes committed so long ago would make that almost impossible to get. He had to approach it from another angle.

All the years he'd worked for Devon, Paul had always kept a blind eye to the goods imported and exported. Devon handled all of the shipments personally through his antique shop. With the amount of money he made, the stuff had to be illegal. He'd only let Paul deal with the financial end of the business. At the very least, he had proof that Devon was guilty of tax fraud.

Paul took a deep breath and slowly let it out. There had to be more crimes, and he'd make it his business to find them. Time to do some investigating.

Leaning over the desk, he turned off the light. Tears slid down his cheeks. His heart ached for Lynn. Had she been asleep when she died? Had the psycho done anything to hurt her before he set the fire?

Devon would pay. Paul would nail him even if it meant implicating himself. He'd do it for Lynn.

CHAPTER 33

WYATT DROVE TO WORK, still on a high since Anne had accepted his proposal last week. He'd sweated it out, and God knew the day hadn't gone as planned, but in the end, the woman he loved now wore a diamond on her finger. He never thought any piece of jewelry could mean more than his Super Bowl ring. Wrong. So much had changed since he'd met her. She'd opened his eyes to what he'd been missing.

His phone rang with John's ringtone. "What's up?"

"Hey. It may be nothing, but we might have found one of the guys who attacked you and Anne."

Wyatt's heart jumped. "How? Who?"

"A body turned up in the river," John said. "The dude must have really pissed someone off because he was missing a hand and half an ear."

"Holy shit." Talk about gruesome. "I guess that stuff happens in the city with gangs and all, but what's the connection to us?"

"I'll explain in a sec. The river rat's name was Louie Capello. Ring any bells?"

"No, never heard of him." Wyatt stopped at a light.

"I did some checking around with the locals after I found out where he lived."

"I'm listening."

"Didn't get any names, but it turns out he has some buddies who are regulars at Jerry's. It's a local bar in Baltimore. Never been in the place, but I know of it."

When the light turned green, Wyatt hit the gas pedal. "Okay."

"Word on the street is they're for-hire hands, almost any job. One of them matches your description with the tattoos and bandana. That got me thinking. Maybe Capello and his friends were your attackers. Might be a dead end, because lots of bikers dress like that, but I'm checking every possible lead."

An image of the guy dragging Anne into the alley flashed in Wyatt's head, and his stomach tossed. He tightened his grip on the steering wheel. "So, what now?"

"I'll send you a picture of Capello. Tell me if you recognize him. They're running a DNA test against the sample they took from under Anne's nails."

"I didn't know they did that." God, anyone could have done anything to her while Wyatt was lying there like a helpless sack-of-shit. His chest burned, and he ground his teeth together.

"Don't blame yourself. You were knocked out. If it's a match, we have one of them, but he won't be talking."

"Yeah, too bad." Wyatt parked in the high school lot.

"It's Friday. Bet they'll show up at Jerry's tonight. How about meeting me at ten, and you can keep an eye out for anyone you recognize from the alley?"

"I'll be there."

"Okay. The bar is in a tough part of town. Dress to fit in, and lock your car."

"Got it. I'll leave the ascot at home."

"Just bring your ass." John hung up.

When the picture message came, Wyatt tapped the screen. The muscles in his neck went rigid. That was the guy, all right.

He typed a quick note back to John.

* * *

Wyatt's phone dinged as he parallel parked on the street near Jerry's.

A text from John. *Stay put. Need to talk before we go in.*

Cutting the engine, Wyatt waited. Maybe a change in plans? Could be anything.

A minute later, John opened the passenger door and got in the car.

Wyatt glanced at him and did a double take. If he didn't know better, he'd swear the mustache was real.

John handed him a Raiders ball cap. "Wear this low to hide your face. I don't want anyone to recognize you. Black and silver will blend in, and no one would expect a Ravens player to wear another team's hat."

A sliver of apprehension wound itself around Wyatt's lungs. "Why the mustache?"

"I work undercover, so no one should make me as a detective, but I don't take chances." He met Wyatt's eyes, the usual glint of humor absent. "I've been at this for a long time. I know how these scumbags think and work. Sometimes I make it up as I go, and I need you to trust me and follow my lead."

Wyatt nodded. Shit was getting real. He'd never seen John in action.

"I think someone hired these creeps. If that's the case, your problems aren't over until we find out who." John glanced at the bar front. "Depending on what happens in there, we might have to let the small fry go to catch the big fish. Are you all right with that? It's a risk."

If John's theory held true, nothing would stop the person behind the attack from striking again. Much as Wyatt wanted all of them in jail, he needed to get to the bottom of things. "I trust whatever you think."

"All right. If they show up, don't talk unless I ask you a question, and keep your cool."

"Got it." Wyatt put on the cap.

John patted his coat. "I'm wired and have a camera. Don't have the resources to keep agents staked out night after night when we have no idea if or when these dicks might show up. If those assholes are in there, I'll call for backup, and we'll make our move once we're covered.

"Sounds like a plan."

They entered the bar and found a table located behind the door. Perfect position for a stakeout. John told Wyatt to sit facing the wall so all people would see was his back. Heavy-metal music blared, and the rowdy crowd at the bar yelled over the noise.

John was right about the place. Full of bikers wearing black shirts, leather vests, wallet chains, and bandanas. He and John almost fit in with their black Tees, ripped jeans, denim jackets, and boots. Close enough.

A few of the bikers had glanced at John and Wyatt when they entered, but either lost interest when they took the small table away from the action, or were intimidated by their size. Hard to say. At least they were tucked back in a dark corner and far enough from the loud speakers to hold a conversation.

Trish approached with a big smile.

Wyatt did a double take. He hadn't seen her working at the Corner Bar for a while. Now he knew why.

"Hey, didn't expect to see you two in here." She flicked a finger at John's mustache. "That's new. I like it."

John sat taller and smiled back. He'd always had a thing for her, but had never got around to asking her out, and then she'd disappeared. A petite brunette with big brown eyes, she was totally his type. Her gaze lingered on his chest, then snapped back to his face. Wyatt bit into a grin as his buddy postured.

"When did you start working here?" John asked.

"Couple of months ago. Right after some jerk got me fired." Her mouth twisted. "He complained to my manager because I didn't leap to his beck and call when he snapped his fingers. I had other tables, and he was a snobby asshole. Full of himself."

"That sucks." Wyatt said.

"Yup. Worked there for three years, busted my ass, and had a bunch of loyal regulars like you guys. Didn't matter. Mr. Big Wig apparently threw his weight around, and next thing I knew, I was out the door." She perched a hand on her hip. "The bastard actually went to the trouble of leaving me a one cent tip that night to make sure I knew he didn't forget."

John shook his head. "Unbelievable. For what it's worth, we miss you there."

"Aww, thanks. Whatcha drinking?"

They ordered a couple of Buds, and Trish went to the bar.

"I'm not going to drink, but I want the bottle in front of me so I don't stand out," John said.

Wyatt scanned the room. His hopes sank. "Don't recognize anyone."

"It's still early."

Trish returned with their beers. "Here ya go. Anything else?"

"No, thanks." John gave her another one of his killer smiles, and Wyatt snorted. His chance to poke some fun at the putz. Wyatt sure as hell had taken his shots the night he'd spilled his drink on Anne.

John's eyes narrowed. "Check out the two bikers who just entered."

Wyatt twisted in his seat, eyeing the guys headed to the bar. A shot of adrenaline raced through Wyatt's body, and he balled his hands into fists. "That's the guy who punched me. The one with the skulls bandana and the Harley Davidson shirt."

"Recognize the other guy?"

Wyatt frowned. "Didn't see him well that night. He's about the right size."

"Stay calm."

The steel glint in John's eyes meant all business now. Wyatt nodded and forced down the urge to throttle the bastards. He had to play by John's rules.

"Time to call for backup." John pulled out his phone, a piece of paper, and a pen from the inside pocket of his jacket. He typed a text message and then scribbled a note.

"What's that?" Wyatt squinted, trying to read the writing upside down.

"A little business proposition. I don't want to confront them at the bar around all their buddies. If they think we want to hire them, they'll come over here." His phone vibrated, and he checked the text. "Backup will be here in five minutes."

Wyatt nodded. Time seemed to freeze as each long second ticked by.

At last, John said, "Roger that." He met Wyatt's eyes. "They're in position, and we're live."

He must have been answering them through his mic. A rush of energy flooded Wyatt's body like it used to before a trick play.

John waved at Trish to get her attention, and she stopped by their table. "Whatcha need?"

He handed her the note. "Can you give this to the guy at the bar wearing the bandana with skulls on it? He's standing next to a dark-haired, bigger man."

Trish's gaze cut to the group of bikers. "That's Moe Dog in the bandana and Charlie beside him."

"You know them?" John asked.

"Yeah." Her nose crinkled like she smelled something foul. "Those two are the worst cheapskates. I'd have to eat dog food for survival if I relied on their tips."

As Trish left, taking the note with her, John faced Wyatt. "Don't turn around. I'll tell you what's going on."

"Got it."

"They're reading the note. Now Trish is pointing to us." John gave them a small nod. "Trish just shrugged and walked away."

Wyatt's heart thumped harder. Damn his banged-up body. If things got physical, he'd rather be in top shape. Christ, how did John do this shit for a living? "Are they coming over?"

"Looks like it. They're headed our way. Remember, don't say anything unless I ask a question and keep your head down."

A voice came from behind Wyatt. "Never seen you in here before. Who told you about us?"

"Word gets around." John waved at the empty seats. "Sit down and we can talk."

Silence.

With them out of his sight, Wyatt had no idea from their expressions what they were thinking.

"We need to check you out first, or tell us who sent you here," the man said.

Shit. Wyatt's hands turned clammy. This could all go sideways.

"I'm not tossing names around until I find out if you're the real deal." John held his hands up in a suit-yourself gesture. "Job can't wait. You don't want it, I'll move on down my list."

The guys muttered something to each other that Wyatt couldn't make out, then said, "All right, we'll talk."

Moe Dog sat beside John, and Charlie next to Wyatt.

John tapped Wyatt's boot under the table. "These the guys?"

Wyatt glanced at them. Both were large, but not fit, with beer bellies and double chins. Wyatt could easily take either of them in a fight. Several scars disfigured Moe Dog's face, including a long, jagged one that ran from his ear to his under his jaw. Doubtful Charlie scored many dates with his beady eyes, crooked oversized nose, and acne-pocked skin. Wyatt fisted a hand against his thigh, controlling the strong desire for revenge. "Yup. These are the guys."

"What's going on?" asked Moe Dog. "Thought we were gonna talk about a job."

"Maybe not." He pointed to Wyatt. "Recognize him?"

Wyatt raised his head so the asshole could see his face.

Moe Dog's eyes widened. He shot a wild look to his friend, then the door.

"Wouldn't do it." John gestured to Wyatt. "With his positive ID, I have enough to arrest and officially question you at the station. We can chat here or you can get locked up there. Your choice."

Moe Dog sneered, "Or we can tell everyone in this place you're the heat. You'll be dead before your body hits the floor."

Wyatt's pulse raced, his muscles tense and ready for anything.

John didn't flinch. He tapped a button on his jacket. "Body cam. Say "hi" to my friends in the van parked on the street." He leaned on the table. "Play nice, and I'll forget the threat."

The two thugs glanced at each other. The stink of body odor came off them, and Wyatt understood why Trish had wrinkled her nose earlier. John had them sweating now.

Finally, Moe Dog cursed and gave a jerky nod.

"Let's start with your names, and don't bullshit me because I can find out easy enough," John said.

He must not have wanted them to know Trish had told him already. Probably best to keep her out of it as much as possible. Wyatt tugged his cap down lower.

"I'm Moe Dog, and he's Charlie."

John whipped his phone out and tapped the screen. He held up a picture of Capello. "You know this guy?"

Moe Dog frowned and huffed out a breath. "Yeah. Used to."

Charlie's forehead glistened with sweat.

"Who hired you to rough him up?" John gestured to Wyatt.

Wyatt held his breath. John was fishing with the question. This was the risk he'd talked about.

Charlie's jaw dropped, and he shook his head hard. "No way. We ain't crossing that crazy ass."

Moe Dog kicked him. "Shut the fuck up."

Wyatt dug his nails into his palm, his pulse zipping. So, someone *had* hired them. John had hit pay dirt. He'd been right all along. But who? And why?

"I don't rat. I got a reputation." Moe Dog crossed his arms.

John smirked. "So do I. People who don't cooperate with me end up in a lot of trouble. I promise you, puppy, if you don't talk to me, I'll make you my personal chew toy. I got vacation time and I'll take it all dancing on your ass. See how much business you can do with a cop as your shadow. Now talk or I'm taking you in."

Red blotches formed on Moe Dog's face. "Okay, okay, I got a lead on a job. No strings, good money, just bust up a guy and get out."

Wyatt's blood simmered. Someone really had it in for him, but he had no idea why.

John leaned forward. "I'll ask again. Who hired you?"

"Don't know his name. Met him in the alley. He paid cash, and I didn't ask questions."

"Paid you full, up front?"

"No motherfucker's that stupid." Moe Dog waved a hand. "Half up front, said the rest would come after."

John nodded. "Describe him."

Moe Dog shook his head. "It was dark, so I didn't see his face. Just a normal size dude."

"Not helpful." John scoffed. "You're giving me nothing. We're done. I'm taking you both in."

Moe Dog grabbed John's arm as he raised out of the chair. "Wait, there's more."

"Thought so. Now stop fucking with me." John eased back down.

"I didn't see much, cuz the dude had on a long coat and a hat. He gave me an envelope. Told us not to hurt the bitch, only the guy."

Rage snapped Wyatt's slim hold on self-control, and he yanked Moe

Dog up by the shirt. Before he could smash his fist into the bastard's face, John caught his arm and shoved him back into his seat. John's eyes flashed, and he scanned the room behind Wyatt.

Moe Dog tugged his shirt down and held a hand up to someone, shaking his head.

Wyatt's body quaked and he took a deep breath. John had warned him to keep his cool. They didn't need a brawl. He gave John a quick I'm-on-board now nod.

Moe Dog glared at Wyatt before turning back to John. "The guy was fucking crazy. We did what he asked. He gave me three-fourths of the pay off and said Louie was gonna get his separately. Next thing we know, Louie's dead."

John rubbed his chin. "You think he killed Louie. Why?"

"Dude was pissed that Louie slapped the bi"—Moe Dog's gaze darted to Wyatt, then back to John—"girl, and said people paid for not following orders. That's all I know, man."

John drummed his fingers on the table. "I'm gonna make a deal with you."

"What kind of deal?"

"I need the name of the fourth guy in your operation. That's not negotiable. And you tell me where your boss is. After you three ID him, we'll discuss your charges."

"What kind of shit deal is that?" A vein bulged in Moe Dog's neck.

"The best offer you're gonna get. So, where is he?"

Moe Dog shrugged. "No idea."

John stared him down, and tension crackled between them.

Charlie finally spoke, "He wasn't from around here, but we can do some digging. And yeah, I'll ID the fucker if you bring him in." He shot a look at Moe Dog, as if daring him to say anything. "Louie was my cousin."

Wyatt's stomach flipped. They'd have at least one sure ID.

John picked up his phone. "Gimme your full names and numbers, including your fourth man who's not here. None of this nickname bull-shit, and don't even think about leaving town. I got eyes all over this place. If I don't get a lead on this guy in a week, I'm taking you both downtown. If I get a fake, you'll be riding wheelchairs instead of bikes."

Moe Dog scowled but gave John the information and slunk out of the bar with Charlie.

Wyatt massaged his temple, his head hurting. "I'm floored. No idea what any of this is about."

"These thugs are scared shitless of whoever killed Capello. That's why they won't give him up. They'll ID him, but they won't be the snitches to turn him in. It'd be suicide." John glanced at the bikers getting louder at the bar. "Time to leave."

Trish came over to their table and stopped next to John. "You guys want another round?"

"Nope. Just the tab," John said.

She wrote something on the bottom of their check and placed it on the table. "Sure thing."

John picked up the bill. He stared at it, and his eyebrows raised.

"What's up?" Wyatt asked.

"I'll tell you outside." John tossed some bills on the table and stood.

Wyatt followed him out the door. What the hell was going on? This was crazier than sandlot football. No rules with split-second decisions that could make or break the game. Constantly on the defense.

John faced him. "Sorry for the smack-down, but I couldn't let you hit that dick in front of me. We had them where we wanted them and were damn lucky no one in the bar went all Hell's Angels on us."

Wyatt's throat constricted. "I know. I lost it. I'm sorry, man."

John blew out a breath. "Let's move on." He pointed to the lit-up signs of a diner a block away. "Trish left a note on the check. Wants to meet us there on her break in ten minutes."

The small hairs on Wyatt's arm stood up. Maybe she'd seen or heard something that could give them a lead.

They entered the diner, sat in a booth with duct tape sealing a rip, and ordered coffees. While John had an exchange with his backup unit, Wyatt warmed his hands over the steaming mug. What did Trish want to talk to them about?

She opened the door and glanced around before approaching. Worry lines wrinkled her brow as she slid into the seat opposite John. "I didn't realize you were a cop."

"How do you know?" John asked.

"I stayed near your table and overheard part of your conversation." Her face turned blood red. "I was worried about you guys because those bikers are rough."

John's mouth twitched. "Well, I'm glad you didn't have to save us."

"Yeah, I feel pretty stupid now." She rubbed her arms.

"Don't." John leaned closer. "You helped us out, and I appreciate your concern. Now what did you want to tell us?"

She straightened. "I might be able to help if you can tell me what you wanted with Moe Dog and Charlie."

John smiled and acted like he was having a fun chat with a friend. "I need to find out who hired them for a recent job."

Trish's mouth pressed into a thin line. "I think I might know."

A spark of hope flared in Wyatt's chest. She had his full attention.

"That Big Wig asshole I told you about who left the penny tip?" She tilted her head. "He came to Jerry's, dressed down. Went out the back door to the alley, and Moe Dog followed him."

Wyatt clamped his teeth together. If Trish recognized him, they'd lied about not seeing his face since he'd walked through the bar before going to the alley. No surprise. Couldn't expect thugs-for-hire to tell the truth.

"What happened next?" John sipped his coffee.

"Moe Dog come back in later and handed Charlie some money. Big Wig never returned. I guess he left through the alley." Trish shrugged.

"What did he look like?" asked John.

"Tall with dark hair and brown eyes. Both times I saw him he wore a suit or coat, so I don't know if he has any tattoos or anything."

John tapped his chin. "Any distinguishing features?"

"No, but I would recognize him if I ever saw him again."

John handed her a business card. "Can you come by the station and work with our sketch artist?"

"Sure. I can fit it in tomorrow afternoon between babysitting and my study group. I'm sorry, that's the soonest I'll be free."

"Study group?" John eased back in the booth.

Trish smiled. "Yeah, I'm in a nursing program up the street at Hopkins. We have a big exam Monday."

"Wow, impressive. That's great, and thanks for your help."

Trish stood and glanced around again before leaving.

"Talk about a damn big break." John pushed his mug aside.

"No kidding." Wyatt wiped his brow and frowned. "I'm not sure what to do about tomorrow."

"What?"

"I have this huge Big Brothers Big Sisters fundraiser. It's an overnight camping trip at Ocean City. I hate to let the kids down, but I think I should cancel."

John shook his head. "Actually, I think you'd be better off going."

"Why?"

"Think about it. Moe Dog and his goons were told specifically to rough you up and leave Anne alone. This was a hit on you. She's probably safer with you *not* around."

Wyatt picked up his mug. "Maybe you're right. I don't know what to think anymore. She's supposed to be spending the night at Emily's with the girls tomorrow. Some wine and cheese party."

"That sounds safe enough. She won't be alone. I'm more concerned about another attempt on you." John glanced out the window. "Keep your eyes and ears open. Hopefully, with Trish's help, we'll get a sketch of the guy and find him. Things can happen fast."

"All right."

Until John figured out what was going on, Wyatt didn't want to say anything to worry Anne. This was his burden. As long as she stayed at Emily's and away from him, she should be okay. His heart twisted into a knot. They were engaged now. He ached to hold her in his arms and make love to her, not be apart.

Much as it hurt, he'd keep his distance to protect her.

CHAPTER 34

ANNE SIPPED a cup of coffee at the kitchen table and gazed at the huge diamond on her finger. Excitement danced in her chest. Wyatt had shocked her with the proposal, but she'd followed her heart and said yes.

His ringtone sounded, and she grabbed the phone. "Good morning. Did you and John have fun last night?"

No response.

"Wyatt? You there?"

"Yeah. It was okay. We're going to be busy at this event, so I figured I'd call now. Is the wine and cheese party still on for tonight?"

"As far as I know. You sure everything was all right with John?" Usually Wyatt laughed or made some joke about the guy.

"He's fine. So, you'll call me if anything changes about you sleeping over at Emily's?"

Anne stood and went to the coffee maker for a refill. "I guess, but why would it?"

"Stuff happens. Like maybe you drink too much and get sick or something."

"When have I ever done that? And if I did, then I would feel like crap the next morning. Besides, I'm still recovering from the concussion, so I'll stick to soda." She poured the coffee but sloshed some over the side, burning her finger. Damn. She ran it under cool water.

Wyatt continued, "Well, you may decide you want to go home, and then someone would have to take you and—"

"Everyone else is going to be drinking. No one would drive me home." She frowned and turned off the faucet.

"They could get an Uber."

"What?" She thrust a hand on her hip. "If I got sick, which is not happening for the record, do you think my friends would shove me into a car with a stranger and send me on my way?"

Wyatt sighed. "I guess not."

"No, they wouldn't." She picked her mug up and returned to the table.

"I know you won't get sick, but something else could happen, like a pipe bursting that floods the place."

Anne choked on her coffee, irritating her throat. What the hell was wrong with him? She held the phone away until her coughing fit subsided. She slowly returned it to her ear, wary of what insanity might come over the line next. "A pipe bursting? Emily's apartment is brand new. This is the stupidest conversation we've ever had. Why are you imagining all this stuff?"

Silence.

She rubbed her neck. "Wyatt?"

"I'm worried because of the attack, and I don't like being out of town," he said, resignation in his tone.

She let out a breath. "I've been fine all week. You can stay over when you get back in—"

"No," he said, sharply.

Anne blinked. "What? I thought you said you were worried—"

"I did, but...I mean...you're right. I'm being paranoid. You're okay without me there."

A dull ache formed in her head. She smoothed the lines over her brow. He was making her crazy now. "Try to enjoy the kids and relax. I promise if anything comes up, I'll call you. If a pipe bursts, a fire alarm sets off all the sprinklers, or a mandatory evacuation is declared, I will let you know. All right?"

"Yeah." He paused, his voice softer. "Remember, I love you."

Like always, her heart did a slow melt when he said those words. "I love you, too. Now, drive safe and see you tomorrow."

She hung up and slid the phone across the table, eyeing the thing as if it were possessed. Between the attack and the proposal, the last week had been super stressful. Anyone could crack a little under all that pressure. She'd give Wyatt a pass.

Shaking her head, she couldn't help but half-smile. Bursting pipes?

CHAPTER 35

THE SUN WARMED Anne's face as she popped the trunk. She'd picked up brie and chardonnay to take to the party, where she absolutely would stay no matter what disaster might happen. With a grin, she shook her head. Maybe that ring on her finger had short-circuited Wyatt's brain.

Emily called, and Anne answered, placing the bags in the car. "What's up?"

"I need to see you right away. Where are you?"

A wave of alarm rose from Anne's belly. Something was wrong. "I'm at the store. What's—"

"Which store?"

"The TJ's near my house. You don't sound right. What's going on?" She got into the car and started the engine.

"I'm at an outside table of Grand Nachos. Can you come right over?"

Anne frowned, her heart picking up pace at Emily's tone and urgency. "I guess. You're scaring me. Are you okay?"

"Y-yes, but I need to talk to you in person. Hurry."

The line went dead.

Jesus. Maybe someone died. Anne backed out and drove to the restaurant, ticking through a mental list of all their friends. There hadn't been any texts or news of any accidents. When she reached the place, she parked and turned off the engine, hands clammy and dread compressing her lungs.

Emily sat rigid at a table, her mouth drawn in a tight line. Her chest rose and fell when she met Anne's gaze. Okay, now she *knew* something was terribly wrong. She hurried over and sat opposite Emily.

"You're freaking me out. What's going on?" Anne leaned forward.

"Shit." Emily leaned her head down, shielding her eyes. "This is even harder than I thought it would be."

Anne's throat thickened, making it hard to breathe. "Please, for God's sake, talk to me. I'm picturing someone dead."

"Okay. I'm sorry, but I think…" Emily raised her head and swallowed. "I think Wyatt might be cheating on you."

What little breath Anne had taken sputtered out like the air in a released balloon. Her body froze, every muscle stiffening. No way. She must have heard wrong. "Why would you think that?"

Emily chewed on her lower lip and nodded to the empty table beside them. "Earlier, I overheard two women talking." Her knuckles turned white in her squeezed hands. "I didn't pay much attention until I heard one of them bragging about how she was back with Wyatt. She said whenever she came to town, they got together."

"There's a million Wyatts. Why would you think—"

"Because her friend said she'd heard that Pearson had gotten engaged." Emily's eyelids slitted. "I glanced at them and recognized the woman. She's Victoria, the model he dated. When they broke up, the tabloids splashed pictures of her."

Anne's heart hardened under a protective shell. No. She wouldn't believe it. Not Wyatt. "That woman had to be lying. I don't care what she said."

"There's more." Emily winced. "I don't want to hurt you, but I have to tell you."

Anne's legs refused to push her up and out of the bench. That's what she needed to do. Get up and go. But she sat there like a rubbernecker on the highway unable to stop looking at a wreck.

Emily's cheeks puffed out, and she exhaled. "She said he was supposed to be out of town this weekend, but since she was here, he changed plans, and they were going to spend the night at his place."

"I don't believe any of it. Why would he do that?" Anne shook her head.

"God, I hate repeating this, but she bragged about their sex life, saying he liked things wilder than he was getting." Emily reached for Anne's hand, but she pulled away, crossing her arms over her chest.

"That woman is a crazy liar."

"It's fucked up, Anne. I couldn't believe what I was hearing, but I really don't know Wyatt very well, and let's face it, you guys haven't dated long. Did he say or do anything to make you think this could be true?"

Anne's temple throbbed as the memory of their last conversation flooded back. Wyatt's intense insistence that Anne stay at Emily's overnight. The ridiculous scenarios of pipes bursting and Ann getting cab rides home...and he'd made her promise to call if anything came up and she had to leave. God, was it because he didn't want to chance her finding him with another woman?

"What is it?" Emily leaned across the table and touched Anne's arm.

"N-nothing." Anne's insides quaked, and every insecurity she had rose to the surface, smothering her. "I-I have to go."

Emily leaped up and rounded the table. "Come to my place and we'll talk—"

"No. I need to be alone." Anne stood.

"Nonsense. I'm cancelling the party, and we'll spend—"

"Please, no." Anne held up a hand and closed her eyes. Her head spun, and her throat was dry as chalk. "Thanks, but I have to get out of here."

"I hate this so much." Emily threw an arm around Anne and hugged her. "I'm here for you. I'll do anything to help. If you want me to drive you to his place or stay with you, or anything, just name it."

Anne managed a stiff nod and headed to her car. This couldn't be happening. Victoria was probably an attention hog who ran around telling wild, made-up stories. That's all.

Except that didn't explain Wyatt's abnormal behavior and downright paranoia over Anne staying at Emily's overnight.

Anne sank into the driver's seat and gazed down at her engagement ring. Tears burned the back of her eyes. She'd thought they had something special, but maybe Wyatt was only content because he had women on the side. Sick to her stomach, she bent over the steering wheel and forced a deep breath.

Now what?

CHAPTER 36

Since Paul had uncovered the deadly fire articles, it had been an agonizing week of waiting for the opportunity to snoop around the antique shop. His blood still simmered. He'd been following the money trail and knew a portrait and lamp were shipping out tomorrow. They must be stashed somewhere on the premises. Devon had mentioned a dinner meeting, so Paul should have the place to himself.

When he entered the building, the grandma's-attic, musty scent of mothballs and old, wooden furniture filled his nostrils. He glanced around, but nothing unusual stood out. Stacked paintings rested against the wall, and antiques adorned tables.

Not sure what he was even looking for, he circled the room, stopping in the middle. He pinched his chin and sized up the area. All open with no closets or attic meant nowhere to hide anything. His gaze dropped to the floor. But what about beneath?

Pulling a flashlight from his pocket, he clicked the button and ran the light along the hardwood floor. No deep cracks, no hinges, no signs of an opening. His heart sank.

Wait, something wasn't right. The boards next to a carpet bearing a heavy armoire were darker than the others, not faded. Maybe the rug usually covered them.

Dropping to his knees, he shined the light under the wardrobe. His stomach jumped. Tiny wheels beneath the legs made it mobile. He pushed the armoire to the edge of the carpet.

His pulse quickened as he rolled up the carpet, revealing a trap door with a recessed handle. Bingo. He grabbed the ring, pulled hard, and the door swung open. Darkness swallowed the descending stairs, and the humming of a machine rose from below.

He beamed his light into the black hole, but the ray only illuminated the steps. Taking a shaky breath, he placed a foot on the first tread and bounced up and down to test the strength of the wood. Seemed solid enough and appeared to be newer than the flooring of the antique shop. Maybe Devon had built the downstairs after he'd purchased the store. This had to be where he kept his exports.

The back of Paul's throat itched, and the flashlight shook in his hand as he slowly descended. When he reached the bottom, he shined the light around the room and located a wall switch. With no windows, he didn't have to worry about people seeing him. He flipped the toggle and the room lit up.

Squinting, he waited for his eyes to adjust to the flickering of fluorescent lights. A metal heater or air conditioning unit buzzed in the background. Piles of various sized boxes, tape, and shipping materials lined the perimeter. A large taped box stamped "fragile" leaned against a wall. Had to be the portrait.

He whipped his phone out and took pictures, documenting the room's contents.

A small table in the corner with gleaming gold drawer handles caught his eye. He crossed the room and stepped onto the thick, black velvet carpet mat in front of it. Nothing weird about that.

A silver candelabra on top held five half-burned tapers. He ran a finger across the smooth, dark wood of the stand. Not a speck of dust. Devon kept the surface polished. An eerie feeling creeped up Paul's backbone. The table, the carpet, the candles—this looked like some sort of shrine.

He opened the cabinet doors and pulled out a crudely made wooden box. Hardened glue gummed up the sides and bound the uneven edges together. "Mom" was scrolled on the top in child-like writing. Paul rotated the box to check the back, which bore the initials "DB." Devon must have made the case for his mother. Hard to imagine he'd ever crafted anything less than perfect.

With trembling fingers, Paul slid the lid off to reveal a yellowed newspaper article about the house fire. He sucked in a breath. Devon had highlighted the line about his brother dying in the fire, trapped in his room. Sick son of a bitch.

Paul set the clipping aside and extracted a ribbon-tied, rolled-up parchment. He slid the band off and unrolled the paper. Devon's college diploma. Odd place to keep it.

Two pieces of gold jewelry winked under the light. Paul picked up a smaller college ring that matched his own. A sick, twisted thought wrapped its arms around his lungs. Oh God, no. Lynn's?

Sweat soaked his shirt despite the chilled room. He adjusted his glasses and read the inscription with Lynn's name and their graduation year.

All the blood drained from his head, and the room spun. He tried to catch his breath, fisting his hand over the ring in his palm. The metal cut into his skin, and hot rage ravaged his body.

He had proof now. Devon had killed Lynn. That sick bastard was going to pay. What did he do, light candles at his psycho shrine and relive the event?

Paul shook his head as a wave of nausea rose from his gut. Focus. He might have already compromised any fingerprints on the ring by touching it. Dumb mistake.

He took a picture of the other piece of jewelry in the box. A gold-studded earring. Maybe a trophy from some other woman Devon had killed. How had he ever thought this man to be a friend? Paul's body shook, and he dabbed the sweat from his brow. He'd call the police. Turn himself in for the tax fraud and send Devon to rot in jail.

A scraping sound came from above as the front door opened.

Paul froze. Panic welled inside, immobilizing him. Devon should still be at dinner, but maybe his plans had changed. He might be coming back to the store to get the shipment ready for tomorrow.

With the trap door wide open and no weapon, Paul was screwed. Caught with the evidence, he'd be killed like the others. He dialed nine-one-one, shoved the wooden box back into the cabinet, and grabbed the candelabra.

No matter what, he wasn't going down without a fight.

CHAPTER 37

ANNE POURED a cup of tea and set it on the counter. Past dinner time, she should eat something, but food wouldn't stay down in a stomach full of knots. The large diamond weighed heavily on her finger, but nowhere near as heavy as her heart.

She'd spent the afternoon in a fog, unable to focus on anything except the bitter bite of betrayal that ripped at the bond of trust she had with Wyatt. Her every instinct screamed that he would never cheat on her.

Emily's ringtone sounded, and Anne answered the phone. She'd been responding to texts with only emojis. She didn't want to worry her friend, but she also wasn't up for much talking. It wouldn't do any good. Not with Emily, anyway. Only Wyatt had the answers.

"I cancelled the party. Come over, or I'll come there," Emily said, concern in her voice.

"I feel so bad you did that, but thanks. I'm upset and really need to be alone," Anne managed to say around the huge lump in her throat.

"I wish there was something I could do. Don't get mad at me, but I called the Big Brothers Big Sisters office to ask if there'd been any changes in the program today. No luck. The place is closed because everyone's at the Ocean City event."

Anne frowned. She'd never even thought of calling them. God, is that what people did to check up on their spouses? "At least you did something productive. I googled Victoria and Wyatt's online pictures. She's like all the others, gorgeous and hanging all over him."

"Girl, don't torture yourself. There's no point."

Tears welled in the corners of Anne's eyes. She blinked them back. "I thought we were past all this. I stopped worrying about the other women because I knew Wyatt loved *me*. Now I'm not sure of anything."

Her phone beeped with another call, and her pulse jumped. Wyatt. Her ears craved to hear his voice, the deep timbre that melted her insides and made her long to sit on his lap. Hard as it was, she tapped "decline." When they talked, it needed to be face to face so she could see his expressions.

"Anne, you there?" Emily asked.

"Sorry, Wyatt just called, but I can't deal with him over the phone. I... I don't know what to say." Anne pressed a fist to her mouth and sucked in a breath. "Part of me wants to go to his place and see for myself, and another part says I shouldn't be wearing his ring if I don't trust him."

"Totally understandable. What if I go—"

"No." Anne brushed a strand of hair back and raised her chin. "I need to handle this on my own."

"All right. Call me if you change your mind about coming over."

"I will. Thanks."

Anne hung up and crossed her arms, hugging herself. Emily was the best friend ever, but she couldn't help with this situation. Anne tried to downplay emotions and focus on logic. Aside from his recent strange behavior, Wyatt hadn't given her any reason to think he was cheating on her.

Anne's phone dinged with a text from Wyatt.

All good here. Make sure to call me if any plans change tonight.

Her belly twisted into a tight coil. Again, another reminder about calling him. He'd never checked on her like this before. Something was definitely up, and the sick feeling wouldn't go away until she confirmed or denied her worst fears.

She called Emily back. "Just wanted to let you know I'm heading to Wyatt's. I'll keep you posted."

CHAPTER 38

WYATT'S CALL to Anne went to voicemail for the fourth time in the last hour. He'd texted and called Emily with no answer as well. Maybe the party was going strong, and no one could hear their phones. What if John was wrong and Wyatt wasn't the target? All he could think about was if anything happened, he wouldn't be in town to help.

He'd signed footballs, taken pictures with the kids, and called a friend to fill in for him tomorrow. Nice to know some of his old buddies still had his back and rallied for a good cause.

His calf cramped as he pressed the brake and exited the highway. John had called to tell him Trish had car trouble and was running late. She should be at the station soon to work with the sketch artist.

Wyatt flipped on the radio. Anything to distract him from the million thoughts buzzing in his head. Now that he was in town, he'd go straight to Emily's. If he saw Anne's car in the lot, he'd drive home and not worry her. She didn't need to know he was on edge after finding out someone had hired Moe Dog and Charlie. Best to keep her out of the loop until John got to the bottom of it all. After that, Wyatt and Anne could get on with life.

His chest warmed as he pictured the glowing smile on her face when he'd slipped the engagement ring on her finger. If he could make her grin like that every day, he'd be a happy man. They had so much ahead of them. He'd started looking at properties that had big yards with running room for Goober and kids one day.

Wyatt shook his head. Hot damn his life had done a one-eighty since he'd met Anne. Never expected to settle down and think about space for swing sets. His heart swelled, pressing against his ribcage.

He pulled into a gas station, filled up the tank, and sent a text to the dog sitter. Might as well pick up the goofy mutt on his way home. With any luck, they'd both be back there in a half hour. Wyatt could use a beer and some chill time. Probably acting a bit paranoid, but he'd trade that for peace of mind.

When he reached Emily's apartment complex, he drove around the lot, searching for Anne's car. Emily's Beetle was parked in a numbered spot. His neck muscles grew taut while he made a second pass. No sign of the Honda.

Shit. A frisson of unease worked its way up his back. Where was Anne? Maybe Emily had picked her up or something. Parking in an empty space, he cut the engine and dialed her number. Again, she didn't answer.

She'd wonder why he wasn't at the event if he knocked on the door, but he'd deal with that after he'd seen her safe and sound. His heartbeat quickened as he climbed the stairs, like he was on a rollercoaster, tick, tick, ticking up the steep incline.

He knocked on Emily's door and stood back. No music or laughter came from the apartment. If they'd cancelled the party, Anne should have called.

The door burst open.

"So, it's true. You *are* in town." Emily glared at him, her mouth twisted.

Wyatt jerked his head back at the venom in her tone. "What? I'm…is Anne here?"

Emily thrust her hands on her hips. "Wouldn't you like to know?".

A red flag waved before his eyes, and his blood pressure rose. What the hell was going on? "Please, I need to talk to Anne. Is she here?"

"No." Emily all but spat the word. "Why aren't you at the shore?"

"I found someone to fill in for me. I—"

"Yup. Just like she said." Emily's nostrils flared, and she shook her head.

"Who said what?" His head hurt as he strained to follow. "I don't know why you're mad at me, but I need to find Anne."

"Oh, I bet you do. To make sure you know where she is at all times tonight."

"Well...yeah." Since the case was under investigation, he couldn't discuss it with Emily, or why he came home. Sweat dripped down the side of his face. "Look, I don't know what's wrong, but she's not answering my calls. Do you know where she is?"

"Yeah, I do as a matter of fact."

"Where?"

"At your apartment, where all the women are," Emily said.

Fuck. A jolt of alarm shot through his system. With a target on his back, the last place he wanted Anne to be was alone at his home. She needed to stay away until they found the guy who'd hired those goons. "Why would she...never mind, when did she go? Can you call her and stop her? I don't know why she won't answer me."

"Too late. She should be there about now." Emily raised her chin, a smug look on her face. "Your tight-end is screwed."

Emily slammed the door and flipped the deadbolt.

What the fuck?

He flinched and dropped his jaw. Christ, he needed a playbook for this. No clue what the hell was happening. Why was he screwed, and why did Anne go to his apartment? Nothing made sense. He didn't have time to get answers out of Emily, who didn't appear to be in a cooperative mood anyway.

Taking the steps two at a time, he raced down the staircase.

CHAPTER 39

ANNE CIRCLED WYATT'S apartment parking lot. No sign of his car anywhere. Her erratic heartbeat evened out a tad. Blowing out a breath, she pulled into his vacant space.

Victoria had lied. No clue why the woman would make up stories, but people had all kinds of issues. A nagging doubt still lingered in Anne's mind, though. Nothing explained Wyatt's bizarre behavior yesterday. And, of course, if he didn't want anyone to know he was home, he wouldn't be stupid enough to park at his place.

The tea she had drunk earlier sloshed in her empty stomach, and perspiration wet her brow. She wouldn't know the truth unless she checked.

All she had to do was go up, find the condo empty, and call it a night. Despite being exhausted, she'd never sleep if she kept picturing Wyatt with Victoria. Once and for all, she'd put an end to the question.

Steeling her nerves, she made her way to the stairs. Every smack of her shoe on the steps reverberated like the imaginary sound of a beating heart under the floorboards of Poe's classic novel. Only she had nothing to feel guilty about. Or did she?

Thump. Thump. Thump.

She and Wyatt didn't knock anymore at each other's doors since their engagement. They used their keys to come and go. This time was different, though. This time when she opened the door, she'd cross the line of trust on which their relationship hung. This time meant she didn't have enough faith in him. And if she didn't have that, they had nothing.

She paused on the landing, her pulse throbbing at the base of her throat.

Couldn't do it. If she was going to marry the man, she had to trust him completely. She refused to spend the rest of her life questioning Wyatt's love and fidelity. He'd done nothing but show how much he loved her. She'd return his call, go home, and put the craziness of the day to rest.

About to leave, she glanced down the hall and stilled. Wyatt's door stood open a crack. That made no sense. He would have locked up. Her shoulders tensed as she treaded lightly to the entrance. She'd call the police and run back to the car if she heard anything suspicious, like someone trashing the place.

She stopped short of the door and craned her head to listen. Soft music played, and someone hummed in the background. Her breath caught, and her stomach lurched. Not *someone*, a woman.

No, no, no. This couldn't be happening. On wooden legs, she stepped to the door and eased it open. She gasped at the sight of Victoria, sipping wine on Wyatt's couch, wearing one of his shirts. Unbuttoned, it gaped apart revealing a black bra and lacy panty.

Shockwaves rocked Anne's body like a magnitude-nine earthquake. She grabbed the door for support and gulped for air. Her dreams crashed around her, crushing her soul. She hadn't believed what Emily overheard, thought Victoria was lying, but here she sat almost naked on Wyatt's sofa. The same one where Anne had spent hours cuddled next to him.

Victoria looked up and formed an "O" with her mouth. She shook her head. "Tsk, tsk, tsk. Wyatt is *not* going to be happy about this. Looks like the cat's out of the bag."

"Where's Wyatt?" Anne choked out the words past her constricted throat.

Running her long, candy-red nails through her hair, Victoria shrugged. "No point in lying now. He went out for more condoms."

The room wavered, and Anne clutched the door. Tears stung her eyes, and the strings that tied her to Wyatt snapped, plummeting her heart to her feet. How could he do this? How?

Victoria made no effort to cover herself or apologize. "This shouldn't be a surprise. Did you really think a man like Wyatt was going to be happy in a boring, comfy marriage?" She crossed her legs and swung a stiletto-clad foot. "No offense, but the man has needs, and you aren't enough to fulfill them, sweetie. He likes things a little wild and dirty."

Anne trembled, her numb brain trying to make sense of it all. *Boring.* The word kept coming back to bite her. She'd believed Wyatt when he'd said he liked to do normal, everyday things with her. Lies, their whole relationship was nothing but lies. He'd played her for a fool, having his bimbos on the side the whole time.

She was blind and stupid. Stupid to believe she could ever trust a sports celebrity. She had to get out of there. The last thing she wanted was to see Wyatt pull up with his jumbo package of condoms. Hands shaking, she yanked off her engagement ring and hurled it across the room. "He's all yours."

Tears blurred her vision as she stumbled down the stairs. Somehow, she managed to get into her car. She covered her face with her hands and cried. Body-wracking, deep sobs she couldn't stop. Salty tears wet her lips before she could brush them away.

She needed to go home and pick up the pieces of her life, which no longer included Wyatt.

As she drove, she couldn't escape the image of Victoria with her breasts falling out of Wyatt's unbuttoned shirt. Voluptuous and wild, what Wyatt secretly still wanted.

She parked in her apartment lot and got out of the car. Lightning flashed, followed by a loud boom of thunder. Nothing compared to the storm raging inside of her. She leaned against the driver's side door, resting her forehead on her arms, and took a deep breath.

Another crash of thunder reverberated as the betrayal played over and over in her mind. She squeezed her eyes shut tight.

A car pulled up beside her, and a door shut.

"Anne?" Devon's voice rang out. "Are you okay?"

CHAPTER 40

DEVON OPENED his umbrella and approached Anne, slumped against her car, her back to him. A bolt of lightning flashed, and sheets of rain dumped from the sky. She didn't move.

Satisfaction slithered through his veins. His plan had worked.

Now he'd close in for the kill.

"What are you doing out here in the storm?" He held the umbrella over Anne's drenched body.

Shivering, she pushed off the car and wiped at swollen, tear-stained eyes, smearing black mascara down her cheeks. "What?"

Disgust twisted in his chest. God, she was a fucking mess.

"Never mind. Let's get you inside. Which apartment is yours?" Like he didn't know. He pulled her closer to keep them both covered.

Her body shook, and her teeth chattered. She didn't answer, but walked stiffly with him toward the staircase.

When they reached her apartment, she fumbled with the key, hands shaking too hard to slide it into the lock. He set the umbrella down and helped her, opening the door. After she entered, he followed her inside.

She glanced at her soaked shoes, and then back up to him. "What are you doing here?"

"I brought some flyers I intended to leave at your door when I figured out which unit was yours, but that doesn't matter now." He placed a hand on her cold arm. "What happened? Are you okay?"

"No, not really." She hugged herself and shivered. "I need to…be alone."

Too bad. That wouldn't work for his plan. "You're chilled to the bone. In good conscience, I can't leave you like this. Why don't you go change? I'll make you some tea, and we can talk?"

Her eyes filled with tears, and she bit her lip. "Honestly, I'm a little shell-shocked right now. I think you should go."

He lowered his voice and patted her arm. "What kind of friend would I be if I did that? I'm a good listener, and you're clearly upset. Please, just go change into dry clothes."

"I can't even think right now." She frowned and shook harder. "Okay, whatever."

His body amped. A step in the right direction.

As she trudged down the hall, he went to the kitchen. He microwaved a mug of water and dropped in a teabag he'd found to steep. Bringing the cup with him, he moved to the living room and took a seat on the couch. Better chance to interact with her if they weren't separated by a table.

She wandered back out a few minutes later, wearing jeans and a flannel shirt.

He scoffed inside. She'd fit right in at a rodeo. "Come sit down. I made you some chamomile."

Dabbing her eyes with a tissue, she walked around the sofa and sat at the far end. Like a zombie, she stared into space. A muscle under his jaw twitched. He might as well not be in the room for all she noticed him.

He picked up the mug and slid closer, holding it out to her. "Drink some of this. It'll warm you."

"What?" She turned to him, brows drawn together. "All I want is to be left alone."

"Please, tell me what's upsetting you so much. I'm worried." But really, he was more confused about why she wasn't appreciating all he'd done for her. He'd brought her inside, made her tea, and acted like he cared. She should be fawning all over him. He placed the untouched cup on the table.

She let out a huge sigh and covered her face with her hands. "God, I can't get it out of my head. How could he have done this?"

"Who? Done what?" Devon placed a hand on her shoulder. "Talk to me."

Anne shrugged his hand off and stood. She paced the room, talking more to herself than him. "Ch-cheated on me. With…this…this horrible woman. It's over. We aren't getting married, and I can't stop thinking about her dressed in—"

"Hold on. Are you saying you walked in on Wyatt Pearson and another woman?" Devon feigned indignation as his gut leaped. The engagement was off.

She swiped hard at the tears on her cheeks and faced the window, apparently lost in her world.

Ugh. Enough with the waterworks. Time to move on. "He's a fool who doesn't deserve you."

Anne turned and yanked a tissue from a box on the side table. After blowing her nose, which was red as a clown's, she swallowed. "I'm sorry, but you need to leave now."

"Nothing to apologize for. I think it's time you saw the truth."

"Oh, I saw it all right."

Stupid bitch was ruining his moment. She should be focused on him. Pearson was history. "I meant the truth that's in front of you, now."

"So blind. How could I have not known?" She pressed her lips together and shook her head again.

Talk about blind. She was in such a fog she wasn't even paying attention to Devon. He clamped his jaw tight as tiny pricks of annoyance stabbed his abdomen. Somehow, he needed to make her see him. He stood and gazed down at her. "I think I know what will help."

"Huh?" She glanced up.

Finally, he had her attention. She'd see what should have been obvious all along. Pearson was a loser. Devon had cleared the table, and now he held the winning hand.

"I told you I'd wait for you." He touched the side of her face. "I'm here right now and have proven I'm the better man. The one you deserve. I can give you everything."

Anne blinked, and her eyes widened. "What?"

"You know it's true. There's only one question to answer."

CHAPTER 41

WYATT'S HEARTRATE raced right along with his car as he sped to his apartment. His brain was a total jumble. Emily had been furious with him. Over what?

She'd made a strange comment about Anne going to his place, where all the women went. Made no sense at all. He switched on the wipers as rain pelted the windshield, forcing him to slow down. Damn it, he didn't have time for this shit.

Whoever hired Moe Dog and Charlie could have paid someone else to harass Wyatt at his apartment, and Anne could be hurt again if she showed up there. Especially alone. He cursed under his breath and pressed the gas pedal. Screw the slick road, he'd take his chances.

When he reached his complex, he parked and ran up the stairwell. He twisted his key in the deadbolt, which turned freely. A zap of adrenaline heightened his senses. The door was unlocked.

Maybe Anne had gone in and not bothered to latch it behind her. Didn't matter. He wasn't going to call the cops and wait for them to show up. She could be in danger. Bracing himself, he swung the door open and charged into the room.

Whoa. He grabbed the back of a chair to stop his momentum and skidded to a halt in front of Victoria, who looked up at him from her seat on the sofa.

"Hi, Wyatt." Her lips curved into an evil smile.

Shock caved his lungs, spiking through his body like caffeine from a triple espresso.

What the hell?

"You don't look happy to see me." She stood and fluffed her hair.

Christ, she was wearing his shirt with some sort of lingerie beneath. Stunned, he stood stock still, struggling to form words. He'd figured out on their second date that she was bat-shit crazy, which she'd proved with all the social media bullshit, but this went beyond.

"What are you doing here and how did you get in?" He gripped the back of the chair until his knuckles turned white.

"Oh, so simple, honey." She shrugged. "I told them at the office that I forgot my key. The super was more than happy to let me in after I showed her pictures of us together."

Wyatt forced a breath. She was fucking insane. Having lunatic, stalking fans went hand in hand with being a celebrity, though. His own fault that he'd dated her. He should have known she wouldn't go away. Probably got jealous over the engagement picture of him and Anne. Victoria had major issues.

Despite the insanity of the situation, his gut-wrenching fear that Anne was in danger dissolved. No one held her at gunpoint in his apartment or had kidnapped her. He just had to deal with this wack job, who had managed to find a shirt of his to wear over not much else.

He shook his head to knock out the image of her sorting through his clothes. "If you leave now and never bother me again, I won't call the police. Do you understand?"

She pouted. "Yeah, I guess. My work here is done. I got what I wanted."

"What does that mean?" He hated to ask, but the smug expression on her face begged the question.

"I met your fiancée tonight." Victoria brought a hand to her mouth and giggled. "Oops. I mean, former fiancée."

Wyatt's heart froze along with every muscle in his frame.

No. Fuck no.

Victoria stroked her chin. "She stopped by and seemed...hmm... what's the word I'm looking for? Surprised?" She frowned. "No, that's not it. Distraught?" She shook her head. "Oh, I know." Moving a step closer, she whispered, "Devastated."

The blood drained from every vessel of Wyatt's body. Anne had to think he'd cheated on her. Devastated didn't begin to cover it.

Before he could respond, Victoria plucked out a ring from the pocket of his shirt. "By the way, she left this for you by the trashcan where it landed." Victoria smirked. "Apparently, you're all mine now. Wanna take me up on it?"

Wyatt bit back his response as his world hurled out of orbit. He had to get to Anne. Explain to her that Victoria was a certified nut case. He closed his hand over the ring and took in a deep, burning breath.

"You have five seconds to get out of here before I call the police." He faced Victoria. "Four...three..."

She snatched her purse, a bag of clothes, and a raincoat from next to the couch. After throwing on the slicker, she trotted out the door on spiked heels. "See ya, baby. This was fun."

Wyatt opened his fist and gazed at the ring. A symbol of his promise for a life together. One Anne thought didn't exist anymore, or she wouldn't have thrown the diamond away.

He had to tell her nothing happened. But would she believe him? She'd seen his ex-girlfriend half naked in his apartment when he was supposed to be out of town, and he'd called for a fill in at the event. Easily documented with news photos. He didn't have a leg to stand on. Except he loved Anne. And none of this was real. Convincing her of that was another story, but one step at a time.

Focus.

He pressed a hand to his aching head. She'd either go home or to Emily's. Neither of them would answer his calls.

Knowing Anne, she'd bear the pain on her own.

He got in his car and gunned his way toward her apartment.

CHAPTER 42

ANNE JERKED her head away from Devon. She didn't want him touching her. For that matter, she didn't want *any* man touching her ever again. And what the hell was he talking about with giving her everything? She must have misunderstood him. "I've asked you several times to leave. You really need to go right now."

"Actually, I think that's the last thing *you* need." He inched closer. "What you need is someone who can take care of you. Give you the good things in life. Someone with a solid reputation in the community who doesn't embarrass you and cause your picture to be constantly blasted on social media."

The strong scent of his cologne gagged her, and she took a step back. Where was he going with this? She didn't have the energy to deal with him. Her mind was still reeling from the shock of betrayal, and nothing Devon could say or do would help. She pointed to the door. "Last time I'm asking."

"I don't think you understand. Pearson isn't good enough for you. I can offer you so much more. I've waited for you to see the light, and I think you finally have." Devon slowly pulled a ring box out of his suit-coat pocket and flipped the lid open, revealing a diamond twice the size of the one Wyatt had given her. "What do you say? Will you marry me?"

Her chest seized, and her overtaxed brain snapped to awareness.

Holy shit.

He had to be kidding, but that ring wasn't from a bubble gum machine, and not a hint of a smile lit his face. Nothing but hard lines and an intense focus on her. For God's sake, they hadn't even dated. He had to be crazy if he thought she'd accept a proposal right after finding out Wyatt had cheated on her.

She held her hands up. "This is nuts. Put that away and go. I'm not kidding."

"I didn't come this far to lose," he gritted out, then smiled and softened his voice. "There's no logical reason for you to refuse me. We'd be perfect together. What's your answer?"

She broke out in a cold sweat. No logical reason? He must be a certifiable lunatic. She headed to door and yanked it open. "Go now."

He crossed the room to her and took the ring out of the box. "Not without an answer. Last chance."

The ominous tone in his voice sent a shiver down her backbone. She needed to be blunt and get him the hell out of her apartment. "No. I've never been interested in you that way and never will be."

His eyes blazed, and heat came off him in waves. For a long moment, he stared at her. His nostrils flared, and his mouth twisted into a sinister, evil snarl. He grabbed her hand and tried to force the ring onto her finger. "Wrong answer."

She curled her fingers into her palm and knocked the diamond to the floor, her breath coming in short bursts. The man had lost his ever-freaking mind.

Devon's pupils dilated as his face turned red.

Her heart short circuited, and her flight-or-fight response kicked in. "I said no. What are you doing? You're scaring me."

"Scaring you?" He slammed the door shut, grabbed her chin, and pinched the flesh, forcing her to look up at him. "You should be scared. You should be *very* scared. I didn't come this far for you to reject me. No one fucking rejects me. You think it was easy setting all this up? The flat tire? The attack in the alley?"

Backed against the door, she couldn't yank free from his grip. Her mind scrambled to keep up, every muscle in her body tense. Devon had saved them in the alley. He wasn't making any sense. "Wh-What do you mean?"

"Planning and more planning. You were so gullible." He scoffed. "That chance meeting we had on the road? I put a nail in your tire so it would go flat. I obtained the leadership role on the stupid walk-a-thon so I could get close to you. I hired guys to jump you and your pitiful excuse for a boyfriend."

Anne's pulse beat wildly in her throat, and fear seeped out of her pores. Devon's words rattled around in her head, but she couldn't understand any of it. Why would he have sabotaged her car, and what did he have against Wyatt?

Panic closed her throat. She'd left her phone and purse in the car. With no way to call anyone, she'd have to deal with this Ted Bundy on her own.

Devon's mouth contorted. "I spent a month eating crappy food at that cockroach-infested restaurant to make an impression on you. It wasn't even my birthday the night we went to dinner. I just told them that. And do you think I actually give a damn about the brats in the hospital? Nothing but a show for you."

Anne gripped the door knob, her heart beating faster than whirring helicopter blades. He'd been lying to her from the moment they'd met. Trying to impress her with crazy, conjured-up scenarios. Why? It's not like she was a celebrity or anybody special. She had to get away from the psycho.

His gaze dropped to her hand, and he growled, a sick, guttural sound.

"Too late, bitch. You had your chance."

He hauled back and slapped her face.

A million lights exploded in her brain as her head smashed against the door.

CHAPTER 43

THE CANDELABRA SHOOK in Paul's hand as footsteps sounded from the store above. His heart pounded, and his shirt stuck to his drenched body.

He whispered answers to the nine-one-one operator and prayed the cops got there before Devon could kill him. Maybe Devon wouldn't want to be caught committing another murder, knowing the police were on the way. That was Paul's only hope. He had no delusions about his inability to win in a fight.

"Hello? Is anyone here?" an elderly female voice rang out from upstairs.

Paul's shoulders sagged, and he brought a hand to his chest, letting out the breath he'd been holding. Thank God. He'd forgotten to lock the door behind him. The store hours weren't posted because they varied based on appointments.

"Just a second, I'll be right up." He set down the candlestick holder and climbed the stairs.

A silver-haired woman peered down as he emerged. "Is the shop open? I'm looking for a hand-made lace tablecloth."

He needed to shut the trap door and get her out of the place in case Devon did show up before the police. The psycho might kill them both and leave them to rot down there. Probably best if they both left. He could wait in his car for the cops, and if Devon did come back, he'd have no reason to suspect Paul had found his secret room. "I'm sorry, we're closed, and we don't have any of those right now. Maybe try back another time."

She frowned. "Phooey. My sister, Mable, is having hernia surgery and she was supposed to find one, but now—"

"You really need to leave. There's...rats in here. That's why I was downstairs."

"Rats?" The woman's eyes widened and she held her purse up higher, her gaze darting around the floor.

Christ, where had that come from? Didn't matter. She seemed freaked.

"I don't think those sandals are the best choice in here right now." He hurried to the door and opened it.

She gasped and glanced down at her feet, curling her toes. "Oh, my. No."

Moving with a speed that belied her age, she whisked out the exit, casting a worried look over her shoulder as if the vermin might be hot on her trail.

Paul rushed to close the trap door and roll the armoire back on top of the carpet. If Devon saw that open, Paul's wedding ring might end up as the next trophy in the wooden box. He shuddered and headed to the entrance as a cruiser pulled into the lot.

His rigid muscles eased. Safe from the psycho.

He opened the door and raised his hands in the air, his heart beating triple time. Two policemen got out of the car and approached, hands on their gun holsters. Paul stepped outside, gave his name, and told them he was the person who'd called nine-one-one.

The policeman with grey hair told him to stay where he was and keep his hands in sight. A much younger cop frisked Paul and waited with him outside while the other officer went into the store. Paul hadn't expected the pat down, but he couldn't blame them for it. They had no idea who to trust walking blind into dangerous situations.

When the "all clear" came, the young cop motioned for Paul to enter the shop and followed him inside. He tugged on his collar, picturing

Lynn with her innocent love and sweet smile. He had to do this. His stomach hardened as he committed himself.

Letting out a tense breath, he faced the policeman. "I have financial records to turn over that will incriminate myself and the owner of this store, Devon Blackwood, with tax fraud."

The cop raised an eyebrow and nodded. "Okay, but that doesn't merit an emergency. The nine-one-one dispatcher said you called in fear for your life."

"I was in the basement when I heard someone enter the store above. I thought Devon had come back while I was downstairs. I never knew this place had a lower level until I found it tonight." A shiver ran up Paul's back. "It turned out to be a customer who'd entered the store, but if it had been Devon, I know he would have killed me."

"Why?"

Paul straightened. Devon had killed Lynn, his family, and who knew how many others? Time to put away the son of a bitch. "Because I found physical evidence down there that should link him to one, if not more, murders."

CHAPTER 44

WYATT KEPT a heavy foot on the accelerator. He had to find Anne and explain they'd both been deceived by crazy Victoria. He'd known she was a few cards short of a full deck, but never expected in his wildest dreams she would do something so insane.

John's ringtone sounded, and Wyatt answered through the blue tooth. "What's up?"

"Do you know where Anne is?"

Wyatt snapped to attention at the abrupt question and the urgency in John's voice. "No. I'm headed to her place. You won't believe what—"

"I gotta make this short because things are happening in real time. Blackwood's the one behind all this. I have a warrant out for his arrest."

Wyatt's stomach rocketed to his throat, and he blinked. "What? Blackwood? I've never even met the guy."

"When I saw the sketch artist's images, I recognized him from the press picture taken at the hospital. Trish ID'd him too, so I sent units to his house and store. We haven't found him yet."

"What beef could he have with me? This makes no fucking sense." Wyatt tried to focus on the road, his body on high alert, and his brain struggling to process the information.

"I don't have time to explain. Anne's not answering her phone and could be in danger. I sent a unit to her place."

A fist slammed into Wyatt's heart. "I'm almost there, but why would Blackwood want to hurt her? I mean, if he's the one who hired Moe Dog and his goons, he gave them instructions *not* to harm Anne."

"Hold on." John's voice muffled as he spoke to someone else, then came back on the line. "I gotta chase down this lead. Listen, officially I have to warn you not to enter Anne's building until after the police have cleared it. Blackwood is capable of anything. Keep in mind what he did to Capello."

Cold sweat formed on Wyatt's forehead, and his insides knotted. Holy fuck. Blackwood had cut off the guy's hand and ear, and now he might have Anne? "All the more reason I'm going in."

"I'll be there as soon as I can. Sorry, gotta go."

John hung up as Wyatt turned down the road leading to Anne's apartment complex. He forced air into his constricted lungs. This night had spun out of orbit. Anne could be at the mercy of that monster. She'd never be able to defend herself against him. Wyatt firmed his grip on the steering wheel. He had to keep it together if he was going to be of any use.

Shit, five minutes ago his biggest worry had been whether he could get Anne to believe he'd never cheated on her. Now, he just wanted to see her alive.

He swung into the lot of Anne's apartment complex. He didn't have time to figure out the answers. All that mattered was getting to her.

When he spotted her car, his heart vaulted.

And then his gaze caught the BMW parked beside it.

CHAPTER 45

ANNE GRABBED THE DOOR FRAME, but slid to the floor, her head pulsing with pain and shock. What kind of psycho was Devon? First he'd proposed, and in the next minute he'd slapped her. None of what he'd told her made any sense.

She screamed as loud as she could, and he laughed. "You think that old bat across the hall is going to hear you over the storm?"

Her head hurt to the point of making her nauseous. She needed to escape.

He yanked her up by her hair. Pain seared her skull. He brought his face close, and his dark eyes bored into hers. "I wasted so much time on your worthless ass. But you know what was actually fun?" He shook her until her teeth rattled. "Hiring Victoria to make you think your precious has-been football player was cheating on you. I overheard her performance, and the crazy bitch nailed it. She enjoyed herself so much I think she'd have done it for free."

A zap of electricity jump started Anne's heart. What performance? This shit got crazier and crazier. Now she had a million questions. "Wh- what are you saying?"

"I picked your lock and bugged this low-rent, piece-of-shit apartment." He shook her again, his fingers digging painfully into her arms.

She tried to break free from his grip, but he held tight.

"Someone isn't paying attention. I told you this took a lot of planning. I paid Victoria and her friend to follow Emily until they found a chance for her to overhear them talking. You had a key in your drawer tagged with Pearson's name. That's so stupid." Devon clicked his tongue. "I made a copy and bugged his place months ago. Then I gave the key to Victoria and called her when you told Emily you were headed to Pearson's."

Holy shit. The diabolical maniac had set up the whole sordid thing. Tears welled in her eyes. Wyatt did love her. He hadn't cheated on her. Their life together still existed, if she could get out of this alive.

"I've stayed one step ahead because I've been listening to you both the whole time." Devon brought his mouth to her ear and whispered, "We've even had sex together, just not in the same room."

Her stomach roiled. Oh, God. Sick bastard. "Why? Why did you do this?"

"Boredom. My friend and I make bets for fun. Been doing it for a long time. I always win. Except for once." Devon twisted his lips into a sadistic frown. "Lynn was a stupid bitch like you. She chose Paulie over me. Paulie…that wimpy little troll."

Anne winced at Devon's raised voice, anticipating another blow from him. But he seemed to be in the midst of some sort of tirade, wanting to gloat. Maybe she could use it to her advantage. If only she could find a way out.

"You know what happened to Lynn?" He sneered, narrowing his eyes. "I torched her. Same way I did my family."

Anne's mouth went dry, and her knees buckled. If he was sick enough to kill his own family, she didn't have a prayer. And he'd confessed to committing murder. Goosebumps trailed up her arms. No way he'd let her live now.

"That's what I do to people who cross me." He let go of her and paced, but not far enough away for her to make a move. "My old man was an abusive alcoholic, and my mother spent all of her time fawning over my brother, the big sports hero. What a joke. Not a brain in his head. But it's okay. I gave them what they all deserved. You see, I'm a fair person, Anne. Wouldn't you agree that I'm fair?"

A splitting headache and fear for her life made it hard to keep up with his rantings. The only thing she'd agree to was that he was completely insane.

He grabbed her, jerking her body close. "I asked you a question. Don't you think I'm fair?"

She trembled. "Please let me go."

"You sound like Louie. Remember him? The scum who slapped you in the alley and messed up your face? He didn't follow my orders and got what he deserved too."

Her lungs flattened, and she strained to breathe. Oh, God no. Not another confession. How many people had Devon murdered? She'd be just another unsolved case.

"I took my time with Louie. He begged me to stop. I made him pay." Devon shook his head slowly. "You all had chances. I gave you a shot at making the right choice, but you didn't. So now the talking is done, and I'm going to give you what you deserve too."

He was going to kill her. It was now or never. She jerked her knee up as hard as she could, aiming for his groin, but Devon was quicker. He jumped back, releasing her just in time.

With a vicious backhand, he knocked her to the ground.

She bit her lip, and her mouth filled with the copper taste of blood.

He yanked her back up. The whites of his eyes shone, and spittle gathered in the corners of his mouth like a rabid animal. "That was pitiful. I'm toying with you right now. You're not too bright, so I'll make this clear. You're about to die."

Every muscle in her body quaked, and she fought to keep control.

Devon brought his face to within an inch of hers. "When I'm done with you, Pearson's next."

No, not Wyatt. He didn't know Devon had a key to his place. The bastard could enter in the middle of the night and kill Wyatt in his sleep. Adrenaline surged through Anne's body. She might not make it, but damn if she'd let this psychopath get away unscathed.

She yanked her head back, then smashed her forehead against his nose. A crunch sounded, and Devon released her, cursing and bringing his hands to his face. Blood gushed from his nostrils. She pivoted and tried to run for the door, but he snaked an arm around her waist, snatching her back.

"Change of plans, bitch. I planned to set a fire, but now I'm going to kill you with my bare hands." He threw her onto the floor. She landed on her back, and her breath whooshed out. Before she could recover, he straddled her and wrapped his hands around her neck.

He pressed his thumbs into her throat, closing off the airway. His eyes bulged, and blood continued to flow from his nose.

She writhed beneath him and clawed at his hands, gasping for air. Pressure built in her head, and little spots of light appeared before her eyes. God, no. This was how she'd die. She'd never see Wyatt again, or her sisters, or their babies. Her entire life she'd taken care of everyone she loved, keeping her pain to herself and handling her own battles. What she wouldn't give now for some help. She couldn't beat this monster on her own.

Tears streamed down the sides of her face, and she thrashed, but nothing loosened Devon's iron grip. Just as the room began to turn black, he let go.

Someone growled, and his body flew off of hers. She gulped for air, clutching her neck, and looked up to see Wyatt hurl Devon across the room.

"Run. Get out of here," Wyatt yelled over his shoulder, pure rage in his eyes.

He grabbed Devon, slammed him into the wall, and punched his stomach.

Anne's heart stopped, and the room blurred as relief quickly turned to dread. Wyatt was still recovering from the last fight. He had two fractures, and now was up against a martial arts expert. She labored to get air through her swollen throat, making her dizzy.

Devon karate chopped Wyatt in the ribs.

Anne cringed. That blow must have landed on his broken one. The bastard had deliberately attacked Wyatt's weak spot, knowing where to hit.

She pushed off the floor, her gaze darting around the room to find anything she could use as a weapon.

Devon delivered a round kick to the back of Wyatt's knees, but Wyatt reared up, using his weight and size to smash Devon once again into the wall.

Anne blinked rapidly to try to bring the room into focus. Blood pounded in her ears, keeping time with her throbbing head. She had to do something.

Her gaze locked on the big conch shell Wyatt had given to her at Ocean City. She fumbled to pick it up from the coffee table.

Damn her trembling fingers. Every second mattered.

At last she managed to get a grip.

Seeing double, she staggered toward the men, who struggled in a hold on each other like the wrestlers in a heavyweight match.

Devon freed an arm and gave a sharp whack to Wyatt's kidneys.

Hot fury fueled Anne's muscles.

Wyatt let go of Devon, took a quick step back, and punched him hard in the gut, dropping him to his knees.

With Devon's back to her, this was her chance. She raised her arm, and with all her might, she bashed the shell down onto his head.

He grunted and went limp, sliding the rest of the way to the ground.

Her body collapsed, every ounce of energy draining from her limbs.

Wyatt caught her as sirens sounded and lights flashed through the windows.

"Help is coming. Hang in there, baby." He wrapped her in his arms, and rocked her, kissing the top of her head. "Oh God. I thought I might have been too late."

She shook uncontrollably, but the thumping of his heart under her cheek assured her they'd survived. Clenching his body, she melted against him. "I love you so much."

Together they'd beaten that soulless beast.

The nightmare was over.

CHAPTER 46

Wyatt gazed down at Anne, snuggled in a blanket on his couch as the first rays of sun shined through the window. His heart wrenched. Last night he could have lost her to that psychopath.

The dark circles under her eyes, bruises on her face, and worry lines etched across her forehead made him wish the sick freak had died. At least he was in custody, and it didn't sound like he'd be driving his high-end cars ever again.

Poor Anne had been whisked off to the hospital, just like the night of the alley assault, and later questioned by the authorities. In the aftermath of that and surviving Devon's attack, she had to be exhausted.

Wyatt eased onto the sofa and wrapped an arm around her. "How are you doing?"

"Okay, but your rib, is it—"

"Shh. I'm fine." He kissed her temple and stroked her arm. "All that matters is you're all right."

"I was so scared. I thought I'd never see you again. Never be able to tell you I loved you and I knew Devon had put Victoria up to that crazy shit." Anne shuddered and nestled against him.

He pulled the engagement ring out of his pocket. "I'm hoping you want this back."

"God, yes." She held her hand out and he slipped it on her finger. "I'm so sorry. I'll never take this off again."

"It's not your fault. I saw what you walked in on. Pretty convincing, not to mention sick." On both Devon and Victoria's parts. She sure seemed to relish every second of what she'd done.

Anne shook her head. "I can't believe all the horrible things Devon did, meanwhile walking around like some sort of patron saint, fooling everybody."

Wyatt's phone dinged, and he stood. "John's here. He promised to brief us as soon as he could."

Anne picked up her mug, and Wyatt opened the door for John. His bloodshot eyes, five o'clock shadow, and wrinkled clothes were clear indicators he hadn't slept either.

"You want some coffee?" Wyatt asked.

John nodded. "More than a junkie craving a fix."

"Have a seat, and I'll bring you some."

"Thanks." John walked to the family room and took the chair across from Anne. Wyatt brought him a cup and sat beside her on the couch.

"How are you holding up?" John asked.

Anne leaned against Wyatt. "Better now that the monster's in custody."

"I'm sorry he got to you. It shouldn't have happened." John frowned.

"Stop. You and Wyatt keep apologizing. No one could have predicted this. Devon was insane. If anything, I'm the one who should have known. I spent the most time with him."

"Well, I can't change it, but I can make sure he never walks free again." John took a sip of coffee. "Everything I'm telling you is off the record because this is an ongoing investigation, so keep it between us."

"Understood." Wyatt squeezed Anne's shoulder.

John continued, "We found the recordings he had from both of your places and what's on them would be enough to put him away even without the physical evidence we have now."

Wyatt's skin crawled, and his hands itched to get another chance to punch the psycho. Twisted fuck had listened to their private conversations. "What physical evidence?"

"Last night, I sent a unit to Blackwood's storeroom, and two cops were already there in response to a nine-one-one call his partner had made. Turns out, the guy had found a box of what we think are souvenirs from people Blackwood killed."

Anne shivered. "Must be the ones he bragged about. His own family, some poor woman, and the guy who attacked me."

"That was Capello. The DNA test came back positive on him from the assault in the alley. Now, we think an earring in the box might have been his. We sent it out to test for matches to him and Blackwood." John glanced at Anne. "We also found out more about the bet."

"Was his partner the one he'd made it with?" Wyatt rubbed Anne's arm.

"Yeah. They go back to college. Been betting on stupid shit for years. He claims he had no idea Blackwood was a psychopath. The wager was that Blackwood could get a ring on Anne's finger in three months." John shifted. "He was running out of time and got desperate."

"You should have seen his face when I turned him down." Anne pressed a shaky hand to her mouth, and Wyatt's heartrate throbbed in his forehead. If only he could have gotten to her faster.

He brushed back a strand of her hair and guided her head to rest on his shoulder.

"You won't have to worry about him ever again." John scrubbed a hand over his chin. "His partner turned over financial records that he says will prove tax fraud as well. And Victoria has been questioned. She's going to pay for her part in all of this, too."

"She never mentioned Blackwood. Just told me the super let her in," Wyatt said.

"Blackwood warned her she wouldn't get paid if she said anything about him hiring her. She used the spare key he'd made to enter and lied to you about the super." John stood. "I gotta get back downtown. They're bringing in Moe Dog and his goons. They aren't getting off scot-free, either."

"I'll walk you out." Wyatt took the mug from John.

John glanced down at Anne. "You put up a hell of a fight against a maniac. I'm glad you're okay."

"It's a good thing Wyatt showed up when he did, but thanks." She gave him a half-smile that didn't reach her sad eyes.

Wyatt's chest tightened. He'd have to fix that.

He followed John out the door, pulling it partially shut behind him.

John stopped on the landing and faced Wyatt. "I'm sorry, man. I didn't account for dealing with a psychopath. If I'd thought for one second that Anne was in danger—"

"Let it go. We're good." Wyatt held up a hand and shook his head. "The important thing is she's safe."

John blew out a breath and nodded. They stood in silence for a while as people came and went from the building, carrying groceries, taking out trash, performing normal everyday tasks.

Wyatt gripped the railing. It would be nice to get back to normal again. "Hey, next time we grab a beer, let's not make it a biker bar."

"Hell, no. And you'll be buying, as usual, loser." John clapped him on the back, keeping his hand there for a second as he looked Wyatt in the eyes.

They'd been friends long enough to not need words.

John smirked and jogged down the stairs, calling over his shoulder, "If you want to keep that classy woman, get a shower and a shave, baboon butt."

Wyatt grinned and leaned back against the cool, hard concrete surface of the wall. With a sigh, he forced away all the what ifs hammering in his head. He'd come so close to losing Anne. Thank God the craziness was over. He pushed off the wall and opened the door.

Time to get back to the woman he loved and start the rest of their lives…together.

CHAPTER 47

PAUL'S PULSE quickened as a guard led Devon, wearing an orange jumpsuit, into the prison visiting room partitioned by a glass wall.

Far cry from his designer threads. The sweet taste of retribution swirled in Paul's mouth. He swallowed and studied Devon, happy for the barrier. No telling what the psychopath would do without one.

Two months incarcerated, and Devon's skin had paled. A couple of cuts on his face looked fresh. Good. Bastard deserved that and more. Probably wasn't playing nice in the sandbox. What a shock.

He slid into the seat across from Paul, and the guard stepped back, crossing his arms. Devon picked up the receiver from the telephone on the counter and Paul did the same.

"Hello, Paulie." Devon leaned closer to the glass. "I almost refused your visit, but I had to hear what you could possibly have left to say after all the talking you did to the police." A muscle in his cheek popped up as he gritted out the words, "And there's something I wanted to tell you."

"My name is Paul, and don't forget it." He held Devon's gaze. How could he have missed the pure evil that radiated off the guy and ever believed they were friends? "We have some unsettled business. But first I want to ask you something."

"Ask away. Clearly I have all the time in the world." A vein on Devon's forehead bulged, belying the calmness of his voice.

"Why did you do it? Kill your family and Lynn?"

Devon scoffed. "Because they deserved it. I punish people who wrong me, Paul-ie."

"You feel nothing? No regrets?"

"Oh, I have regrets, but not over any of them." He pointed a finger at Paul. "What I regret is ever bringing you onboard. I paid you enough to keep your mouth permanently shut. Why did you turn me in, and why aren't you in jail?"

"They cut me a deal, so at least I'm free, unlike you." Paul shook his head, his heart an empty shell. "I'm bankrupt after all the fines and taxes. House and car taken. My wife left me, and I'm starting from scratch." He waved his hand in dismissal. "But I don't care. It's just money and stuff." Leaning closer to the glass, he narrowed his eyes. "I did it for Lynn, and now, you're finally getting what you deserve, you bastard."

Devon's body shook as his face turned red.

"Now what is it you wanted to tell me?" Paul sat back and adjusted his glasses.

Devon's hand balled into a fist. "I'm going to get out of here, and when I do, you're the first one I'm coming after." His voice raised, and his mouth twisted. "There'll be nothing left of you when I'm done." He slammed his fist on the table, and the guard stepped toward him with cuffs. "You're a fucking dead man. You hear me?"

Paul stood and smiled. "I won the bet, and now you owe me a beer. It's okay. I know you won't be able to pay up, because the only bars you will ever be around again are the ones in front of your face."

Devon lunged at the glass, his face contorted in rage as he yelled, "I'm gonna fucking kill you."

The guard grabbed him, yanking his arms back to cuff.

"Tsk tsk. No time off for good behavior now." Paul hung up the phone and walked away, chin held high as the room reverberated with the sound of a scuffle, a thump, and then...

Silence.

EPILOGUE

MOUTH DRY, sweat trickling down between his shoulder blades, Wyatt stood at the altar, staring at the closed doors Anne would soon walk through. As promised when he proposed, he hadn't rushed her to get married. He'd waited seven months for this, so what was a few more minutes? Felt like an eternity.

Time had flown with wedding planning and the new home under construction. The house would be ready and waiting for them when they got back from their honeymoon. Falling in love had changed his life, for the better.

He slipped two fingers under his collar and tugged the bow tie out to get some air. Standing beside him, John cleared his throat in an obvious attempt to cover a laugh. Wyatt shot a look at him and caught John's smirk before he put on his appropriately solemn, poker face.

Music played, and the church doors opened. The ring bearer and flower girl walked down the aisle, distracted and needing some prodding from Maddie, who followed. Everyone oohed and aahed at the children. Emily and Sarah came next, escorted by Wyatt's friends.

The wedding march cued, and Anne appeared in the doorway, holding her father's arm. Wyatt swallowed hard and held his breath as she floated down the aisle, her face hidden behind a sheer veil. The dress suited her perfectly. Classy, conservative, and elegant with a lacy front that encircled her throat. Beautiful.

Her father lifted the veil and kissed her on the cheek. She turned to Wyatt and beamed a smile, her gorgeous blue eyes radiating love. His heart swelled. He took her hand, and his fingers tingled at the touch of her smooth, soft skin.

Their relationship had been challenged and threatened, but she'd kept coming back to him. Her strength and loyalty had overcome every obstacle. Having gone through that ordeal, they'd become stronger together. Now she stood before him, about to pledge her love to him forever.

No one and nothing could make him a happier man.

* * *

Emily clinked her glass with a spoon, and the tinkle of silver against fine crystal filled the room as everyone followed suit. Anne smiled at Wyatt, seated next to her at the banquet table. He leaned over and kissed her with champagne-laced lips, causing hers to tickle in a delicious way.

A boisterous round of applause erupted, and he squeezed her thigh under the table. "Better eat something. You're going to need your energy later."

"I hope so." She grinned and gazed around the hall. Soft music played in the background as servers glided about the room in synchrony, carrying silver platters.

John picked up his beer and tapped Wyatt on the shoulder. "Good grub. Now I need to go rescue Trish."

Anne cocked her head and scanned the room. She bit her cheek and stifled a laugh. Trish leaned back in her chair as a skinny, young guy with a crimson-red face tried to mop up a spilled beer with his napkin. Unsteady on his feet, he nearly took out another drink. Poor kid probably thought he had a chance with her. Might be his first taste of liquor.

Wyatt shook his head. "Glad John finally grew a pair and asked Trish out."

"I think the two of them are just tough enough to make things work out together." Anne nodded.

Wyatt squeezed her hand, and she took another sip of champagne. She gazed at her family. Her dad winked at her, his arm slung around the back of her mother's chair. Scott laughed at something Bruce said as he hoisted his daughter onto his lap and handed her a juice box. Maddie and Sarah chatted, holding their babies.

Anne glanced at Wyatt, her heart so full it threatened to explode. He brought a hand to her cheek, and his eyes softened. "Yeah, like I told you before, I want that, too."

Happy tears blurred her vision, and she kissed him.

Cameras flashed, and for once, she didn't care. All they could possibly catch was a beautiful, tender moment. Let the whole world see it. She loved this man with all her heart and couldn't wait to share the rest of her life with him.

* * *

Thank you for reading! Did you enjoy? Please add your review because nothing helps an author more and encourages readers to take a chance on a book than a review.

And don't miss more from Diane Holiday with ROCK BOTTOM ROMANCE, available now. Turn the page for a sneak peek!

You can also sign up for the City Owl Press newsletter to receive notice of all book releases!

SNEAK PEEK OF ROCK BOTTOM ROMANCE

Crystal Lovechild would rather be caught without makeup by paparazzi than scout another wretched location for a campground-set reality show. From the passenger seat of a dented SUV, she tugged at the seatbelt, chafing her neck. She checked her fresh manicure and let out a breath. All good. The tips and polish would have to last throughout filming. How she longed for the days when she arrived at a gig in a chauffeured limo with her own hair, makeup, and wardrobe team.

"You gotta be shitting me. More wild turkeys?" Sydney, her field producer, leaned on the horn. She blew her purple-streaked bangs up and slapped the steering wheel. The flock jerked, separated, and trotted off the road.

"Are we almost there?" Crystal gazed out the window. They sure as hell weren't in Hollywood anymore. Cows grazed behind miles of fences. This spot in the Midlands of South Carolina took the prize for the most remote of the four locations they'd scouted and showed the least promise. Nothing but farms, fruit stands, and blood-thirsty mosquitos. She shuddered and scratched her now itchy arm.

"We're close." Sydney's pierced lips twisted. "Not exactly what you're used to, is it?"

"I'll be fine." Crystal hoped.

Sydney was a real pain in the ass with a chip on her shoulder a mile high, knowing the star of the show would be a fallen celebrity. From the moment they'd met, the woman had doled out one backhanded insult after another. People loved to see a famous person out of their element. The concept of a celebrity learning to rough it camping had thrilled test audiences, but Sydney's production company couldn't afford an A-list actor. She'd made sure Crystal knew she'd been their *last* choice in the low-budget production.

Since subletting her Hollywood penthouse wasn't enough to put a dent in Crystal's bills, it was the reality show or wait tables. So not happening. She cringed at the mere thought.

She glanced at her silent phone, and a pit formed in her stomach. No texts, messages, or calls, aside from Jenna, Crystal's long-time friend, the one person who hadn't ghosted her.

Sydney slowed for yet another turn in the road. "I hope you like hot dogs and beans because there's no caviar on the island."

"It's two months. I'll survive." A bead of sweat trickled down Crystal's back. Her agent had made it clear it was this gig or nothing. Crystal needed a spark to get people talking about her again, and any screen time counted. Besides, how hard could camping be?

At last, they reached the gate. A sign that read "Stone Island Park" marked the entrance. Sydney stopped at the admissions booth and opened the window.

Hot humid air rushed in. The temperature topped ninety and it was only the first week of June.

A short, stout woman, wearing a khaki safari shirt and shorts, stepped out of the booth.

Sydney handed her a business card. "We're with the production company for *Celebrity Trials*."

"Yeah, I heard y'all were coming to check out the island. You're gonna love it." The park attendant bent and peered at Crystal's glittery halter tank, miniskirt, and stilettos. Her lips twitched and her eyebrows knitted. "That's...quite the outfit."

"Thank you." Crystal's chest inflated and rose like a hot-air balloon. She'd glammed up for scouting the sites. In the end, she might decide she didn't want them to use any of the footage, but if she did, she'd give her fans a glimpse of the star they knew and loved. Couldn't hurt to start off with some confidence, and it might be a while before she could dress in her fashion line of clothes again.

The attendant straightened, scratched her head, and checked the road behind them. "I expected a row of cars. You know, full of bodyguards and reporters."

"I don't think she has to worry about paparazzi anymore." Sydney smirked.

Crystal's blood heated. The truth stung. Even if she had the money to pay for a bodyguard, she wouldn't need one. She'd lost mega followers and subscribers on social media. No one tried to sneak candid shots anymore.

The park attendant grabbed a pamphlet from the booth and handed it to Sydney with a big smile. "Here's a map. Feel free to stop back and ask any questions. We're excited for y'all to be here."

Sydney thanked the woman and pulled forward. "Trevor is meeting us at the campsite for the opening shoot. I hope the cameras are all set up because I need him to capture your arrival. If not, I'll have to help him again like the last time when he was running behind."

"Don't look at me," Crystal replied. "I only know one side of the lens."

"I wasn't holding my breath, hoping for your assistance." Sydney's cheeks puffed.

They crossed a long bridge over the lake with water rippling on both sides. Random small boats peppered the shoreline as fishermen cast near the rocks. What fish was worth baking in the sun and bouncing around in the water all day? No thanks. Plated and served was more Crystal's style.

She gazed at the woods on either side of the single-lane road beyond the bridge and shook her head. "Why don't we save us all some time and turn around? This is too remote."

"You haven't even seen the camp yet."

"I've seen enough." Crystal dusted her hands of the place. "Go back. We're done here."

Sydney hit the brakes and turned to Crystal, her face bright red. "I've had it with you. I busted my ass for four years to work my way up to producer, and this is my big chance. I'm not about to let some washed-up child star living off her past celebrity status blow it. The contract says the company picks the site, not you. Got it?"

Crystal's throat constricted. Damn. She hadn't read the contract. That's why she had an agent, who should have told her about the stipulation.

She huffed. "Fine. Let's get it over with then."

Sydney pulled into a shady parking spot on a campsite loop. "Looks like Trevor is ready for us."

He stood by a cement slab surrounded by woods with a trail that led to the lake. Just like at the other locations, people pitched tents on concrete here. Crystal's hips and elbows ached at the thought. She'd hoped for a more comfortable arrangement. Maybe she'd buy a foam pad like the one she had for her bed. The thicker, the better. As soon as she had money for one, she'd order it.

With her well-practiced, red-carpet smile pasted on, she opened the car door. She pushed out of the SUV, making sure to pause as her heels hit the ground for the best toned-legs shot. Not that it mattered, because she had no intention of working on this island.

For now, she'd play along.

She crinkled her nose and shrugged. "I think my viewers will be bored with this remote place. The other sites had way more campers and action."

The roar of an engine cut through the silence. She spun around as some sort of jeep or four-wheeler thingy came to a halt next to them.

A mountain of a man jumped off the vehicle wearing camo pants and an olive T-shirt stretched to the max over his broad shoulders. The fabric clung to the rippled muscles of his stomach. He radiated pure strength with corded veins in his neck and not an ounce of fat on him. She judged him to be about her age, late twenties.

He had a buzz cut and a couple of days of stubble on a chiseled face. His prominent, strong jawline clenched as he strode toward them. This guy moved with purpose and power, like a big black bear on its hind legs defending his territory.

Crystal swallowed and tried to ignore the fluttering under her ribs. The unfamiliar feeling caught her off guard. Sure, she'd worked with macho types in the movies, but Hollywood used special effects and cosmetics to make them appear larger than life.

Aviator glasses hid his eyes, yet she sensed anger emanating from him. What was his problem?

Sydney made a keep-the-cameras-rolling hand gesture to Trevor.

Great. Sydney and Trevor couldn't be on film, so it was up to Crystal to deal with the man.

He stopped in front of her, planting his feet in a wide stance. "I'm Zach Stone. Obviously, you are the celebrity whatever crew." The sides of his mouth turned down. "I run this campground."

Not the most welcoming hello. And either he didn't care enough to know the name of the production company, or he'd dissed it on purpose. She smoothed back her hair and shrugged. "Doesn't look like much to manage. A bunch of woods and tents. What's the worst problem? Sunburn?"

He snorted and his chest expanded.

She tore her gaze from his pecs to his face, and her own reflected in his mirrored sunglasses. Her cheeks heated, and they turned pink before her eyes. What the hell? She didn't blush. Then again, she'd never been this close to someone so…daunting.

"What's this getup?" He waved a hand from her head to her feet. "You plan to camp in that?"

Her skin prickled. Getup? He should be thrilled she'd even considered wearing one of her designer outfits to his Podunk grounds. From the corner of her eye, she noted Trevor had moved closer, zooming in on them.

"I'll have you know this is the latest in my line." She smoothed a hand down her side and squared her shoulders. "It's so popular I can't even keep up with the orders." If only that were true.

Zach's head dipped and snapped back up. Was he checking her out?

"Cut." Trevor lowered the camera. "This thing's on the fritz again. I have to get the other one from the villa."

"That's fine. I need more coffee anyway." Sydney checked her watch. "We'll grab some at the general store and meet again in half an hour?"

Trevor nodded.

"I'll make sure I'm here," Zach said.

Crystal raised her chin. "We don't need you to be. Why don't you do whatever you do while we check out the place?"

"Keeping people like you from getting hurt while stomping around my territory unsupervised *is* what I do. I'll be back."

Crystal glared at him as he stalked to his vehicle. Her face burned. The guy had a bad attitude and a load of arrogance to go with it.

Just another reason to make sure they chose a different location.

Like hell he'd have the last word. She had a thing or two to say to him before she left him in the dust.

***

Don't stop now. Keep reading with your copy of ROCK BOTTOM ROMANCE.

And sign up for Diane's newsletter to get all the news, giveaways, excerpts, and more!

All reviews are **welcome** and **appreciated**. Please consider leaving one on your favorite social media and book buying sites.

Escape Your World. Get Lost in Ours! City Owl Press at www.cityowlpress.com.

ACKNOWLEDGMENTS

My heartfelt thanks go out to all of the amazing people in my life who support me and make it possible for my books to be published:

To my husband, Steve. He's my rock and also a pretty darn good critiquer now! I have to laugh at his lack of a filter sometimes. "Really? How many times is she going to smell his cologne?" But seriously, he reads every chapter and gives me great input. One of my writing friends even has him read some of her chapters for his input. He might have to quit his pontoon boat tour job to keep up with the critiquing demands.

To my daughter, Kelsey, for all her support getting her friends hooked on my books.

To my son, Brent, for having a farm full of animals up in Maine that make excellent photo opportunities with my books for advertising.

To Mary Cain, my content editor. I don't have enough words to explain how wonderful she is and how much she strives to help me reach my full potential. She pushes me to take my characters to that next deeper level.

To Tina Moss and Yelena Castle, co-founders of City Owl Press. I love the transparency of our press and all that these women do to support their authors. They are constantly exploring the latest, best marketing and opportunities for us.

To my fantastic critique partners who I can't thank enough for their time and dedication. We all help each other. It's tough love, but we're in it together.

To Investigator George Simmons from Richland County Sheriff's Department, Columbia, SC. Thanks for answering so many of my questions about police procedure. Any misinterpretations or mistakes are my own.

To Brooke Arthur for being my local cheerleader, taking pictures of my books with her animals, and giving out my bookmarks to customers at The Color Bar where she works.

To Jerry, the owner of The Coffee Shelf in Chapin, for hosting book signings and carrying my books in the store.

To all military members past and present. You and your families sacrifice so much to keep us safe. Every book sold adds to the personal donations I make to a non-profit organization that supports veterans.

ABOUT THE AUTHOR

DIANE HOLIDAY is an award-winning author who writes romantic suspense and contemporary romance with a healthy dose of humor. Her characters will make you laugh, cry, and root for them to the end. If you are sleep deprived because you couldn't put her book down, then she's achieved her goal. She and her husband, a retired Navy Captain, who  is her go-to for colorful slang and guy-talk, live in South Carolina on beautiful Lake Murray. Diane loves dogs and features one in each of her books. In her spare time, she volunteers at a rescue farm for large-breed dogs and another no-kill shelter national organization.

www.dianeholiday.com

f facebook.com/DianeHolidayBooks

instagram.com/diholiday333

ABOUT THE PUBLISHER

City Owl Press is a cutting edge indie publishing company, bringing the world of romance and speculative fiction to discerning readers.

Escape Your World. Get Lost in Ours!

www.cityowlpress.com

 facebook.com / CityOwlPress
 x.com / cityowlpress
 instagram.com / cityowlbooks
 pinterest.com / cityowlpress
 tiktok.com / @cityowlpress